Rich Man Road

Ann Glamuzina

First edition published in New Zealand by Eunoia Publishing Limited (NZ) 2015
For more information about our titles go to www.eunoiapublishing.com

Copyright © 2015 by Ann Glamuzina
The moral right of the author has been asserted

Cover design and illustration by Keely O'Shannessy
Text design and layout by Elin Termannsen

NZ Map 6274 reproduced on cover with permission from Sir George Grey Special Collections, Auckland Libraries ref:2014-278

All characters and events in this publication, other than historical figures and those clearly in the public domain, are fictitious and any resemblance to real persons, living or dead, is purely coincidental.

ALL RIGHTS RESERVED.
This book contains material protected under International, New Zealand, and United States Federal Copyright Laws and Treaties. Any unauthorised reprint or use of this material is prohibited. No part of this book may be reproduced or transmitted in any form or by any means, electronic or mechanical, including photocopying, recording, or by any information storage and retrieval system without express written permission from the author/publisher. For permission requests, write to the publisher at the address below.

ISBN-978-0-9941047-3-1

Eunoia Publishing Limited
PO Box 33890, Takapuna
Auckland 0740
New Zealand
Level 13, WHK Tower
51-53 Shortland St
Auckland 1140
New Zealand

www.eunoiapublishing.com

Printed in China by Asia Pacific Offset
Also available as an eBook

1 3 5 7 9 10 8 6 4 2

In memory of Sylvia Glamuzina

(14 June 1928 – 27 February 2011)

Počivala u Miru

Inā kei te mohio koe ko wai koe, I anga mai koe i hea, kei te mohio koe.
Kei te anga atu ki hea.

If you know who you are and where you are from,
then you will know where you are going.

Maori Proverb

RICH MAN ROAD

CHAPTER 1

AUCKLAND, JUNE 2012

In the dream little haloes of light explode like stars against the night sky. The girl stands on the footpath, sweat beading on her forehead as she watches the Lincoln Continental crawl along the curb towards her. She cannot see the man in the driver's seat, but she knows he is there and that he is wearing a sombre suit with a silk paisley tie and the look of someone who knows how to get what he wants.

As the car gets closer, the girl tightens her grip on the ticket she is holding, twisting it into a ball of damp paper.

The dream is all trickery and shifting light and there is a sense that she is both the girl on the sidewalk and the observer from above: the eye of God who sees the car approaching and the girl becoming ever more agitated.

It is the observer who comes to the girl's aid, telling her to leave quickly. She tries to move but her feet have become heavy and when she looks down, her toes have burrowed like roots into the asphalt. The sedan moves closer.

There are people nearby who could help her. She opens her mouth, but there is no sound in this dream, and she stands there, calling out silently into the darkness.

☙

She awakes with a start, her mouth dry, her body bathed in sweat and curled in on itself like a question mark. Pushing onto her elbows, she kicks her feet free from the tangle of sheets. It has been years since she has dreamed of the man. She wonders what has brought him back to her. She yawns, annoyed that he has disturbed her sleep and that it is still before dawn.

Another letter arrived yesterday from her mother and she holds the unopened envelope in her hand. She is sure that she can recite its words as if she had written them herself. Perhaps the letter has made her think of the past, allowing the man to work his way back into her subconscious.

She dismisses him from her mind, and her thoughts turn to her family. She has a clear picture of her mother waiting in the village with chickens and pigs swarming around her like a brood of children demanding to be fed. Her mother ignores her surrogate children, looking instead into the distance, waiting for her daughter to return home. But the daughter struggles with the question of where *home* is, and so, like every other morning, she sets about getting on with the day just as the birds in the tree outside her window begin to herald the approaching dawn.

She places the letter on top of the others, stretching a rubber band around the bundle, letting it *snap* before placing the letters under her pillow.

In a few steps she is across the room to where her habit lies. She lifts the woven scapular over her head, letting it slide down over her slight body. She carefully fastens her headdress and then, just as she steps into her house slippers, it occurs to Sister Mary Pualele Sina Auva'a that she hasn't heard a sound from her friend in the next door room.

ଓଃ

She opens the door and within seconds is at the window pulling the curtains apart. The room is a replica of her own and her gaze quickly passes over the bare walls and the tallboy standing next to the bed and comes to rest on her friend. Sister Teresa Olga Mastrovic is sleeping, and Pualele smiles at how peaceful the older nun appears, lying on her back in the growing light, hands folded delicately across her middle as if praying in her sleep. She is tempted to leave Olga be, but she knows that she must wake her and help her to dress.

Olga! It's me. Pualele, she whispers, cupping the older nun's shoulder.

The room is very still as she waits for the familiar warmth to filter through to her waiting hand. Her own breathing and the blood pulsing loudly in her ears are the only sounds Pualele hears as she wills the thin body of her friend to move. She places both hands on Olga's shoulders and gently shakes the old woman. She looks more closely – the few stubborn scraps of hair still hanging on to her scalp, the high forehead, wide cheekbones and the closed eyelids with familiar dark half circles beneath them.

It's almost reluctantly that she notices the blue-tinged lips.

Pualele's heart thumps as she looks around the room, taking in the curtains and the medicine bottles that sit undisturbed on top of the dresser. Everything seems as it should be. She blesses herself and hangs her head for a moment, trying to steady her breathing. She can't look at her friend's face again, and instead looks at the hands, the arthritic knuckles. And there, poking out from between her fingers, is a doll's head.

Pualele carefully closes her hand around the tiny head and pulls gently. The doll doesn't move; it is stuck firmly in the grasp of rigor mortis. She tries again, this time tugging with more force as she prises the fingers apart with her other hand. There is a sharp crack as Olga's index finger snaps and the doll comes free. Pualele is horrified at what she has done and prays silently for forgiveness as she presses the stiff fingers back into place.

The novice nun examines the crude rope-doll, its coarse threads having blackened over time. As it swings like a crucifix over its owner, she wonders where it came from. But that's something to think about later. Now there's no time, and she places the doll in her pocket as she opens the drawer.

Lifting an ageing Bible, she searches amongst the neatly folded undergarments, her fingers finding a bulging paper packet. She withdraws it from its hiding place, careful to replace both the clothing and the Bible so that they appear undisturbed. She opens the flap and pulls out the envelope that lies on top, placing it in her pocket with the doll. The bigger package she slides beneath the belt of her habit before breaking into a run, stumbling briefly as her skirts wrap like seaweed around her legs as she goes in search of the prioress.

It seems that siesta time takes for ever to arrive on the day of her friend's passing. The morning falls into disarray as news of Sister Teresa's death spreads through the convent. The normal quiet is shattered as first, Doctor Sutherland arrives, and then, soon after, the undertakers come to take the body away. With Lauds missed and Silent Communal Prayer disturbed by concealed sobs and whispering, prayers are abandoned altogether until Mass is finally called and some semblance of order returns to the day.

Pualele prays for patience. It isn't until early afternoon that she has an opportunity to break away from the others and retire to her room alone.

She shuts the door and sits on her bed, removing the packet from under her clothing. She slides her index finger under the paper flap and eases the envelope open to reveal the letter on top.

Dear Pualele,

I wouldn't be writing to you if I could find the courage to speak to you face to face. But it is not the first time in my life that courage has escaped me. You see, I have a confession to make – I am a fraud. I never planned on becoming a nun, but rightly or wrongly it was my choice and although I regretted it sometimes it has been a good life and my privilege to have been a part of this Order of wonderful women.

I hope that as you read through my journal, you will come to understand my reasons for joining the Order, and why it's so important to me that you know my story. You might think I am suffering some sort of spiritual crisis because of my illness, but nothing could be further from the truth. Cancer has given me the clarity to be honest for the first time in many years. I watch you struggle with your coming vows, and I want you to understand that you have choices – choices that perhaps I never saw for myself.

Olga

She turns the letter over, wondering if Olga is watching, urging her on. It seems like a long time since they first met, and Pualele suddenly wishes that she could remember all the things the older nun has ever told her.

As a young girl, Pualele learnt to protect herself by keeping to the crevices and shadows of life, like the octopus she remembers from her childhood in Samoa. But when Pualele took on the mantle of Sister Mary, wearing the white headdress with pride, she and Sister Teresa had quickly become friends, calling each other by their given names and spending their spare time together. It was Pualele who followed Sister Teresa's every movement – the way she held herself, her calmness and the way she spoke only when necessary. God showed her the way through the older nun. All she has to do is stick by her friend and believe. That was all very well when Sister Teresa was alive. Now Pualele can't even rely on her memories, for the old woman has by her own hand admitted that she was a fraud.

The packet lies on her lap. She opens it to find an amber lump of translucent rock. She frowns as she turns it over and over in her hands, her eyes focussing on an insect that has been preserved within, its wings forever trapped in mid-flight. She places the rock on the bed next to her and lets her fingers wander back inside the envelope.

A small cloth sampler is next. Its white background has discoloured over time, but the purple, red and green of the embroidery is still as vibrant as the day the needle had carefully been pulled through the cotton swatch.

She holds the cloth up to her face and inhales. There is a hint of an odour she can't quite identify – something woody, not unlike rosemary. Maybe thyme. Lavender! It's lavender. She is pleased with herself as she inspects the embroidery more intently. It is a simple piece, something that a young girl might make on her first attempt. The embroiderer has made a series of Ms, with lavender sprigs at each end – all straight lines for the stalks and letters, with feathery purple petals for the flowers. *MMM* – like a contented sigh.

Underneath the sampler are two black and white photos. The first is of two men leaning on shovels, their feet planted in swampy ground that looks as if it is trying to suck them downwards. The other is an arresting portrait of a small boy with enormous dark eyes that seem to look right inside her.

Pualele is transfixed by the boy's gaze and doesn't turn away until a noise from the hallway breaks the spell. She holds her breath and her heartbeat quickens, but the footsteps pass and she exhales in relief, her body relaxing as she lies back on her bed. Her eyes close. She wishes she could talk to Sister Teresa one more time and say to her all the things that are swimming around inside her head. She loved her friend, but feels an unexpected rush of anger towards her as she thinks how cruel it has been of Sister Teresa to have hidden the truth from her.

Tears pool in her eyes as she pulls the last item out of the envelope. It is a journal, hard-backed with a maroon cover and stiff spine – it's an uninspiring sort of book that a shopkeeper might use as a ledger. She flips back the cover and flicks the pages – they are covered in tightly packed script with the odd paper clipping pasted onto a page or a drawing here and there throughout. She turns to the first page and stares without seeing the words.

She slaps the book closed and throws it onto the floor as she collapses back onto the bed sobbing, as much in anger as with grief. Slowly, the sobs subside. A numbness spreads through her. Once again she feels alone in the world, believing that there is not one thing she can do about it.

She pushes herself upright with Sister Teresa's things scattered around her. She picks the diary up off the floor and contemplates what to do next. Sister Teresa had wanted her to read the diary and to be sure of her reasons for wanting to become a Carmelite. Pualele knows that she should go immediately to the prioress and hand over the trinkets and photos and the old nun's diary. Then she could focus on her upcoming vows and her future life in the convent, leaving Sister Teresa and her treacherous words in the past.

At least, that's what she *should* do.

CHAPTER 2

AUCKLAND HOSPITAL, 1 APRIL 2012
OLGA'S JOURNAL

It's April Fool's day and what an old fool I am, Pualele. I remembered to bring this book I am now writing in, but I forgot to bring something to write with! Luckily the nurse who's looking after us this morning has found me a lovely pen that she took from a consultant's table, and although I'm glad I can write I'm nervous every time someone walks past me, in case they're the owner of this pen.

I'm not sure what to tell you or where to start, except that here I am sitting in this ward and what a truly strange place it is. The atmosphere here is a little bit hopeful and a little bit frightening, although I'm not exactly sure how I feel.

There's eight of us here today, all hooked up to drips so that the chemical concoctions can enter our bodies through the ports in our chests, and we're all, I guess, hoping that it will be for some good. A girl in the next chair has her back half turned to me and a man in a suit on the other side is holding her hand. I don't think she wants to be here at all and certainly not sitting next to me as we take our poison, but I can't blame her. I know how I must look.

I understand that people are uncomfortable around me. Yesterday, a man across from me was wearing a T-shirt. I couldn't help but notice it – I see the image in the mirror every day – short, bald, wrinkled and ugly!

I asked the man. *What is that on your T-shirt?*

It's Gollum, he replied.

Funny, I said to him, *it looks just like me!*

He gave me a strained smile and I wasn't sure whether it was from pain or pity, but I suspect that I am more Gollum than Mother Theresa (God rest her soul).

When the girl came into the room today the seat next to me was the last space free, and I watched her hover in the doorway with a look of panic as she caught sight of me. The man in the suit was there with her. He whispered something into her ear before guiding her to the chair, smiling briefly at me as the girl reluctantly sat down on the La-Z-Boy. I imagine she must be about your age, yet here we are battling the same illness. It doesn't seem right that one so young should have this disease and I pray that she has a brighter prognosis than I do. The girl and the man don't see the Gollum sitting next to them now, and I think this is how it has been for a long time.

But it wasn't always like this. I haven't ever spoken to anyone about what happened, and even now I cannot look you in the eye and tell you what I must say, but instead I will write it down here like a coward, not even sure where to start. But start I must.

ଦ

DALMATIA, 1944

Our small village clung to the side of the mountains that crowded around the Adriatic. Over the centuries, we'd been invaded by the Ottomans, the Hun and the Venetians. Most often they came by sea, and although they raped the land and its people, they could no more remove us from our place in the world than they could destroy the mountains.

Stone walls hugged the hillside and they were like girdles around them, stopping the hillside from spilling into the sea. Further down, where the water lapped at the feet of the village, were the russet-tiled roofs of our church and the houses in the village proper. The church lay on the town square that from afar, looked like a sheet of discoloured paper by the side of the dirt road that connected us to the rest of the coast. That was my home.

World War II was well under way and our country was in the thick of it. I was almost thirteen, and until that last winter we spent in our village I really had no idea that things could go so wrong. Everything might have been different if we had run from the war earlier, or had emigrated with my father and older brother. But it's easy to sit here now and wonder *what if*?

Back then my friends and I still ranged across the rocky mountainside as if we hadn't a care in the world. Sometimes we played children's games like hide-and-go-seek. Other times, while we were supposed to be watching the sheep and goats or tending to garden plots, we would instead sit and talk. I loved that best of all.

And of all my friends, the one I loved most was Mila. I wish I had a picture of her, a coloured photograph. You would see how her dark hair fell down around her shoulders in waves of velvet. How, if you got close enough, you would see that her hazel eyes were flecked with gold and green. And you could imagine how she inhabited the world – like a magic fairy-woman, a vila come to honour us by just *being*.

She was a few years older than me, but it wasn't her age, it was her beauty that made her stand out like a nugget of gold in a prospector's pan. Next to her, I was nothing. My hair was that shade of brown you see for only a few brief days when the corn stalks turn from green to golden yellow. No one can ever remember it until they see it again. And then there was my oval face and sallow skin that I always thought made me look like an egg!

But it would be wrong of me to let you think my childhood was some sort of Balkan fairy tale. Yugoslavia was at war, with its people fighting amongst themselves, killing each other under the banner of one flag or another, all of them believing they were on the side of the just. I was ignorant in the way that children often are, knowing nothing until years later of the massacres by one side over the other, or the transport of Jews and gypsies to the East.

There were things I remember being afraid of – like the rumours about what might happen if the Partisans couldn't stop the Germans and the Ustashe. The adults talked amongst themselves of plans and contingencies – about the *what ifs* and the *how tos*. But it seemed to me that all of this was something the adults would sort out. I never really believed that any of these things would ever affect me.

I had my own plans. I hoped that one day I would be one of those who would leave for a better life in a foreign land. I had my sights firmly set on America and St Louis with its golden arches. The Americans called the city *The Gateway to the West*. That's where Mila's sister lived and we planned to follow just as soon as we could. My mother, on the other hand, had no intention of ever leaving our village. Mama had lived through one war already, and she had never contemplated leaving or living anywhere else, even as fear drove other people away. She often complained that I spent too much time dreaming about what I didn't understand and couldn't change. She said to me that I would do better if I accepted what God had in store for me instead of dreaming about things that would never happen and places I would never see. For Mama, dreams only made you sad for what you could never have. They were an extravagance for those who could afford to squander time dreaming, and in her words, *Dreaming never fed a family*.

When I write this now, I wish I could go back and find that girl with the tawny hair and the green eyes. I would take her hand and tell her that it is good to dream. I would let her know that sometimes bad things happen to decent people, and I would make her see that she was a good girl who never meant anyone any harm.

◯�

On a day when my mother had sent me in search of wild dandelion and parsnip, I foraged high above the village in the hope that I would find Mila and her twin brother, Oliver, tending their few sheep. I made it to the upper reaches of the mountain and my eyes scanned the landscape below for my friends. In the distance I could see the villages further along the coast with their own white stone houses and church spires.

As I rushed forward, my foot slipped and I fell onto the rocky path, peeling the skin on my knee back and making a small tear in my dress. I brushed away the blood with an already-muddied sleeve as a sweet-smelling hand clamped itself over my mouth. There wasn't time to think before Mila leaned forward in front of me and put her finger to her lips. I nodded as she removed her hand from my mouth and pulled me behind some boulders.

We heard loose stones sliding and then bouncing off the bigger rocks from somewhere above us, then nothing. Mila pressed in closer to me so that I was sandwiched between the boulder and her body. I felt the length of her against me, her hip bone pressing into my back and one of her legs hooked around mine. Through the softness of her chest pressed to my arm I could feel her fast-beating heart and I dared not move in case she should get up and leave. She leaned towards me, her face coming as close to my ear as she could without actually touching it.

Don't move. I held my breath waiting for more. I could've stayed there forever just like that, lying next to her on the mountain.

Got you!

There was a thump as someone landed on the ground below us and our screams echoed across the hillside.

My hand flew to my chest as I knelt on the ground, trying to catch my breath. Oliver was standing in front of us grinning, and as Mila struggled to her feet beside me she joined in the mirth. I watched the twins laughing at their own private joke and felt my face contort with anger. My eyebrows drew together and I pursed my lips in an effort to stop myself shouting at them.

Smile, Ola. Oliver stood next to his sister, both of them with wide grins on their faces. *You look like a cat's bum*.

Hand on my heart, those are the exact words he said to me – and me, well, I didn't feel like smiling. I wanted to be lying back where I was a minute before he had landed next to us. I didn't know how to explain to Oliver that he shouldn't be here with his crude jokes and idiotic smile, or how I would tell Mila that I'd rather be alone next to her and have her whisper to me again.

Oliver's eyes were on me and I felt my skin grow hot. I was naïve and didn't understand why my body betrayed me, blushing under his gaze. He'd stared right at me before and on those occasions I had turned away. But that day I returned the stare until embarrassment got the better of me and I looked away first. I heard him laugh and he said, *Let's go*. Without speaking Mila took hold of my wrist and with that one gesture I forgave her everything. I trailed behind her, her fingers like a bracelet around my arm.

☙

We headed off across the hillside, passing sheep that were oblivious to our movements. Where the patches of grass disappeared, the hillside spewed up lumpy formations from the stony ground, and Mila let go of my arm.

I followed them to the entrance of a cave we had found years before. I ducked my head as we entered, and waited a moment while my eyes adjusted to the light inside. It smelt of damp earth and rodent droppings.

Inside the cave, my cousin Dragan hovered over a glowing candle. His head was cocked to one side and his wild hair hung limply, casting spidery shadows across the long bundles lying in front of him. He was sixteen and over six feet in height, although you couldn't really tell how tall he was because of a stoop and a lame leg he dragged behind him. He often appeared as if he was trying to slip through the world unseen and I admit that there was something about him that was unsettling.

The bundles on the ground were wrapped in sheets of canvas. Out of the corner of one of them poked the butt of a rifle. I was afraid then of what we had stumbled into. Dragan nudged the canvas with his foot and we all heard the sound of glass bottles rolling against each other. Mila leant forward towards him.

Do you think it's Ustashe?

Death to Fascism! Freedom to the people! Dragan shouted, punching the air with his fist. *This has to be Partisans.*

Could be Germans.

They're thirty kilometres away. What do girls know about that stuff anyway!

Mila punched him on the arm and Dragan feigned great pain and rolled onto the floor.

Fool.

He sniffed and hauled himself up, the candle catching his grinning face.

So much for brotherhood and unity.

We saw Oliver at the back of the cave, lying down, his arm and upper body under a ledge that ran the length of the cave.

He called back at us. *Smells like piss in here.*

Oliver. Mila sounded more like Mama than herself.

Dragan made his way over to Oliver. *If it's sweet it'll be Partisans, if it's not it'll be Ustashe.* The boys snickered at Dragan's joke as Mila crouched down beside Dragan. The three of them carried on as if I wasn't there. I felt like an outsider. I didn't really understand the politics of the time, only that our people were Communists and Partisans. I was certain that if I was quiet I could slip out and head home without them noticing. But something stopped me. I watched in fascination in the candle light as Dragan rested his hand in the hollow of Mila's back, before she wriggled sideways away from him and his arm fell away.

Oliver backed out from under the ledge and craned his head towards the entrance.

Did you hear that?
Hear what?
Listen! Mila hissed.

Oliver and Dragan pushed the bundles back under the ledge. Oliver extinguished the candle and in the darkness we fanned the air with our arms to disperse the candle smoke. Mila hissed at us again and we hid wherever we could find cover. I dropped to the floor, landing on my grazed knee, and slid into a recess, not knowing exactly where the others were in the cave.

Men's voices could be heard growing louder.

The talking stopped as the light that illuminated the first few metres inside the cave was blocked. There was a clatter of metal, as if heavy bags were being dumped on the floor, and then grunting as the figures hefted the bags further inside, their bodies in profile against the outside light.

My foot was becoming numb as I pressed it into the wall of the cave. I hoped the men wouldn't stay long, but their movements were slow and careful, and I supposed they were ensuring that whatever they had brought with them was stowed safely out of sight.

My heart pumped harder as the grunting and pulling came nearer to my hiding place. I tried to hold as still as the rock I was pushed up against, but something was tickling my bare leg. I reached down with my free hand and felt the brush of fur on the back of my hand. I gasped and my legs moved involuntarily away from the rat. The pulling stopped, and for a moment there was stillness in the cave.

What was that?

There was a rattling of glass and the striking of a match then an oil lamp sprang into life. A man I didn't recognise swung the lamp around, an arc of light grazing the top of Mila's bowed head. The rat was sitting on the cave floor a few centimetres from where I was hiding. It froze momentarily in the lamplight before scurrying off towards the far wall of the cave.

Rats!

He turned back to his companion, who was bending over the bags. I watched their backs as they pushed them under a gap between the cave floor and the overhang, spending some time ensuring that everything was hidden from sight before extinguishing the lamp.

At last we heard them leave, and when there were no more sounds from outside, I felt myself relax, the pins and needles pricking my sleeping foot awake.

We emerged from our hiding spots. Amongst the search and the discussions of what to do next, nobody noticed the approaching footsteps until the light at the entrance of the cave was once again blocked by someone.

What . . . ?

Dragan and Oliver were closest to the entrance. Oliver ran straight at the figure silhouetted in the mouth of the cave before Mila and I had a chance to react. I saw the bigger frame fall to the side as the two smaller figures shot out into the sunlight. I ducked down into my hiding place as Mila sprang over the fallen man's legs. The man groaned, his feet scraping as he tried to stand. There was a pause before I heard him leaving the cave. I knew that I didn't have long before he would be back, so I quickly got to my feet and ran.

Outside, daylight burned into my eyes and paralysed me for a few seconds while I adjusted to the brightness. Before I could move, a large hand grabbed my shoulder and spun me around.

What in God's name do you think you're doing?

Father Bilić's fleshy red face shook as he spoke down at me. He was a tall man, his shape like that of a sack of grain hanging on a hook, and he squeezed my shoulder until I winced with the pain.

Please. You're hurting me.

That's nothing to what Ustashe would do to you. Who else was with you? Tell me! He shook me and I shut my eyes while tears leaked out. I tried to swallow but I was choking.

Tell me, Olga. His grip softened. But his voice stayed firm.

Ol . . . Oliver . . . and Dragan.

He released me, satisfied with the names I'd given, and tilted my head so I was forced to look at him again.

I'll walk you back to your mother.

☙

Father Bilić followed me down the stone path leading to my house. We picked our way between giant boulders and the homes that had been abandoned over time as our people had moved down the hillside towards the sea. The houses were like old men who had shrunk with age, their bones warping until there wasn't a straight line to be seen. The walls bore deep wrinkles as vines strangled the last of the life out of the buildings. If we'd paused we might have heard a rustling of leaves and sticks as some animal scuttled further into the belly of the houses. But the priest showed no sign of stopping until we were in front of my mother.

By the time we reached the end of the track, I was feeling ill. Father Bilić hadn't said a word. I wondered what he would tell my mother. It was hard for me to imagine which would be worse – being caught in a cave far above the point on the hillside that I was forbidden to cross on my own, or that I'd been in a cave alone with Dragan and Oliver. I couldn't decide which would enrage her the more. I had wild thoughts of running to Uncle Jure and telling him that we'd caught the priest hiding food away from everyone. That seemed my only hope of escaping my mother's anger and a beating with a switch, although a beating was nothing compared to the sharpness of her tongue.

One of the first things I learnt from Mama was that words could be more painful than any beating. I sometimes wished that I'd been born a boy. I thought that then she would have loved me more. She had endless time for my little brother, but she was impatient where I was concerned. The story I knew of my mother at that point was that she was a strong woman who had chosen my father over his younger brother. I know that Jure and she had much in common, not the least being that they were both Communists who were fierce supporters of an independent Croatia. Father was different. He had sought to build a life for us on the other side of the world and was committed to a capitalist future in New Zealand while my mother was resolute in her refusal to move. My father was a patient man and he bided his time, going back and forth from New

Zealand while trying to persuade my mother to join him. Despite their differences, my mother had made the decision to make a life with my father and she never wavered in her loyalty. I begrudgingly respected her for that.

I know some people would think their relationship unconventional – my father living and working in New Zealand while my mother stayed behind in Croatia. But I know you understand the situation our family found itself in, Pualele. There were many families like ours where fathers and older brothers had left to find a better, easier life. In that respect my family was no different to many. The only difference was my mother. She was inscrutable – she never complained or wailed the way some women did about their situations, she merely set her shoulder to the world and pushed on.

As Father Bilić and I reached the stands of pine and cypress, my feet dragged, knowing that I would no more run off to Uncle Jure than my mother would leave our village. Instead I hung my head and worried about what she would say. We'd been told it was dangerous to venture so far up the mountainside, that Ustashe or Germans might arrive and they'd slit our throats and leave our bodies for the birds and foxes.

As we neared our house, I could see the door open. The chickens fossicked for scraps in the yard while Mama worked in the vegetable patch, pulling the dark green leaves of blitve for our dinner. She stood up as we arrived, placing her hands on her hips. I felt Mama's gaze on me but I refused to meet her eye, hoping that she wouldn't notice the blood on my leg or the rip in my dress.

Could I have a word, Ana?

Of course.

I trailed Father Bilić and Mama to the door, following the worn shoe steps. Mama turned, blocking my way inside.

Go and find Ivica. He went fishing. He might have some srdele for us.

❦

I made my way to Ivica's house, all the while wondering what Father Bilić was saying to my mother. It wasn't so much what he would say as what my mother would believe I had been doing. She fawned over him and I believed she always imagined the worst of me. If Father Bilić said I was stealing, telling lies or cavorting with boys, Mama would believe him, as would the entire village. He was *always* right, no matter what. Everyone in the village accepted his advice as if he were an expert on everything, from the cultivation of crops to the gender of unborn babies. I didn't understand the power some men could wield in the world at that time, but I knew he held a position in our lives that I could never challenge.

Adults were a mystery to me, except for Uncle Jure. He was the most patient, calm human being I have ever known and, most importantly, he never made me feel bad. I spent many hours with him talking about my dreams of going with Mila to America. Despite his politics, he would nod wisely and join me in imagining my life in big foreign cities where everyone was rich. Jure was also my link to my father and brother in New Zealand. They had been gone so long that I could barely remember them; their faces had faded in my memory to a point where I couldn't see them any more. That is, until I heard Jure laugh his big belly laugh. It was a sound that filled the room and lifted you up till you felt you were floating. If I closed my eyes quickly before the laughter died away, for a moment I could see Papa's face. I meant no disrespect to Papa, but I admit that more often than not I pretended that Jure was my real father.

There was nobody at Ivica's when I got there, so I headed down to the small bay where the flotilla of small fishing boats waited in the shallows. I ran down the path, through trees and past gardens towards the sea. *Ola! Come help!* The old man had no relatives left in the village – we were his adopted family. He helped my mother on our small holding whenever he could, and in exchange she mended his clothes and provided him with her best bread.

Ivica was standing in knee-deep water and had a length of twine in one hand. In the other he held a crab between his middle finger and thumb. I took one end of the coiled twine while he tied the loose end around the crab, placing a flat stone on its underside. The crab waved its pincers in the air, trying desperately to escape Ivica's hand.

There! I'll throw. You pull it in.

I nodded as he swung the crab above his head, releasing the twine so that it flew out into the water where it landed with a *slap*, slowly sinking beneath the surface. He handed me the rope and I pulled it in slowly, hand over hand over hand.

The end of the rope was at my feet, the crab tied firmly and still trying to snip anything within its reach. Ivica picked it up and we repeated the throw and pull again. Hand over hand over . . .

Now I felt the insistent pull of the octopus, as every tentacle sucked onto the crab. A few more pulls and we could see the mottled orange and brown creature as it trailed through the water. Ivica stepped further into the sea and yanked the twine up in the air, grabbing the octopus at the base of its head above the tentacles. As he held it, the colours drained from the frightened octopus until its skin turned white. He stabbed it between the eyes before flipping its head inside out, exposing the slimy yellow-white interior.

He held it high in the air and we laughed.

Your mama will be pleased with you.

My joy evaporated.

Wait here. I'll get the fish.

As Ivica walked back towards his boat, I felt sick to my stomach. I was dreading going home, regardless of whether I had srdele and octopus for Mama.

As I waited for Ivica, angry voices floated down from the hill above. I couldn't hear what they were saying, but I could see Mila and Dragan arguing beneath an almond tree. He was holding her by her wrists and, as they continued to face each other, their voices dropped until they were a silent picture framed by trees and land. A few seconds passed and then Mila rose up onto her toes and kissed Dragan on the cheek. She pulled away from him and disappeared into the trees. Dragan took a step after her before changing direction and limping away.

I was puzzled by the exchange, but I quickly returned to thinking about my own situation. I wondered if the priest had finished telling my mother where I had been that afternoon, and if he had already moved on to look for the others. As I watched Dragan disappear into the distance, I hoped that he wouldn't be angry with me when Father Bilić found him.

When I returned home the priest had indeed gone, and my mother was peeling potatoes. She glanced my way when I came in but didn't stop paring the potato in her hand.

Clean the fish.

The terse words and firm set of her mouth told me all I needed to know. I kept my head bent over the fish as I picked up a knife and twirled it in my fingers. I crouched down on the floor over a wooden board and laid out the fish and octopus. I started by scraping off the filmy covering on the octopus, then cutting out its black beak and its innards full of tiny crabs from its last meal. I chopped the tentacles into lengths, the suction caps staring up at me like a hundred little eyes before I cast them into an iron pot. The rest of the octopus I sliced into strips, flicking them into the pot to cover the eyes. I turned to the fish while Mama started chopping onion and garlic. The only other sounds I could hear were from the animals outside. As I gutted the fish, my face grew hot. I tried not to cry.

There had been rumours in the village that the German army was advancing and might soon arrive on the coast. But it wasn't the first time this had happened to us. We had been occupied by the Italians and when they had finally capitulated, many villagers had chosen to evacuate and leave the Partisans to fight. But some, like my mother, weren't so easily moved.

Pero wandered across from where he'd been sleeping on the floor, dragging a blanket behind him and rubbing his knuckles into his eyes.

Mama?

She put the knife down and opened her arms to him before scooping him up and leaving the house. Tears came as I continued with dinner preparations, wishing that I could follow them. When they returned with Uncle Jure, the octopus was stewing in its pot, the potatoes were boiling and the cleaned fish sat on the bench ready to be grilled over the fire.

Smells good! Jure winked at me. *Octopus, my favourite.*

Pero ran up to me and held out his hand.

Look what Barba Jure made me! It was a whistle made from a hollowed stick. He put it to his lips and let out a shrill note that pierced the air.

Outside, Pero. My mother pointed at the door and my little brother ran out, still blowing the whistle as he went.

Why do you make such awful things?

It's fun for them, Ana! You're so tense. Jure placed a hand on her shoulder. She stepped away from under the hand and swivelled around to face him.

How can I relax knowing that there are Ustashe everywhere and maybe Germans? And now Olga is running all over the countryside like a wild animal. She turned on me, her hands waving in the air and spit flying from her mouth as she spoke. *Do you have any idea what they do to young girls?*

Stop it. It was Jure's turn to shout. He paused as he calmed himself, letting out a long slow breath through his nose. When he spoke again his voice was firm but quiet. *She won't go up there again – will you, Ola?*

Mama was pacing and becoming more agitated. Her face was red and blotchy and she looked ready to explode. Pero stood in the doorway, his mouth open. His lips started to quiver.

Ana, Uncle Jure continued, *I can get you and the children away. Somewhere safer.* He held her hands and coaxed her across the room to a stool.

He carried Pero to the table. Mama reached out, touching my brother's cheek. He clasped her hand and crawled into her lap. I put the food on the table and somehow found the words as I looked at my mother.

Sorry.

No, I'm sorry . . . I . . . Her voice trailed off as Jure squeezed her arm, placing a glass in front of her. She cradled the wine in her trembling hands, her anger visibly weakening.

Just don't go up there again.

෬

God forgive me as I write this, but I have committed to writing the truth down here, and so I admit that I was a reluctant churchgoer. I remember Sundays, walking with my mother and Pero to Mass. I hated the sermons preaching fear and guilt, especially when I had done something to be guilty about. But I was obedient, if nothing else, and recited the prayers by rote and ensured that no one ever knew I believed anything other than what was expected of me. Even then I was a kind of fraud.

My mother was a different story – she was both Communist and Catholic at the same time. You might find this hard to believe, but my mother was a complex woman. I can't tell you whether she was having a bet both ways or simply that she saw no conflict in being a churchgoer and Communist, but she showed no signs of giving up the church. At Mass I could watch her being carried along to a different place by the prayers and incantations. It was as if she truly believed that God would protect us and that he would tell her what to do. She was a contradiction in terms – that was another thing I knew about her.

The following Sunday after Mass I went in search of Oliver and Mila. I found the twins watching over their flock of sheep grazing above the village. In the trees surrounding them there were hundreds of lastavice sitting on the branches, small black birds with split tails. The twittering was so loud in the trees that my friends didn't hear me enter the clearing. Mila jumped when she noticed me.

You gave me a fright.

Sorry. I sat down next to them.

Oliver looked my way. *Thanks for sending the priest my way.*

I felt the creep of pink rising up my neck and onto my face. No one spoke. We stared at the few sheep that were milling around a clump of grass.

I got such a hiding. This is the first time I've been able to sit down since yesterday.

Mila rolled her eyes.

I promised Mama I wouldn't go up there again.

But Ola, that's just it! Oliver jumped to his feet, frightening the lastavice from their perches and sending them skyward. *We're scavenging for food and minding these bags of bones while there's plenty hidden away – but she didn't want to hear about that!*

Oliver picked up a stick off the grass and threw it at the sheep, scattering them.

What happened to Dragan?

Oliver stood still, watching his sister. *Ask her.*

Mila shook her head, glaring back at her brother as he walked away.

I waited for Mila to speak, but she just chewed her bottom lip and stared into the distance. I yearned to grab her hand and ask her things. I wished we could talk in the easy way we always had, but I felt that easiness slipping away. I searched desperately for the words to bring her back to me. But it seemed at that moment my friend was as separate from me as the swallows waiting in the trees. I looked intently down at my bare feet, dread flooding my body as she turned away. She had gone only a few steps before she looked back.

Thanks . . . for not telling about me.

I thought she might say more and we both stayed where we were for a while, with me willing her to come back.

I'll see you later maybe.

I stood there mute as I watched her moving away through the grass. The fading blue dress clung to her slim waist and pulled across the swell of her buttocks as she took long strides towards the trees and the path home. As she disappeared from sight, it occurred to me that I didn't know her at all.

I headed towards home, walking through a group of fig trees, catching a whiff of the humus rising up from the damp earth. As I walked on, I felt a sting on my neck and I raised my hand to brush the insect away. Then something hit the back of my arm and another landed my dress with a thud. I twisted around and scanned the trees.

Where are you? The tiny shots kept coming, but they were missing me now as I moved for shelter behind a tree. I saw a dried kernel of corn fall down at the foot of the tree.

Dragan. If that's you, stop it. The corn kept coming and I sank down on my haunches and waited. *Please.*

He dropped down from one of the trees, landing with a squishing sound. I moved out from behind my hiding place.

That was for the other day, cousin. He grinned at me, a slingshot in one hand and a bag of corn kernels in the other.

How'd you know it was me?

He shrugged.

Dragan had had a hard life with his father, Tome. The story goes that Tome, famous for felling a brown bear in the forests of Bosnia with a slingshot and an iron ball, disappeared with the gypsies one summer, only to return with the travelling Ciganin caravan the following year accompanied by a wife, Biljana, and their baby, Dragan.

When Biljana died giving birth to their second child, a stillborn baby boy, Tome took comfort in drink. Even when he almost lost Dragan to polio, he left the boy to raise himself as the next drink became the most important thing to him. Tome's greatest – and possibly his only – gift to his son was to ensure that Dragan knew how to use a slingshot.

Have you seen Mila? Dragan moved too close to me and I stepped away. Something was tugging at me, pulling me away from his question. I was suddenly protective of Mila and decided to ignore him.

Did you get into trouble? I enquired innocently.

No. By the time your friend Bilić got to our front door, Papa was already throwing anything he could get his hands on. He called him a fat Jesus whore with a donkey's ass for a face. He laughed.

I didn't know how to respond to Dragan's delight in this. I had nothing against his father myself, I just didn't want to cross him, and so I stood there staring blankly at Dragan.

I'm going back up there to get some wine and stuff . . .

What if you get caught?

I can protect myself.

What? A boy with a slingshot and a bad leg?

Dragan huffed and turned away.

What do you know? He stood up straight and I was suddenly aware of how much older he appeared. His dark blond hair was swept back off his face and it curled over the back of his collar. There was something threatening in the shadow on his jawline and in the muscles that flexed in his arms as he balled his hands into fists, a sneer pulling at his face. I had to stop myself from stepping away from him, but before I could move he stormed away with his distinctive lolloping walk through the figs and down the hillside. For reasons I didn't understand, everything I did or said made people angry with me.

Feeling a gentle breeze, I stood there alone. The last few lastavice were dancing from tree to tree and I watched them as they flitted into the pines and vanished behind me. If something happened that they didn't like, they just flew off into the sky. I wished I was a bird. I wanted to grow giant black wings and take to the air and not stop until I made it to America.

ଔ

The Jugo wind came, blowing from the south and bringing with it an ill-temperedness that had everyone out of sorts. I was feeding Šuša when I heard the sound of boots – *clump-clump, clump-clump* – as they headed towards us along the lane. I dropped the bowl, which bounced off Šuša's head and landed in the mud, sending the goat scurrying back into her stall. I ran too, inside to my mother, hearing my own heart thumping in time with the marching outside.

Mama was sitting with Pero, her eyes unblinking as she looked past me to the approaching soldiers. She got up and pushed Pero into my arms. He and I clung to each other as she walked to the doorway and stood there, her arms by her side, back straight and perfectly still.

One of the soldiers stepped forward, as fair skinned as we were olive toned, a pale creature in a grey uniform. He looked as though he had never been outdoors before, with hair as white as a goat's coat, and translucent eyes like the scales of a fish. He cleared his throat and spoke in halting Dalmatian as he read from the papers clutched in his hand.

Gospodje Mastrović?

I saw Mama incline her head forward as the soldier went on, informing us that the Germans were requisitioning our house.

We remained exactly where we were. I tried to make sense of what was happening, and I hid my fear just as Mama hid a piece of kauri gum in a small wooden box under her bed.

I thought I should move, stand with my mother, but I was paralysed by a fear that trapped me there on the floor.

Pero let out a whimper. Mama turned her back on the soldiers and moved towards us. Her face was expressionless, but her eyes were blazing like a cat ready to pounce. She bent and picked up Pero, hugging him to her, talking quietly and running her hand over his silky hair. I sat, willing her to notice me.

Come. We must get our things. I stood while she walked towards the doorway, but in the few moments that her back had been turned, the soldier had moved too and was now standing in front of her at the door.

You. Wait. She spat the words at the fish-eyed soldier and tried to close the door in his face. His foot shot out and stopped the door before it could shut. The soldier stood there, his cheeks the colour of claret.

YOU. WILL. WAIT. My mother stared at the man. She barely came up to the soldier's shoulder, but the authority in her voice made him stop right where he was standing.

I'd not a word of German in me, then or now, but I understood what the fish-eyed soldier was saying as he held up his open hand showing five fingers, keeping his foot in the doorway. We had five minutes.

CHAPTER 3

SAMOA, AUGUST 1979
PUALELE

For Pualele Sina Auva'a, life is changing for ever, to the sound of the howls of her mother and aunties. Her father pulls her away before she drowns in all the tears, pushing her on board the bus that will take them from their coastal village into Apia. Pualele is installed in the back seat between her father and her brother Kasi, her bag tucked under her legs. One last look out the back window: she catches a glimpse of her maternal grandfather, Papavai, who stands behind the crying women, his hand raised like an Indian chief's goodbye.

She swallows the lump in her throat and unintentionally takes a deep breath of the diesel fumes that have filled the idling bus. She feels sick. They pull out of the village and she looks away from the people, focussing instead on the rising sun that sends out orange and yellow and pink crêpe-paper-like streamers of light that fall festively across the island.

The south-eastern coast road turns inland and the bus climbs the road to Le Mafa Pass, creaking from the weight of all the people and their luggage. At the top Pualele sees the ocean in the distance and, for the very first time, the valley behind them and the surrounding hillsides. The area overflows with tree ferns as tall as the spire on the Lotofaga Catholic Church. Coconut palms hide their bounty under green umbrellas while towering banyan trees send roots to the ground like wax dripping from a candle. Sprinkled throughout are teak trees, their leaves the size of doormats with a weave of vines and ferns hidden beneath. The island is a vibrant green with a sapphire sky and white cumulus-sheep clouds that scud through the valley as if searching for a way out.

Her father wakes her. Pualele has never been to Apia and she cannot believe the scene in front of them, streets turning every which way and so many buildings and houses – she could never have imagined that such a place existed. She is nine years old and has never left the south side of the island, and yet here she is in Apia, on her way to New Zealand. Her father has told her that they will be taking a boat to the Fiji Islands, and then they will take a plane. A plane! She stops listening because it just does not seem possible that someone as insignificant as Pualele Sina Auva'a should be going on boats and aeroplanes to New Zealand. Sister Xavier has given her some rosary beads that the Irish nun says came all the way from Rome. Pualele laces them in-between her fingers as she mutely walks a few paces behind her father and brother through the streets of Apia.

They put on their best clothes for the walk; they are city people now. Pualele fusses with her lavalava. She suspects that it has come from someone else, but it is so beautiful, with enormous crimson hibiscus flowers splashed across it, that she doesn't care. She winds it around her body, concealing the plain black skirt and white shirt that were also leaving gifts. She imagines herself to be just like the English Queen in her stylish touring outfit in the photo Sio brought back to the village. It was taken by a photographer from the *Samoan Times* and shows the palagi Queen waving from the gangway of the royal yacht *Britannia*. A hat and gloves are what Pualele needs.

As she thinks about what kind of hat she'd choose if she were given the chance, she sees it: an enormous royal blue and white cruise liner waiting harbour side. Just like the Queen's. There are people pouring out of it onto the street ahead of them, men and women talking loudly with big boxy cameras swinging around their necks. Pualele feels shy as they laugh and chatter. Her English is not yet good enough to catch everything, but she can hear them asking for directions to Aggie Grey's and how could they get transport to the Robert Louis Stevenson Museum on the outskirts of the city. She avoids their eyes, keeping her head bowed and counting her rosary beads.

As the Auva'a family walk along in their finery, fat droplets of water start to fall from the sky. They fall slowly at first and then pick up speed, hitting the ground and splashing up onto Pualele's hibiscus-patterned lavalava. She is alarmed as spots soak into the fabric.

Father immediately pulls his new fawn cotton shirt over his head; her brother does the same with his until they are both bare-chested. Kasi turns and grabs at Pualele's lavalava. She gapes at the length of material with its water freckles as Kasi spins her around until she stands there in the street – plain, simple Pualele standing in the nun's clothes, looking every bit a girl from the village.

The palagi laugh as they watch the Samoans rip off their clothes and run for cover. A few of them even lift their cameras from under huge black umbrellas and snap away as the Auva'as head back to their modest accommodation, their best clothes saved from the offending rain.

꩜

Pualele's wide feet slap the wet road as they make their way past the *Queen Elizabeth 2*. Kasi grins at his little sister's full bottom lip, pushed out and turning down at the edges. *We'll be getting on our boat soon.*

When? She looks at the liner with its royal blue strip sitting alongside the port. She hopes that people on board won't remember her as she plods along in her missionary garb.

Tomorrow.

It's sooo big. Pualele tilts her head right back so that she can see all the way up to the upper decks of the *QE2*.

Not that boat, silly. That *boat*.

She follows her brother's gaze and her eyes fall on another smaller vessel. Where the *QE2* floats like a grand Cathedral, this vessel looks like a fale. *Samoan Reefer* is a refrigerated cargo ship. It transports bananas, but between the decks there is enough room for passengers. This is their *QE2*.

Pualele waits for Kasi to laugh as she imagines being loaded into the hold with the bananas. She watches as the stevedores carry enormous green bunches of the fruit into the hold. There is no gangplank decorated with bunting, simply an open port side, like a gash in the ship's belly. Its hull is painted white, the better to reflect the sun's heat, but it isn't the bright shiny colour of the *QE2*'s upper decks or Kasi's new shirt – it is the colour of crushed shells on a beach.

The Auva'as board the *Samoan Reefer* early the next morning. As they stand on the deck waiting for the ship's hold doors to be secured ready for sailing, the giant *QE2* pulls away from port and heads out into the harbour. Pualele watches with glassy eyes, her nose streaming, as the foreign tourists on board the cruise liner wave goodbye to Apia, their thoughts having already turned to the next place on their itinerary, another South Pacific paradise full of its own Aggie Greys and Stevenson monuments.

The Auva'as' ship sails from Upolu, island-hopping all the way from Samoa to Tonga and Niue and then onto Nadi. The whole journey takes two weeks and Pualele spends most of the time at sea in the small four-berth cabin vomiting. At Nuku'alofa they are joined by an old Tongan man. The ship isn't due to sail again until that evening, and knowing she won't get any sleep once the *Reefer* hits the open ocean, Pualele lies on her bunk resting and thinking about what might be happening in the village while her brother and father wait up on deck. She notices the new arrival only when she hears him strike a match. She turns her head on the pillow of the lower bunk and observes him as he lights his pipe. As the wisps of smoke float through the air towards her, she feels ill and is soon bent in half over a waiting bucket. They haven't yet set sail, but she is already vomiting, and not for the first time she wishes she hadn't been the one chosen to go to Auckland.

The man watches her from across the cabin, continuing to puff on his pipe. Finally she stops retching and crawls back onto her bunk, where she faces the wall and stares at the graffiti carved into the cabin wall. *Ito was here Dec '76*. She tentatively reaches out and lets her fingers run over the grooves. *Island Girls R Da Best! Salu loves KeKe*.

Pualele hears the man tap the remains of the pipe onto the floor and grind the ash into the wood with the toe of his shoe. There are a few shuffled steps and then he is standing by her bed. She can feel the heat of him. She wills the man to go away. She can hear his clothing rustling near her ear and she considers screaming, but her cracked lips are fused together and no matter how much she tries to part them they remain sealed.

His hand skims over her slight body without touching, and then in front of her he drops a boiled sweet wrapped in cellophane. He shuffles back to his bunk and Pualele stares at the orange lolly. She wants to thank the man, but she feels guilty at having been afraid of him when all he had wanted to do was to show her kindness. Life in the Auva'as' village was much easier than all of this. Pualele knew what was expected of her back there, but out here in the world she finds it impossible to know how to behave. Mama would know what she should do, but Pualele doesn't want to know the rules for living in the world, she simply wants to be back home where she belongs.

ଓଃ

In Nadi the Tongan man leaves them and Pualele begins to feel better. Her father arranges for her travelling skirt and blouse to be laundered and she is comforted by the smell of starch and soap. It is with enthusiasm that she boards the flight to New Zealand, noticing that palagi travel on planes too. She might have been less eager if she had known that the journey would take just over four bumping hours. But it isn't Pualele's way to complain about anything.

ଓଃ

Over the roar of the engine, there is a loud bang followed by a continual whirring sound coming from the underbelly of the plane, as if it might explode any second. She has listened carefully to the air hostess, who has explained the basic emergency procedures on departure, so Pualele looks up at where the emergency oxygen masks are ready to be deployed and prepares herself, but no masks descend from the ceiling and there is no sign of the hostess. The other passengers seem unconcerned. They simply continue reading, or sit back with their eyes closed. Even her father is calm as he holds the Bible in front of him and mouths the words as he reads. Kasi is asleep, leaning into the side of the plane and dribbling slightly as a low rumble comes from his throat.

Pualele sits between her father and brother, her anxiety growing in direct proportion to the excitement she senses in the air crew and the other passengers. Perhaps this is what you do when you are about to die – you accept His plan and grow excited at the prospect of entering eternal life. But such acceptance is not what Pualele feels at this moment; instead, she wants to see her mother one last time before she dies. Terror rises up through the vibrating fuselage and Pualele grasps Iosefo Auva'a's fleshy arm as the air hostess passes by. *Ten minutes until landing.* Her father squeezes her hand and then returns to his Bible, this time speaking the words out loud.

'... *and some fell among thorns; and the thorns sprung up, and choked them. But others fell onto good ground, and brought forth fruit* ...'

Pualele stops hearing the words after a while. Instead, she concentrates on not crying as she tries in vain to stop the warmth that is leaking out between her legs onto the seat.

☙

The plane taxis to the terminal and the Auva'as alight in varying states of enthusiasm. Father is observant and slow moving, as if he wants to savour everything: the cool breeze that comes off the mangroves and mingles with the plane's fumes; the ground staff shepherding the new arrivals towards the building; and the other passengers, chattering about their Pacific adventures. Kasi is sombre, scuffing his feet as he walks along the tarmac.

Pualele bends her head and walks several paces behind her father and brother, her first steps in New Zealand being full of shame and self-loathing. She is fearful that someone will notice the wet patch at the back of her lavalava and hopes that the white men and women won't send her back for her indiscretion. Little flashes of shame shoot through her as she imagines the people who own the plane finding her sodden seat – and then the almost paralysing fear of having Aunty Sefi discover that she has peed her pants. Perhaps she will be sent back so that one of the other Auva'a children can take her place. It never occurs to her to question why she is going to New Zealand instead of one of her other siblings. The twins are too small to be leaving Mama, but she isn't pretty like Lani or clever like Sione. She is just plain old Pualele.

Eventually they find their luggage, the biggest bag having exploded. The twine used to tether it together has snapped and the clothes within the woven mat have spilled over the concrete floor of the luggage claim area. Pualele is mortified to see her underwear lying on the ground in full view of the other passengers, and she can no longer hold the tears back. Father struggles to place all the clothes back into the middle of the mat and he speaks urgently to Kasi, who sits on top of the pile while Father ties the twine. The other passengers walk around them, carefully avoiding the small family in case they should be asked to help them collect their scattered possessions. The palagi don't realise that the new immigrants would never dream of asking anyone for anything.

Finally the bags and assorted luggage are loaded onto a trolley and trundled towards the Customs officials. The Auva'as' passports are stamped: *Three months – visitor's permit*. Father leads the way, head held high with pride, as he and his two children walk through the doors towards their new life.

Welcome to Auckland. Aunty Sefi is as large as two men put together and she approaches her brother-in-law and his children with a smile that threatens to split her face in half. There are kisses and hugs all round. Aunty grabs Pualele and hugs her so that the small girl almost suffocates between her aunt's enormous breasts. Pualele gasps for breath as Aunty clutches her upper arms and holds her out for inspection.

You're too skinny, she laughs. *I'll feed you up.*

Aunty keeps laughing as a horn hoots and makes Pualele jump. The front of a long black Lincoln Continental hearse swings up to the footpath and Uncle Sam hops out of the driver's seat. He looks like a younger version of his brother, and Pualele is amazed to note that one of Uncle Sam's ears sits slightly higher than the other – just like her father's. Sam is half Sefi's size, but he is measured in his movements and walks towards them with no sense of urgency, leaving the jitterbug excitement to Sefi.

It's a work car. Aunty grins and nods. *Soooo proud,* she breathes, clutching her hand to her chest.

Pualele isn't sure whether Aunty is proud of the car or Uncle.

Let's go! We live in Richmond Road, Grey Lynn. One day we buy the house – Richmond Road – very good place to live.

Pualele's jaw falls open. She isn't certain she's heard it right the first time, as Aunty's speech slips between Samoan and English and the words become mangled together. Then Pualele becomes convinced of what she's heard. Aunty says the name of the road twice – *Rich Man Road*! Pualele's spoken English isn't very good, but she understands these words and that she is going to live in *Rich Man Road!*

The thrill she felt when she first started the journey to New Zealand returns. It even helps her forget about the wet lavalava, until Uncle speaks to her.

You sit with us in the front.

Pualele stares at the front bench seat with its fine leather upholstery and lingering smell of incense. She considers running back towards the plane.

Come, Pualele. We're very happy you're here.

Father gives Pualele a push in the small of her back.

Reluctantly, she walks towards the car and stands by the passenger door, the drive to the house in Rich Man Road suddenly more terrifying than any of the boat or plane journeys in the world. Kasi is already in the back behind the driver's seat, his feet on the leather as he reaches into the boot where their bags are piled and where a coffin would normally be.

Feet off, Aunty screeches at him, her face crumpling into a frown.

She is at the door now and grabs Kasi by his waistband, pulling him out of the car, his backside leading the way. Aunty releases him and Kasi struggles to stand as she seizes his arm, her head shaking as she makes a clicking sound with her tongue.

You're not in Samoa now, Afakasi.

He squirms as she pinches the back of his arm.

What do you want with that? She nods with her head at the fala mat he has tucked under his free arm.

To sit on.

Aunty snatches it away. The Auva'a siblings remain motionless while Aunty drums her fingers on the pandanus weave, considering her options.

It will keep such a beautiful car clean from our travelling clothes. We will all sit on one. Father's voice is firm as he steps forward.

Aunty's frown deepens and her mouth opens, forming an 'o' as she turns towards Father, her shoulders pulling back so her chest reaches forward to confront him. Pualele holds her breath and inspects the white rims of the Lincoln's wheels while Aunty and Father hold their positions on the pavement. She prays that Father will say something, and as she lifts her gaze to see what is happening, she spots Kasi standing calmly by the car. He gives her a quick nod and Pualele starts to breathe again.

Father waits patiently, his face soft and open. *Come now, Sefi. You don't want our village bums on these seats, do you?*

Aunty clears her throat, wobbling where she stands just as Uncle arrives back from returning the airport trolley. *Sefi?*

Her scowl vanishes and in its place her happy, beaming face reappears. She glances at Uncle Sam before turning back to Father, laughing now as if he has just told her the funniest joke she's ever heard. *That's right, brother – village backsides. We will all sit on one.* She turns back towards the car, laughing still as she thrusts the mat towards Pualele, who wants to take it and jump in the back, snuggling in between her father and Kasi. Instead she takes the criss-cross pandanus leaves from Aunty and places the laufala on the tan leather seat between the driver's and passenger's seats, promptly depositing her backside on top. Uncle raises an eyebrow at Aunty. She shrugs and sits next to Pualele, as Uncle starts the car and heads for *Rich Man Road*.

CHAPTER 4

OLGA'S JOURNAL

My mouth waters as I think about all the food my mother piled into the middle of that old blanket. There was olive oil, goat's cheese wrapped in muslin, a hunk of bread and the last of our pršut.

But there was no thinking to be had on that day. I threw what clothes I could lay my hands on into the middle of another blanket and we tied them in knots. Mother inserted a broom handle under the knots and we each held an end as we walked back towards the door with the bundles swinging between us.

Wait. Mother put her end of the stick down. She walked back towards the deep window sill that opened out to the chicken coop behind our house. From the sill, she snatched up the only photograph we had of my father and brother, slipping it inside her hip pocket. The image was grainy, and staring back in sepia tones were the two unsmiling men leaning on their gum-digger shovels. There was a watermark stain across the top of their heads, and someone had written on the bottom of the photo – *Awanui, Northland, Novi Zeland, 1939*.

Outside, three German soldiers milled around the yard and laughed as they taunted the goat. They tempted her with fresh leaves from an olive branch, and then flicked her in the face as she came near. They turned when they heard us at the door. The soldier who had spoken to my mother earlier stepped forward. His eyes were on the dried ham leg under my mother's arm.

Nein! Nein! Sie müssen bleiben!

My mother dropped her end of the stick again and walked forward until she was standing alone in front of the gathered men. She pushed through them and they watched as she walked into the stable where Šuša and Darko, the donkey, were sheltering. She tethered the animals together and led them out into the yard. The young soldier was becoming apoplectic.

Nein!

As he continued to shout, another soldier walked into the yard flanked by two others.

Entschuldigen Sie bitte, Frau Mastrović. The man who spoke seemed a little older than the others, and wore a slightly different grey uniform. He sported a moustache in the style of the time and, below a greying widow's peak and moist forehead, were eyes the same colour as his uniform. He walked to the front of the group.

Please, he said in Croatian. *Food stays, bitte.*

I'd an uneasy feeling. He was smiling, this man, but the smile had not reached his voice, and as his lips parted I could see the glint of gold in his teeth. The other soldier had been demanding in his recited Dalmatian, but this man was measured and confident. From the doorway, I watched my mother and the man facing off like roosters in a cock fight.

I didn't hear the sound, but I saw the lob of spittle land on the man's face. It slid down his cheek and for a moment I thought I might have been imagining things. No one moved.

Pero started to giggle. The soldier turned his head and focussed on my little brother and Pero hid his face in the folds of my dress. The soldier reached into his pocket, pulled out a white handkerchief and very slowly wiped the spittle off his face. He refolded the handkerchief carefully, and placed it back into his pocket.

His face was impassive and his eyes were steady on my mother. His hand slowly moved and rested on the Luger nestled in the holster hanging at his side. As he undid the clip, it sounded like the flick of a whip. I winced.

Is there a problem?

Uncle Jure stepped out of the trees that lined the lane. His eyes darted from my mother to the German. He walked forward slowly but without hesitation to Mama's side, resting his hand on her shoulder.
Meine . . . Schwester.

Sprechen sie Deutsch?

Ein bischen. I was a sailor. Captain was German.

Then my Croatian is better than your German. Tell your sister that if she spits in my face again – I won't be so friendly.

Entschuldigung. There must be a mistake. She is . . . alone, you can see . . . my brother . . .

A Partisan.

No. Mama's fight turned to panic.

Why should I believe you people? You are liars. Where is he?

I have a letter. He's in New Zealand.

Mama retrieved a letter from the house, smoothing down the grey and red stamps that were peeling off. The soldier took the letter from her and examined the postmarks and stamps, which had started to curl away from the paper. He opened the envelope and cast his eye over my father's handwriting, raising an eyebrow as a smirk played at his lips. He held the envelope in his hands, and as he looked at my mother, he ripped it slowly in half. Jure's grip on her shoulder increased at the tearing sound of the envelope.

We are peaceful people here at the blessing of your government. You would do well to remember that, madam.

My mother muttered something under her breath as her body seemed to be about to launch itself forward at the soldier. I was cowering behind and I squeezed my eyes shut, waiting for what terrible thing would happen next.

Please, Ana, Uncle Jure spoke quickly to her.

They're taking the house.

Enough. Your sister and the children will leave. Food will stay. He paused and I watched as his chest rose and fell as if in an effort to draw in as much air as possible.

There was a shuffling as someone else approached.

Please, sir. Take my home. I am an old man. It is bigger and I have more supplies. Take it all. Ivica's words whistled out, singing from a mouth that had lost most of its teeth. His words sounded reverential, but as he lifted his head and uncurled his crumpled form he was more like a benevolent king come to give alms to the poor.

The German's hand caressed the gun at his hip. *You,* pointing at my uncle. *What's this man saying?*

He says take his house. He has lots of food. Bigger house. More food. Please. Jure was stumbling over the words, distracted by my mother, who appeared to be on the verge of snapping. We all waited for the German – Mama biting back words, Jure and Ivica trying to appear benign – while I bit my lower lip as Pero embedded himself in my side.

If your . . . sister . . . should forget who is in charge here, I will not be so lenient next time.

He clicked his heels together and walked stiffly away. He spoke quickly to the other men waiting behind him, and then in a flurry of one-armed salutes he stalked off back down the laneway. Another unsmiling soldier came forward. He had a large khaki canvas bag in one hand and a knapsack on his back. He barely hesitated as he tore the ham away from my mother to the sound of his comrades' laughter. He turned to Ivica and shouted in German, pushing Ivica in the small of his back so that he almost fell over. Another soldier took some rope and led the goat and donkey out of their pen.

Ivica led the way and the soldiers followed, but not before pulling open our blanketed parcels and taking the cheese and bread with them, leaving the rest of our possessions scattered on the ground. They marched two abreast along the lane, back towards my uncle's house and the rest of our small village, while I stood there and watched.

It was a terrible thing to be standing there powerless. I wanted someone, anyone, to do *something*, to stop the soldiers and to make them bring our animals back. Most of all I wanted those soldiers to go away and for life to be as it was before they came. Jure stayed with us for a while and I remember him mussing up my hair as my mother stood there with her mouth pinched shut. But then he too left us.

Wait here. I'll go and make sure Ivica is okay. I'll be back with food.

We watched him leave, our precious belongings lying at our feet. I noticed how the trees and shrubs were now covered in a light film of dust from the Germans' boots with their rounded black leather toes and thick tread. I thought I heard their guttural voices on the breeze. And I wondered how many others would also be receiving unsolicited houseguests. As I walked over to stare into the empty animal stalls, I saw the outlines in the dirt of the standard issue soles that had trampled uninvited all over our village.

☙

Large anvil-shaped clouds tinged with pale yellow and mauve hung over the Adriatic, like fading bruises on the delicate sky. Mama sent Pero and me to the chicken coop and we searched out several fresh eggs, grateful we hadn't collected them earlier in the day. We placed the eggs carefully in a basket, the chickens gathering around us hoping for scraps from the kitchen, while Mama busied herself collecting our belongings from the yard and returning them to the house. Pero and I remained outside. He picked up a branch and drew in the dirt while I sat on my heels and leant against the wall of the house and wondered where we would go if we left here.

I'd never been more than ten kilometres away from the place I'd been born, but it hadn't stopped me dreaming. Mama had always said she would never leave our village, not even to join Papa and Ivan in New Zealand. She said they would come back, and then we'd be a family again. But they had been gone since just before Pero was born, and although I missed them I didn't really know them any more.

Somewhere in the years between Papa and Ivan leaving, I had lost the ability to recall their faces and they had become little more than a memory brought forth by Jure's laughter or the tilt of Pero's head when he was listening. The grainy photo Mama held dear to her was little more than a fiction to me and those unsmiling men looking back at me could have been any two men in some foreign land. When I thought about it, I felt guilty that I had somehow 'lost' them. I felt guilty that I hadn't tried harder to maintain a clear picture in my mind of who they were. Uncle Jure had stepped into their shoes and I had never felt alone or unsafe. I came to accept that Papa and Ivan were gone for now, and that was alright.

Come on, Pero.

He hesitated. He looked up at the closed kitchen window and then back at me. I reached out to him and he slipped his grubby hand into mine and I dragged him along the lane before Mama could stop us. We took the small track that led to Mila's house and I hummed a tuneless song. The winter sun was hitting the tops of the olive trees, turning the leaves from green to silver.

Mila was carrying an armful of dark-green blitve back towards her house when we arrived. She stopped when she saw us enter the yard.

I called out to her and lifted my hand to wave, but she stared back at me with such a solemn look on her face that I lowered my arm. Her eyes shifted from my face to something behind me and I turned my head to follow the direction of her gaze. Close behind, the fish-eyed soldier was walking towards us.

Guten Morgen, Fräulein. He inched towards Mila, his lips parting as he ogled. I felt Pero's grip on my hand tighten as Mila slipped in next to me.

They've taken Father Bilić and some other men. They're taking all our food too, Mila whispered to me.

The soldier stepped closer and spoke to Mila. *Kein sprechen.* His skin was almost transparent; it seemed the blood would burst through its filmy covering.

Pero whimpered at my side and edged behind me so that I was between him and the soldier.

Was geht hier vor? Out of the front door of Mila's house strode another soldier, his harsh voice flooding the yard. *Sie sind nur Mädchen. Schnell. Starren sie nicht, Wagner. Wir brauchen mehr Speise.* He turned and looked directly at me. *Kommen Sie.* He held out his long arm and snapped his fingers at me. I kept my eyes fixed on a small black pebble on the ground. I thought that if I ignored him long enough he would stop talking at us and Pero and I could slip away.

I heard the German's footsteps grinding across the yard. He stood directly in front of me. He reached out and tilted my head upwards until I could not avoid his eyes any longer. Everything about him seemed oversized: his hands like opened cabbage leaves; his thick, perfectly formed lips; and his body a giant from one of Uncle Jure's stories. He wet his lips and then let his hand fall away from my chin to my forearm. He placed his other hand on Pero's head, turning us both around until we were facing the direction from which we'd come. I glanced towards Mila, the fish-eyed soldier standing close to her, his eyes wandering over her body. Oliver was on the other side of her, his face slack.

In the doorway of the house I caught sight of Roza, Mila and Oliver's mother. Her hands were trembling as her fingers tried to button up her blouse.

The soldier pushed me in the small of my back, and while still crushing Pero's hand in mine I started the walk towards our house. As we moved away from Mila and her family, a dog whined in the grove of almond trees at the head of the pathway. Along with our breathing and the stomp of the German's boots, these were the only sounds to be heard as we were marched back to our house.

☙

By the time we reached home Pero was having trouble breathing, wheezing and stumbling as I pulled him along. I didn't want to stop. If we kept going, if we paid the soldier no attention, perhaps *he* would disappear.

Mama came to the door as we crossed the yard. She stiffened when she saw the soldier behind us and stepped out of the house. Her cheeks were flushed. She was in no mood for a German on her doorstep.

Cabbagehands herded us towards Mama and the front door. Pero was gasping and we stumbled forward until we were enveloped in Mama's arms. But I felt little comfort in her embrace.

Food and wine. His lips parted to let out the stilted request.

Get whatever's left inside. My mother spoke quietly, her head turned to me, but her eyes stayed on the soldier. *And the eggs. There's a skin of wine hanging on the hook too. Go!*

I got the food and wine together as quickly as possible. The eggs we had collected were in the basket on the table. I slipped three out and placed them under an overturned copper before piling the last of the bread and some cheese into the basket. I plucked the wine skin off the hook with my free hand and went back to Mama's side. She nudged me towards the waiting man.

I stopped in front of him and bent to place the basket and wine skin on the ground. As I let go of the handle and started to turn away I felt his hand clamp around my wrist, pulling me towards him. I knocked the basket, scattering the food over the ground like chicken feed, my foot crushing an egg as I went. I fell against his body, struggling to escape as his grip tightened.

Let her go, my mother was screaming.

Laughing, Cabbagehands lifted my arm and tried to spin me around as if we were dancing. He spun me again and again until I was dizzy, disorientated, tumbling into him once again. This time he stopped and leaned down until his hazel eyes were level with mine. I turned my face away as he exhaled his soured breath. My belly churned uncomfortably. He tried to twist my head back towards him, his hand on my cheek.

I reacted without thinking of the consequences. I turned my face aside and bit the soldier's palm. He let out a yell that I almost didn't hear over the gunshot.

He cursed loudly as he yanked his hand away from my mouth. More gunfire followed – back and forth, talking to each other on the hillside. The German examined me with such hatred I became even more afraid. He reached for the Luger at his side and I was frozen to the spot as we locked eyes. Gunfire started again and he looked away, surveying the surrounding trees. Then, ignoring us, he ran off towards the guns, sending loose stones clattering off the path.

There were indistinct voices in the distance, but we didn't wait to hear what they were shouting. Mama dragged us inside and leaned against the solid door as she closed her eyes and exhaled.

Tell me what happened. Mama was busy pouring rakija into a bowl of hot water before setting Pero in front of it with a blanket over his head to ease his breathing.

They were at Mila's house. One of them was inside with Rosa . . . he marched us back here. I didn't know what to do!

Mama moved from Pero to where I was standing by the closed door. She stroked my head, her face tight with concern.

Are we going to leave like the others?

She ignored my question and stepped away from me.

What if they come back, Mama?

As my eyes rested on her, I thought that she appeared much older. Deep lines fanned out from the corners of her eyes and mouth and her skin had started to sag around her chin and neck. My mouth was dry and I couldn't swallow even though I needed to. I thought she was going to say something, but she turned back to Pero, who was still crouched over the steaming bowl of water, breathing in deeply the fumes of the rakija.

☙❧

Uncle Jure arrived as the late afternoon light gave way to the creeping evening darkness. He was agitated and anxious to speak to Mama on his own. Pero was now in better spirits and sidled up to Jure.

I don't have anything for you. He gently ran his hand over Pero's head, but instead of picking him up as he did normally, he moved over to Mama and motioned for her to follow him. They slipped out and stood talking outside the closed door. I tiptoed across the room, putting my finger to my lips. Pero copied me. I smiled at him and he followed, sitting on the floor next to me as I knelt and tried to catch snippets of their conversation through the door. Cold air whistled in through the keyhole against my cheek and I shivered as it blew right through me.

We can't go without you. My mother's voice pleading.

You'll be OK.

I thought I heard him sigh, and then nothing. As the silence stretched out, I pulled Pero across the room to the beds where we slept. He snuggled under the blankets and soon fell into a deep sleep next to me. Much later Mama came inside and went to her own bed.

I could not stop thinking about having to leave our home again. There were times with the Italians when we hid in the caves, but we'd always come back. The thought that we might now have to abandon our mountains sent a shiver through me, not from fear but from excitement.

If I could speak to Mila, maybe this was our chance to get to her sister in St Louis. Thoughts crept like night shadows across my mind – we had no money and there had been no passenger boats since the war began. Food was another problem – now that our supplies were being plundered by the Germans we would starve to death before we ever got out of Dalmatia. But I was a determined young thing, so I pushed aside the dark thoughts and convinced myself that if I could talk to Mila we'd be able to come up with a plan. After all, hadn't we found food and guns in the cave? There must be a way, I kept telling myself.

CHAPTER 5

PUALELE

Pualele lies in bed that first night staring at the room around her. There are thin curtains of white cotton over the windows that don't stop the moon from creating a dancing pattern of shadows across the ceiling and walls. Outside, the jacaranda tree's arms tap on the windowpane. Pualele pulls the blankets and candlewick bedspread up under her chin, wondering who is looking after Leti the pig. She knows that her other brothers and sisters have no time for Leti. Sione only likes to chase the pig and give it a good kick if it is too slow, and Lani avoids going near it in case it flicks muck onto her. The other siblings are too old to be fussing with a mere pig, so it was Pualele who ensured that Leti was the best cared-for swine in Samoa.

She puts Leti out of her mind. Her eyes come to rest on the picture of a young girl hanging on the wall. It is surrounded by flowers made from silk and draped with a string of rosary beads. On the table a candle glows weakly from behind a cylinder of glass. Next to it, propped up against a frame, is a prayer card, curling in at the corners and attached to the frame by yellowing Sellotape that is starting to crack and flake away.

Pualele Sina Auva'a
12 May 1962 – 7 June 1970
May the Lord grant unto her eternal rest
And may perpetual light shine upon her
May she rest in peace

She knows all about the second Pualele, her New Zealand-born cousin, named after their paternal grandmother. That Pualele had died four weeks before she was born. And so here she is, Pualele Sina Auva'a from Samoa, lying in the bed of her dead cousin, and staring at the shrine that Aunt Sefi has kept for the last nine years, the candle lit every night as the sun disappears behind the multicoloured wooden houses of Grey Lynn.

Pualele worries that the candle might fall over and set the tablecloth on fire. And she is afraid of what might happen if the perpetual light ever goes out in the night. She imagines poor dead cousin Pualele stumbling through Purgatory and falling off into the eternal flames of hell. She's not sure what to do about that and all the other questions she has floating around in her head. Her mother would know the answer to all her questions. All Pualele has to do is write a letter to her as soon as she can get hold of some paper and a pencil, and pray to God nothing will happen before she gets a reply.

Further around the room Pualele makes out the pattern of the brown fleur de lis on the wallpaper. There are rectangular patches where some old paintings or photographs have been taken down, mapped out by the New Zealand sun that has bleached any wallpaper or coverings left exposed for too long. Fleur de lis. She learnt about it when the French nun, Sister Emmanuelle, came to the village to teach for a time, and Pualele was chosen to help her unpack. The inside of the nun's travel bag was silk-lined with a uniform pattern of hundreds of tiny dagger blades with drooping leaves on either side. The nun had told her it represented the Holy Trinity, and Pualele had liked that it symbolised something so important. She stares at the symmetry of the pattern on the walls of her bedroom, and as her eyes finally close the fleur de lis merges with the image of Leti being chased around the village by Sione.

Kasi is standing over her bed. *Wake up! You're going to school.* Pualele squeezes her eyes shut and turns her face towards the wall. Even though she has known that she will be going to school in New Zealand, she is terrified by the reality of actually walking into a classroom full of unfamiliar children. Any confidence she had in her modest English has disappeared after listening to the chatter of the palagi at the airport. She was unable to make out a word they said. They may as well have been speaking in Chinese, like Leilani Lam's grandfather. She can read and write in English, but she doesn't want to speak to anyone, much less educated palagi who would surely laugh at her. She knows that as soon as she opens her mouth they will know that she doesn't belong here.

Kasi points to the uniform. Someone has left it on the end of her bed while she slept. He pulls the blankets off her, tugging on her arm so that she half falls out of bed. She stumbles to her feet and Kasi vanishes out into the hallway. Tentatively she runs the back of her hand over the heavy navy tunic, the wool fibres prickling her skin. A label sticks out from the collar and she turns it over to find that someone has written her name on it in black pen. A warm glow spreads through her body as she picks up her very own uniform; maybe she does belong after all. She presses the dress to her cheek, the row of buttons at the back leaving their imprint on her skin.

She holds the tunic up against her and notes that the hem falls almost to her ankles. It is then that she notices the small thatch of darning just below the knee. She holds the tunic up to her nose and smells the mustiness that no amount of airing could remove. On the bed, brown socks and a white shirt wait for her. She hears Aunty call out to her to hurry up but she moves slowly as she dresses for her very first day at school.

ଓ

St Mary's Primary School sits on the curve of the road as it rises up towards Westmere. Aunty Sefi is on one side, Father on the other, as they march Pualele across the school playground towards the single-level weatherboard buildings. Children race around yelling at each other as a ball bounces in front of the Auva'as and then sails over their heads. A posse of boys and girls chases the rogue ball as it speeds towards the gates. Aunty moves into the lead as Pualele and her father traverse this foreign landscape, aware of the eyes following their progress.

A large, dour-looking palagi nun materialises in the doorway of the administration block. Aunty Sefi lowers her head as she pulls Pualele in front of her.

Good morning, Sister Carmel. This is Pualele Sina Auva'a.

Aunty pushes Pualele forward until she is suspended between her aunty and her father and the enormous nun. She stands motionless in front of the nun's round belly, focussing on the belt that rises up and down with every breath. She considers what might happen if the belt comes undone, and imagines Sister Carmel spilling out onto the playground.

Does the child speak English? The voice flows out in a soft Irish lilt, in complete contrast to the body it comes from.

Her father is whispering to her in Samoan. *You must talk. Say 'Hello'.*

She swallows and the word squeaks out of her, barely above a whisper.

The nun's sausage fingers lift Pualele's chin until she is staring directly into her face. *And you will call me Sister Carmel.* 'Good morning Sister Carmel.'

Good morning Sister Carmel. She thinks she might be sick.

Right then. In you go. Elizabeth Dillon will show you to your desk.

Pualele steps forward towards the door of the classroom, away from Aunty and Father. She turns her head, seeking reassurance.

We're very proud, Pualele. Aunty smiles and grows taller again, while Father looks on, hands behind his back, his face immobile.

Inside the classroom, Elizabeth Dillon comes right up to Pualele and stands uncomfortably close to her. Pualele steps back.

You're the new girl. How come you're wearing one of those old uniforms? Mine's new! I'm Elizabeth, like Elizabeth Taylor. That's my mum's favourite actress, ever since she saw her in National Velvet. I like Olivia Newton-John in Grease. Have you seen it? I have and it's my favourite movie ever!

Pualele wants to ask where she should sit, but the girl keeps talking on and on. She can't follow it all because Elizabeth speaks so quickly. It sounds like one big stream of noise. Elizabeth twirls her ringlets around her fingers as she speaks and then lets them go. The curls bounce in the air like orange springs. Pualele has never seen anyone with such hair before. Nor heard anyone talk so much nor for so long without stopping to breathe.

. . . and Sister Carmel said you're to sit by me so that you can learn faster. I'm top of the class you know. Just like my Daddy. He owns the Four Square up the road and the stationery shop and one day, he said, he's going to buy me my very own shop that sells ice creams. Do you like ice cream? My favourite's Jelly Tip. Do you like them? Jelly Tips?

Elizabeth finally pauses long enough to notice Pualele is staring down at the floor. Pualele feels a panic rising in her. She has no idea how to respond to Elizabeth. She's never eaten a Jelly Tip, doesn't even know what one is, but if Pualele admits that she doesn't know what Elizabeth is talking about, she will laugh at her. Perhaps it is better to say nothing and let Elizabeth talk again. Pualele's face starts to grow hot, and she can hear her own heart pounding in her head. She tries to look at Elizabeth, but can only manage to focus on the freckles sprinkled across her nose and cheeks as she wonders what to do next.

Oh! Elizabeth's eyebrows rise and her jaw drops open. *DO . . . YOU . . . UNDERSTAND?* she shouts with what seems to Pualele to be excitement. *Oh my goodness! You can't understand a word I'm saying. Fancy that! But your mother speaks such good English. For an Islander, at least. Wait 'til I tell Sister, she'll probably want to put you in the slow class with Thomas Malone and the Mancini girl. She's got a funny name too, you know – Annunzia, or something like that anyway. You'd think her parents would have thought a little more before calling her that! And that's not even mentioning Maria Sutich . . . she's not a dummy, but she came to school spelling her name M-a-r-i-j-a. Imagine it! With a 'J'. Couldn't even spell her own name properly . . .*

Pualele understands perfectly. She wonders when she'll meet these others who are more like her. Perhaps they might talk less than Elizabeth Dillon and maybe they will understand that she is frightened. She wants to tell Elizabeth that her Mama is very far away – that Aunty Sefi isn't her mother, can't she see that? But the room that smells of unfamiliar things, like glue and blank paper and floor polish, is already a swirl of children babbling and giggling and jostling about as they weave through the rows of desks.

A bell is ringing, and Elizabeth is talking again as she ushers Pualele towards a wooden chair and desk. Pualele sits down and places her hands on the desk, letting her fingers run over the half-words and numbers like a blind girl reading braille. As she reads the snatches of poems and half-completed arithmetic, Pualele remembers why she is sitting at this desk, in this schoolroom, in this city called Auckland.

The bell stops as a new nun enters the room. She is a large woman with thick ankles and kind eyes. There is a scraping of chairs as the children scramble to their feet. Pualele follows suit. She stands quickly, pushing back her chair with its wooden seat and metal legs. The rubber stoppers scrape along the floorboards and one catches a groove in the wood, sending the chair crashing. There are muffled giggles from some of the children while Pualele blushes, and she struggles to turn around to right the chair without falling.

As she reaches back, a brown hand brushes against hers and grasps the chair, returning it to an upright position behind her. Her eyes travel up the arm of the helping hand, past the grey shirt sleeve and collar right up to a double chin and generous eyes that nestle in the boy's soft brown face. A flash of recognition travels between the two. An acknowledgement of sorts; it is a look that says *I know you*. For an instant, Pualele forgets that she is frightened.

Turn around, please. The nun's voice is firm but kind.

Without pausing, the nun and the rest of the class launch into 'The Lord's Prayer'. Pualele bows her head and recites the words to herself, feeling a sense of calm starting to seep through her body as the words fall into their comforting rhythm. She glances furtively at the nun. Apart from her navy habit, everything about her is pale, almost ghostly – from the tendril of hair that pokes out from under her headdress, to the skin of her face and her fine-boned hands. Unconsciously Pualele steps back, stopping only when she feels the edge of her chair pressing against the back of her legs.

At the end of the prayer everyone sits and Pualele follows. Elizabeth Dillon is now completely still, her eyes firmly fixed on the nun at the front of the class.

This morning we have a new student in class. Pua-lee-lee Oow-var. The nun exhales, glad to have got the name out. Her face becomes animated as she goes on. *Before we begin, I welcome you to our class. I am Sister Margaret.* She speaks softly to Pualele and beams, her eyes crinkling around the corners. Pualele gives a tentative smile in return before the nun carries on. *Elizabeth, Sister Carmel has said you are to help Pua-lee-lee.*

Elizabeth nods vigorously and looks possessively at her charge. Pualele feels panicked by Elizabeth's enthusiasm for the job and starts to breathe quickly. The rest of the class have turned in their seats to take a good look at the new girl. Twenty-five pairs of eyes examine her, categorise her and, mostly, dismiss her. She flushes again. If only they would stop staring.

Eyes this way please, children. I think we will start the day with writing something about yourselves so Pua-lee-lee can get to know us. You'll need to write your name, age, how many in your family, pets and what you like to do after school. You have half an hour then we will read them out. Quiet now, Michael Davis.

A boy at the back of the class is whispering and laughing behind his hand. The children are all staring at Pualele, a private joke tweaking their mouths into smirks.

You too Pua-lee-lee! You will write something so that we can get to know you. Pualele gulps. She would prefer not to say anything about herself. She doesn't want to boast, but she always tries to do the right thing, and despite her first thoughts about the teacher's vapid appearance Sister Margaret seems to be kind.

I have a pencil you can borrow. Elizabeth passes her a brand new 4b red pencil. *It's from my father's stationery shop.* Elizabeth then bends her head over the page in front of her and starts to write carefully on the page: each stroke a precise and measured movement. Pualele opens her bag and withdraws an A4 lined workbook whose edges have discoloured with age. The cover is striped black and red and in the white window her name has been printed in a child's scrawl in blue biro. She opens it to the first page and tries to assemble her thoughts. Then slowly she begins to write. 'My name is Pualele Sina Auva'a and I am nine years old . . . '

CHAPTER 6

OLGA'S JOURNAL

Pero was curled up like a small dog at my back, radiating a welcome warmth that would have sent me off to sleep if I hadn't been so sure about what I needed to do. I waited impatiently to hear the steady breathing of my mother. By the time I could be sure it was safe for me to move without waking either of them, the moon was already high in the night sky, giving the stone of Biokovka a luminous white sheen. It made me hesitate. I felt the unseen threat of the soldiers. I imagined them everywhere watching me, waiting for me.

I decided to take a route through the trees to avoid the shimmering stone paths. I'd taken an oil lamp and some flints, along with a jute sack. If I could wake Mila up I'd tell her about our leaving. We could talk and make plans.

My nerve started to fail me as soon as I reached the olive grove with its gnarled and twisted trees. Normally the sight of the ancient boughs gave me a sense of belonging. We had survived here on this mountainside for hundreds of years, the olives providing us with our precious oil, year upon year. Thunderstorms could bombard the mountainside and lightning set trees on fire, but always the blackened trees would sprout green shoots and the trees would live on. Now, in the moonlight that bounced off their silvery foliage, the branches were leaning down, giant arms with leafy fingers, reaching for me.

The ground was soft underfoot as I hurried towards Mila's house, the only sound the rattle of the oil lamp in my hand. I paused at the head of the path that hugged the curve of the mountain. On the upper side of the path lay a scramble of bushes and creeping brambles. On the lower, pines mixed with cypress that stretched up towards the night sky. I thought I could hear voices travelling along the path towards me. I listened, but only the trees whispered to each other on the wind.

Then I heard it again. The sound of voices.

I stepped off the track onto a carpet of pine needles that absorbed the sound of my footsteps amongst the trees and extinguished the lamp. I held my breath as I peered around each tree trunk. The voices growing louder. Dalmatian voices. Voices I knew.

They stood in a small space between an overhang and several giant cypresses. The round moon balanced on top of the trees, its light sending spiky shadows dancing across the luminescent rock. Dragan had his back to me, legs slightly apart and hands at his side. As he moved, I caught sight of Mila in front of him, her back against the rock.

I felt as if the cold night air was pushing me down into the ground and I slid onto my haunches, listening.

It doesn't have to be like this. We could be happy. Dragan's voice was soft, but insistent.

There's a war on – if you hadn't noticed.

What better reason. We could join the Partisans together.

No. I can't, Dragan. We should wait.

There was a pause as he seemed to reconsider. Then he went on. *Why wait?*

She said nothing for a moment and I willed her to say *No*. I wished I could un-hear the words they had said, and tell Mila to walk away.

I can't just go, leave Mama.

His body appeared to tense at her words and his voice was louder this time.

It's her isn't it? Thinks I'm not good enough.

She never said that.

No – but she thinks it and she'll say anything to keep us apart.

Stop it, Dragan. I'm sick of arguing. She sighed as if she was very tired, her body seeming to shrink away from the argument while Dragan clenched and unclenched his hands hanging by his sides.

It's true, Mila. You just don't want to believe it. She hates me.

This isn't about my mother. I just can't.

Can't what? Meet me in the daylight? So long as no one sees. That's it, isn't it Mila?

You're being ridiculous.

Dragan stepped in towards her. All I could see was his back. He reached forward.

Stop it. You're hurting me.

Dragan wobbled to the side as they grappled with each other, both of them grunting as Mila tried to twist away. I was up on my feet immediately. I don't know what I thought I was going to do, but I couldn't let him hurt her. I started to move forward then stopped as his head bent down towards hers. Muffled sounds reached me as they stood locked together. I stepped back behind the tree. Dragan's head lifted and there was a brief pause before he cried out in pain.

Ooowww! He bent down and clasped his shin.

I said 'No'.

Why not? Or would you rather have a German like your mother?

There was a pause before she spoke, and her cold words reached my ears. *You're nothing but a Ciganin.*

Dragan didn't move.

She went on. *You're the son of a gypsy whore. And your father no better.* She spat the words at him. *You're not a man. You're nothing! You're a crippled gypsy bastard.*

They stood facing each other, both breathing loudly. I could see they were waiting for the other to do something. I saw Dragan's body hunch forward, as if Mila had punched him in the stomach and all the air had gone out of him.

I'm sorry. She said the words as if she meant them – but he was already gone.

The scene darkened as a cloud moved across the moon. My heart was thumping. I stayed where I was, leaning with my head against the tree trunk, trying to make sense of what I'd just witnessed. I had thought I knew everything about Mila – thought I could see right into her soul. But this girl-woman was no one that I knew.

How long have you been here?

Now she was standing over me and I was frightened by her. I knew I could have said nothing and run away, but I was frozen against the tree.

You and him – is it true?

I wanted to take back the words the second I'd said them, for if she didn't reply I could still believe what I wanted to believe. I was crying and couldn't stop. Mila just watched me. *But . . . what about us . . . and . . .* I blubbered.

For God's sake, Olga. You don't understand anything – there is no 'us'.

The words were like a thousand tiny daggers piercing my heart and the pain I felt was the raw pain of my heart breaking for the very first time. I was sure that my life was ruined and I could not understand how life could possibly go on as it once had. I was Mila's best friend. We'd made plans – together. How could I make her understand that she was making a terrible mistake? I meant to say that I didn't believe her, that I knew she was just angry. But my own confused emotions made the words come out all wrong.

Is it true what he said about your mother . . . and the German?

I don't know if it was what I had said or a shadow cast by the moon, but her face became a grotesque half-face, sneering at me with an elongated nose and a single black eye. I thought she might hit me. Her voice was very low and steady. *Just get out of here, Olga! GO!*

I backed away until I was sure I'd merged with the forest before breaking into a run. I was oblivious to the noise of my feet slamming through the bushes, snapping twigs and trampling pine cones into the pulpy earth. By the time I reached home my thoughts were a jumble and I wished I'd never left to find her that night.

Back at my house I slipped the latch and waited a moment, convinced my breathing would give me away and waken my mother. I carefully slid into bed next to Pero, and wrapped my arms around him. He tried to wriggle free as I clutched him to me, cold and shivering, desperate to go back to the world I knew before I'd left the bed. But the image of Mila and Dragan was stamped on my eyelids, and Mila's words played on in my head: *There is no us, there is no us . . .*

☙

Pero and I were running.

Flocks of tracker birds flapped overhead, sending a downward draft that almost blew us over, stopping us in our tracks.

We dived under bushes to avoid the birds' eyes that shone like searchlights down upon the forest.

Then we were running again – scrambling through the tearing brambles that clawed at our clothing, trying to pull us down. But as we tried to escape it was Mila who was trying to stop us.

She was the thorns that tore at us, the vines that looped around our arms and legs. It was her unfathomable eyes that accused us and her finger-like talons that clawed at my eyes and grabbed at Pero as I tried to protect him.

Her gnarled hands had Pero in their grip, her mouth gaping. Wave upon wave of birds, their blue-black feathers shimmering in a crescent of moonlight, flew out of her mouth at me.

As I stood there paralysed, Pero's calls for help grew fainter until I could hear them no longer.

Then out of the vast blackness came words. Thereisnous– thereisnous. I tried to move but couldn't as the words turned into the unmistakable rhythm of the Ciganins' music.

ଔ

I woke gasping as if I were being crushed. Pero's arm lay across my chest and I threw it off. I tried to steady my breathing as he turned next to me, eyelids fluttering.

I lay there next to my brother as the dawn crept across the sea, inching its way up the mountainside. The light slipped into our room and I convinced myself that I should find Mila and say sorry. I wanted her to forgive me for the silly things I'd said and for her to realise that she had made a mistake too. It was all a terrible misunderstanding and I knew if I went to her house I would be sure to find her happily doing chores.

I pictured Mila taking me aside and looking through the letters from her sister. We'd talk about what it would be like to live in a city where you didn't know everyone and in a house that might not even have a garden. But what I really wanted was for Mila to tell me that I was her best friend. That it was me she cared for and that we would one day run away together. But the more I tried to deny it, the more it became true – she wasn't that kind of friend after all.

☙

The girl hasn't come today and I'm sick with worry. What could be the reason for her not being here? You see, once you start your course of chemotherapy you have to come every day until the course is complete. You have a week's break and the cycle starts again. I am certain that she should be here as we started the same week. She should be here with me. There must be something wrong. Oh Pualele, I want to ask what has become of her, but I'm afraid what the answer might be.

I cannot write today.

CHAPTER 7

PUALELE

Pualele is ready to run away long before the session is over. She hears the murmurs and the muffled laughs as they scribble their stories. Occasionally Sister Margaret moves down the rows of desks, stalling the whispering before returning to the front of the class and her marking. But Pualele can't concentrate on writing, knowing that the whispering will start again.

Her focus wavers. She wishes she was back in Samoa with her mother and the rest of her family. The open-sided fale that was their schoolhouse had no desks. The children sat on the floor while the nuns taught them about Jesus and the Apostles and, by extension, how to read and write. Pualele and Sione were often asked to read in their New Zealand English with its swallowed vowels and indistinct consonants. The Irish nuns, and even the French nun, Sister Emmanuelle, corrected the pronunciation that their mother, Olina, had given them.

In late 1961 Monsignor O'Reilly from the Diocese of Auckland had wandered through their village. A round man perched on stick legs, he had been brought to a sudden halt. He had clutched his chest and gasped in such a way that his companions had started towards him, fearing the worst for the corpulent priest. But it wasn't some physical collapse that had almost stopped his heart. It was an angel's voice coming from a small fale. He soon arranged for Olina to be sent to Auckland, where she studied under Sister Mary Leo. But the Auckland climate and her asthma made it impossible for her to excel – so in 1965 she returned to her village, fluent in written and spoken English and in Italian and German opera.

Pualele wants nothing more than to hear her mother now. She wishes she could close her eyes and be transported by her mother's voice, a sound so enchanting that it could draw the whole village to her, even if they didn't understand the words that she sang. And then Pualele remembers what her mother said to her the night before she had taken the bus to Apia: *Make me proud, Pualele. Make me proud.*

Pua-lee-lee! Let's hear what you have written. The entire class is staring at her. Waiting. She looks down at the few lines she has written and wishes that God would open up the ground and swallow her whole.

Come along Pua-lee-lee. Everyone's waiting. The nun thrum-thrums her fingers on the desk impatiently. *Why don't you come up to the front of the class so we can all see you? Quickly now!*

Pualele pushes herself to her feet and shuffles towards the teacher's desk. She stops in front of the blackboard and turns to face the children, keeping her eyes on her neatly drawn words. She sneaks a glance at Sister Margaret, who looks slightly irritated, then clears her throat and tries to read out loud the words she has written.

I am Pualele Sina . . .

Louder, Pua-lee-lee. Nice and clearly now, so the children at the back can hear you.

It is like torture – the children staring directly at her, listening to her talk about her family and animals and how the whole village works hard to support each other, and all the while Pualele can hear some children snickering and others shifting, bored in their seats. Finally it is over and she hangs her head, waiting to be dismissed by the teacher.

Thank you, says Sister Margaret. *You must be very happy to have left all that behind you.*

No, she wants to shout. She isn't happy at all. If she was a bolder child, like Kasi, she might stand up at her desk and tell the class that she'd rather be in Samoa than in New Zealand any day. That a pigsty won out every time over this classroom and these unkind children. But Pualele will never dare tell anyone how she truly feels.

Her thoughts are interrupted by the school bell ringing for morning tea time. Elizabeth materialises by her side and marshalls her towards the cloakroom, and once again Pualele finds herself being swept further and further away.

☙

Pualele does not know what to do. Elizabeth has temporarily abandoned her on the wooden benches that run along the sides of the school building and is now running around with the other girls, throwing a large ball up and down the playground. Every now and then they get to one end and some of them throw the ball around until someone finally gets it through a hoop on top of a pole, while the others try to snatch the ball away. It doesn't seem like a very clever game to Pualele. She can't understand why they don't just kick it, at least that way it would get to the end faster.

Across the field the boys are playing soccer. Now that is a game she understands. She was good at dribbling the ball past other children in the village, and she could run almost as fast as the boys of her age. She wanders over towards the grass and stands watching, waiting for someone to notice her.

She sees the players swarming around the ball like bees around a honey pot. Michael Davis breaks free, heading towards the unguarded goal. He loses his balance and kicks the ball with his left foot, skewing his shot across the field before the ball bounces several times on the soft turf, finally coming to a stop under Pualele's foot. Without thinking, she slides the toe of her shoe underneath the ball, flicking it up in the air before kicking it back onto the pitch. It arcs beautifully through the air and hangs there for a long time before dropping right back in front of the boy. He is close enough for Pualele to see him glaring back at her as another boy yells out.

Even a girl can do better than you, Davis.

She feels their eyes upon her. Dropping her chin to her chest, she turns away. She doesn't know what possessed her to kick the ball like that when they obviously don't want her there. But she loved the feeling of kicking the ball as hard as she could and is pleased that she is skilful enough to volley the ball back to Michael Davis. She doesn't understand what he has against her. She wonders if it is the uniform not being quite right, or maybe she did or said something wrong in class. Whatever it is, it drives her away from the soccer field back towards the girls and the hard, grey, tarsealed playground.

There you are. Elizabeth's face is an unnatural red that makes the freckles darken across her cheeks.

Come and play – you can be goal keep. Betty Seumalu used to be goal keeper. But she and her family got sent back to Samoa. Elizabeth leans in closer and whispers *overstayers,* looking knowingly at Pualele.

She nods mutely back and follows, happy to get as far away from Michael as she can. She means to ask what *overstayers* are, but Elizabeth pushes her towards the goalpost before moving off down the court. Another smaller girl with a familiar appearance comes and stands next to Pualele, giving her a lopsided grin.

You're on the other team. You need to stop me shooting a goal.

The girl has kind eyes that might be blue or grey and a nose that curls up at the end.

My name's Catherine. You can call me Cate. Pualele summons up her best smile. She wants to thank her for talking to her as if she is just another girl, but before she has a chance to speak, Cate jumps to the right, catching the ball in both hands. Pualele watches her as she concentrates. Cate sticks out her bottom lip as she blows a strand of light brown hair out of her eyes and shoots the ball through the hoop.

Pualele! You have to move! She nods briefly at Elizabeth and goes back to trying to make Cate her friend and promising, at least in her own head, that she will try to get the ball next time.

☙

By the end of the day Pualele is exhausted and not looking forward to the walk back to her new home. She can't imagine coming back to school the next day, or the one after that. Apart from Cate and maybe Sister Margaret, she feels totally alone. There is of course Elizabeth, but she doesn't count in Pualele's estimation as she is being *made* to be her friend. In her heart, Puelele knows that some of the children don't like their new Samoan classmate at all. She feels guilty thinking these thoughts, especially as she is aware that a great gift has been bestowed upon her. She doesn't want to be ungrateful, but as she walks towards her new home she can't help longing for her mother and the safety of their village and the wonderful, welcoming sea.

ぐ℞

In Samoa, Father worked in the plantations that encircled the village. On one side there were lines of coconut palms for copra. On the other side were bananas. At the top flowed the stream and together they formed a trio of protectors – the banana plantation, the copra plantation and the stream that laughed at the children as they fell more often than not when trying to cross it. The stones in the stream were moss-green with slime that made them more slippery than a banana peel. At one end the boys made a dam of sorts from pieces of forgotten wood and fallen logs that caused the water to eddy into a muddy pool.

Sometimes they swam there in the muddy waters, and other times they would navigate a paopao along the stream and out over the multi-coloured coral reefs where, if you looked down, you could see the fish swimming over the patchwork patterns of the reef below. The patterns were like the quilt sent to her grandmother by Aunty Sefi. It seemed Sefi had forgotten that there was little need for a woollen crocheted blanket in Samoa, but her mother had given it pride of place in their fale so that all visitors should know they had family in New Zealand.

The village and the plantations of Pualele's memory are replaced by the concrete footpaths that run from St Mary's to their rented house on Rich Man Road. There is no need in this new place to forage for food or raise pigs in your yard. The Auva'as' food is bought from the butcher and Four Square, supplemented by taro from the garden and eggs from the Magasivas. The joy of exploring has been taken away from Pualele. Instead of being roads to freedom and adventure, the streets around her new home are ropes tying her to a suburban section.

ぐ℞

She is almost home when she feels a sting on the exposed flesh between her socks and the hem of her uniform. She turns around as a small piece of scoria glances off her cheek and makes her cry out in pain. She puts a hand to her cheek and scans the street. A Morris Minor comes around the corner, whipping up an empty chip packet and sending it cartwheeling across the road like tumbleweed. As the car rounds the next bend, she spots a dark-haired boy crouching behind a hedge. And there on the footpath stands Michael Davis. His schoolbag sits at his feet and his arms hang loosely at his side as he eyeballs her. She gulps as he snarls at her. *What're you staring at?*

He sniffs and lifts his chin and Pualele finds she can't look away. There is something unsettling about the boy. His blue eyes draw her in and his nose flicks up at the end. She has a distinct feeling of déjà vu, although it is most probably just that many of the palagi children all look the same to her. She hears Michael summon up saliva and sees the spit land on the ground between them.

Cat got your tongue? Or you just stupid?

There is laughing from behind the hedge. She is too frightened to move as Michael Davis picks up his bag and starts to advance towards her. He is a few feet away when another car rounds the corner. It brakes suddenly and the driver gives a few short toots on the horn as the car pulls over to the side of the road.

MICHAEL!

A woman with light-brown hair neatly pulled back off her face gestures through the open window for Michael to hurry across to the car. He gets into the back seat and the woman turns to talk to him. Pualele can now see that there is a girl sitting in the passenger's seat. She gapes at her, not quite believing it is really her. But then the girl in the car calls out to her and she knows she is not mistaken.

PUALEELEE!

Cate waves madly at her. In contrast to her brother's glowering look from the back of the car, she is smiling a wide, beautiful smile. Pualele waits until the car pulls away and finally vanishes around the next bend in the road. Her heart is pounding as she looks around for the other boy, but he too has disappeared.

When she reaches the gate, the tears that she has held in check all day start to prick at her eyes. She looks at the wooden letterbox that sits at a jaunty angle, nailed to the fence by two hastily attached planks of wood. Through blurry eyes she spots the corner of a pale-blue envelope poking out of the box. Pualele snatches up the envelope and reads her own name before bolting up the steps to the front door.

Inside, she runs to her room, throwing her bag on the floor and ripping the letter open as she falls onto her bed.

Dear Pualele,

You have only been gone a few days, but I had to write to you immediately! We are just back from Church and you won't believe it, Leti has had eight fat little piglets! You would be so happy if you were here, after all she was really your pig. Sione is looking after Leti and the babies, and I have already sold four of them! When they are weaned they will be off and we will have some extra money in our pocket – but I shouldn't count the money before they are sold, as the Lord knows that all sorts of things could happen between now and then to a new piglet. But I prayed for them all this morning, right after we said special prayers for you all in New Zealand.

But what am I writing. You won't be thinking about such things now that you are in New Zealand – silly me writing about an old sow. You will be bored by such news now that you are a big city girl. There is little to tell you that you don't already know. We are all happy and well, even grandma's rheumatism seems a little better.

I have been talking to Father Lafiaiga and he says that he knows of the school you will be attending and that it is one of the finest in Auckland. I never went there of course, but I know that you will be doing your very best to make us all proud. Your brothers and sisters are doing well at the village school, but maybe you can send some extra books back to us so that they can know something of what you are learning too?

I hope Sefi and Sam are well and that your father and brother are already working hard. We send you all our love and prayers. May God keep you safe.

Mama

Mama is wrong – she wants to know about everything. Pualele will write to her and tell her that she wants to hear about every conversation and know about every trifling incident that happens in her mother's day. And Leti! Pualele had suspected she was pregnant. She had laid her ear against the pig's belly and run her hands over Leti's sides sticky with slop, but she'd been unsure and hadn't wanted to ask anyone how you knew if it was true.

Pualele reads the letter again, lingering over every word, trying to squeeze out every last ounce of love, but the rereading only leaves her eager for more – and, worse than that, she is now more homesick than before. She doesn't want to know that they are well and happy. She wants them to be as miserable as she is and for Mama to want her back. Mama sends love and prayers. But what she really wants is for Mama to send a ticket so that Pualele can go back home.

CHAPTER 8

OLGA'S JOURNAL

She's not here again.

I asked the nurse this morning if she knew where she was. (It was the same nurse who found this pen for me – the pen I've never returned and that I feel the weight of in my bag every day.)

The nurse said *She's not here.* I tried to ask her what that meant – *not here* – but she had already rushed off down the corridor, her shoes squeaking on the linoleum. I got the feeling the nurse didn't want to talk to me and now I am imagining the worst. *Not here.* It could mean she's lying in a bed in the cancer ward dying. Or, God forbid, it could mean she's already dead. But it could mean something else, couldn't it? *Not here* could mean she's not in the city, that she's moved to be closer to her family, although where they are I don't know. I have no idea where she's from and I've never even thought to ask her, but suddenly it's very important for me to know.

And another thing: the last two days before she disappeared the girl has been alone. I should've asked her where the man was, but I was so wrapped up in writing about the past that I haven't really been in the present.

I hope they are together, the man and the girl. Perhaps the two of them have gone on holiday – a break with reality would be good for her, better than any drug.

And now I'm unsure whether the nurse said she was *not here* or if in fact she said something else.

I'm not sure what to do.

I will pray.

ॐ

She is back and I have spoken to her!

It wasn't a conversation, I only told her that I had missed her these last few days, and she tried to smile before her eyes welled up and she looked away. I put my hand over hers and squeezed as hard as I could. I wasn't sure if I should take my hand away, so I left it there on top of hers. She let it stay that way for a long time.

She is alone, like me, although I am only by myself until you have parked the car and have navigated the many corridors and doors to come and collect me. I don't know what I would do without you, Pualele.

I need to focus and to keep writing because time's running out and I must tell you everything, even if the past is more painful than the present.

ॐ

With my head full of thoughts about Mila and the night before, the day began like any other. Mama stirred and was soon out of the house to tend to the animals. I woke Pero and helped him to get dressed. I prepared breakfast. Some bread and hard cheese that Uncle Jure found for us. The daily routine rolled on.

The tension rose when Mama returned. She and I danced a strange ballet that day, each pirouetting around the other. I was never sure if it was because she knew I'd been out the night before or if she too had her own problems, her own private thoughts and demons. I wished I could have confided in her like Mila did with her mother, but I didn't know how to. She wasn't a cruel person, not at all. But there was something about her manner that always kept me at a distance. Even when she bent down to show me how to darn a stocking, or how to embroider some detail on a shirt, there was never that feeling of closeness that other girls have with their mothers. It was as if some invisible barrier had been erected that allowed only a certain level of intimacy and no more.

To her credit, I knew how to cook a soup with wild parsnip and a chicken. I could clean a house that had dirt floors and stone walls. I knew how to grow cabbage and silver beet in the rocky mountain soil and I could keep our few sheep safe from the wild foxes that roamed the hillside. It is only now that I wonder if it would have been better for her to have shown me how to love her, but I guess teaching me how to survive was the closest she could get.

She sent me to school to learn to read and write so that I wouldn't be like her – having to take the letters my father wrote to her to Uncle Jure to read. I often wondered what my father thought about another man reading the thoughts and longings meant only for his wife, even if the person reading them was his own brother.

But school had ended for me when Ivan had gone to New Zealand. Mama needed another pair of hands to help with the chores of survival, so I was forced to leave the classroom behind.

I loved everything about school: the teacher with his wire-rimmed glasses and his impressive Oxford don gown (or so he said, and certainly no one ever challenged him as to the truth of this claim, mainly because none of us had any idea who or what an Oxford don was); the chalk dust that settled on all the desks as the teacher scribbled equations and quotes and ideas across the chalkboard; and most of all the books – bound in leather or with hardboard covers with well-thumbed pages. With every word read and every page turned it became a pathway into a magical world me. Before long I was the one reading Father's letters to Mama, and I felt important – I felt like more than just another mouth to feed.

When I read to her she closed her eyes and gently rocked back and forth in time with the rhythm of the words. I could see her relax into the story of my father and brother, see her drink in their successes and hear her sigh when they struggled. I tried to crack the shell around her so I might gain access to the gentlewoman I glimpsed beneath, but once the letter reading was over she refused to be drawn into conversations.

I would ask, *Mama, will we ever go to New Zealand?*

And she'd reply. *Only God knows.*

I didn't know how to respond to this vague response, this brushing me away like some annoying fly on a summer's day. And while I was busy formulating another question, she'd be up and gone before I was able to say anything else. I'd become angry with myself for asking such foolish questions, and angry with her for not seeing that I lived my life in reaction to her indifference.

Even though it was difficult to draw out that gentlewoman, there was one thing that I knew for certain: Mama had an unwavering acceptance of her place as a wife to an absent husband. It was obvious that there was outwardly nothing else that was as important to her as raising her children and living life as if my father would step off a boat some afternoon with my brother and be home for dinner that same evening. I loved her for that – for the reliability of her nature – when around me there were the likes of Dragan's father, who could be depended upon only to be drunk by noon.

But I couldn't help hating her sometimes.

I despised her for her refusal to consider a more exciting and richer existence. I thought that *we* should decide what happened to us – not God. Mama's dry replies and her acceptance sometimes made me want to lash out and scream at her and push her away, but at other times I wanted her to hold me fast and have her stroke my head the way she did with Pero. I wanted her to tell me that everything was going to be alright – but I didn't understand then that the future is unknowable.

☙

The morning slowly passed into afternoon as I contemplated what had happened the night before. When the last of the inside jobs had been completed, I left the house to wash and hang the laundry. I became anxious, peering towards the path that led to Uncle Jure's house and then to Mila's, wondering what had happened after I'd left her last night. I imagined her appearing on the dirt lane, Dragan by her side, and my heart lurched at the thought as I scrubbed the bed linen against a wooden washboard, wringing out the last drops of water onto the ground.

I folded the sheets over the line suspended between the house and the trees. The smell of Sunlight soap that my father had sent from New Zealand filled the air as I fought to hold onto the washing against the growing wind. As I struggled to pin the sheets to the line, I saw Jure approaching.

He hadn't spotted me, and I stayed and watched him from behind the billowing sheets that licked around me. I moved backwards until I was amongst the laurel bushes that surrounded the almond tree, watching as Jure stood at the front door and spoke to Mama.

Olga! Mama looked towards the laundry.

Olga! Jure had a look of concern on his face. I don't know why I stayed silent. My tummy tightened as I melted into the bushes, not flinching as the small thorns worked their way in through the thick weave of my dress. Mama and Jure spoke a little longer before they embraced and he headed off. She turned and went back inside. My body relaxed and I flipped over the wash bucket and sat on it as the sheets snapped in the breeze.

I heard someone coming and looked out to find Oliver peering back at me. *I need to talk to you,* he said.

He stepped towards me, behind the drying sheets. *Were you with Mila last night?* I shook my head, hoping the tears wouldn't come.

You need to tell me. She's gone.

I don't know what you're talking about. My voice rose as I stood up. *Why're you asking me?*

Oliver grasped my hand in his as I tried to control my voice and stop from crying. He gave me a steady look and his voice was soft when he spoke. *If something happened, you need to tell me.*

I stared at the ground trying to breathe. I wanted to tell him, but I knew he would be angry with his sister and his best friend. I wanted to do the right thing.

I saw him. The words caught in my throat.

Who?

I saw him. With Mila.

His hands were now gripping my arms, rattling the words out of me.

The other day when I came to find you . . . he was . . . I saw how he was looking at her.

What did he do?

They were fighting . . . he kissed her.

No!

Oliver was breathing heavily, his eyes darting around. He covered his face with his hands as he repeated something over and over.

I'm sorry. I should have said something before.

He dropped his hands and growled at me. *I'll get one of those guns from the cave and shoot that bastard.*

Don't Oliver. Please!

It's what my father would've done.

Don't. Please. I heard my voice whining. *Maybe if you talk to Dragan . . .*
Dragan's gone. I'll handle this myself.
But who are you going to shoot?

My words were lost as Oliver ran towards his house, leaving me with muddled thoughts and a pounding head.

I was tired from the night before and still so angry with Mila that I didn't care what Oliver was going to do, or even think seriously about what it all meant. If I had thought about it right then and there, I might have run after him to tell him exactly what I'd seen that night. But something held me back. The devil in me delighted in Mila's disappearance – and God forgive me but at that moment I hoped she would never come back.

CHAPTER 9

PUALELE

Within weeks, Kasi and Father have jobs with the Ministry of Works. *We help fix the roads*, Kasi says.

To Pualele it sounds a very important job, but she doesn't understand what a ministry has to do with building roads – perhaps these people that fix roads are Baptists. It is hard to imagine that they have to pray to repair the roads, but she doesn't question what Kasi says and in the end she doesn't suppose it matters, so long as they have a job (even if it is with Baptists). Mama is very pleased when she hears they have work, and as a regular stream of money starts to arrive in Samoa, her fortnightly letters are luminescent with pride.

For Pualele, the weeks fall into a predictable monotony. Every day after school she comes home to an empty house. With the men all working and Aunty on permanent afternoon shifts at the hospital, Pualele runs all the way from St Mary's without stopping and lets herself into the rectangular box that is her New Zealand home. There are two panes of coloured glass inset into the front door. When you look through the glass everything takes on a distorted bluish hue. Pualele likes the way it makes things appear squat and ghoulish. She is always very careful to close the door gently for fear of cracking the delicate panes that are thicker at the bottom than they are at the top.

Once inside, a long corridor dissects the house. Pualele goes to the room that has the TV in it, the same room where Kasi and Father sleep. There is a mattress on the floor that leaves no space to walk in, and the room is littered with their clothes. She drops her bag in the doorway and moves the clothes to one side, sinking into the hollow of the mattress. Pulling her knees up, she reaches her arm over to turn on the TV that is wedged between the makeshift bed and the wall. She waits as the box hums into life, a glow starting to radiate from it. Then slowly black and white images dance across the screen.

Pualele is very pleased with herself. She isn't supposed to be in the room, but she likes the children's programmes, and they help her understand more of the conversations around her at school. *Keep cool 'til after school*, the man on the TV says every afternoon. She thought it very funny at first. Why would you want to be 'cool' when almost everyone she sees on the streets wears thick jumpers and coats? New Zealand isn't hot at all. But it is a very strange country.

The programme ends and she struggles to her feet, kicking the pile of clothes back over the bed. She knows that she should get her school work out and start before her uncle and then Kasi and Father appear. Once they get home, they will be hungry and wanting the dinner that she is expected to prepare for them. She is amazed at all the food you can get in New Zealand. Tonight they will have pork sausages, and chop suey too. It is like every day here in Auckland is a special occasion. She can imagine how envious her brothers and sisters would be if they could see how they eat in New Zealand.

As she pulls her school bag towards her, there is a knock at the door. She turns off the TV and holds her breath, listening to the sound of the wooden joinery creaking and the mynah birds squabbling in the backyard. There is a second knock, more insistent this time. She looks out of the room and down the hallway to where the afternoon sun is shining through the glass, sending ribbons of coloured light along the wooden floor. Her heart thumps in her chest and her shoulders rise up around her ears as she stares at the front door. On the other side of the glass, Pualele can see the shape of a dwarf. She watches, horrified, as it pulls a coil from its oversized head and then lets it go. She doesn't move as the thing put its face up to the glass.

Pua-lee-lee! Open up!

Her body relaxes and she trips down the hallway, slipping the latch on the door to reveal Elizabeth swinging a pink vinyl bag in front of her.

Would you like to come to our shop and get something?

Pualele isn't sure what to say. She should probably say no and do her maths and spelling. It won't be long before she will have to get the dinner on, but it is a tempting offer. The first of its kind – and she won't be long.

The door clicks behind her as she follows Elizabeth onto the footpath, where she sees Cate and Michael waiting. Pualele stops at the gate. She's not sure she wants to go anywhere with Michael. He kicks the wooden fence post, leaving black scuff marks on the white palings. She should tell him to stop. Aunty Sefi wouldn't like it. But Cate smiles at her expectantly and so Pualele says nothing.

Pualele falls into step between Cate and Elizabeth. Michael trails behind as the three girls walk towards the shops on Ponsonby Road. Aunty promised to bring Pualele up to the shops, but with school and Aunty's shift work they have never quite made it. They reach their destination and Pualele reads the faded sign that hangs over the door: *Dillon's Convenience Store.* The door is wide enough for a car to drive through. She follows the girls inside onto the chequered linoleum floor.

Pualele feels like Ali Baba entering a giant cave of treasures. She marvels at the aisles of goods all neatly arranged like pews in a church. Tins and plastic packages and boxes, and even fruit and vegetables all lined up. She doesn't know where to start first, and as she has no money she decides she will just look.

There are so many different things that she has never seen before. The four aisles stretch the length of the building, and that's not even taking into account the lollies and other sweets in the cabinets under the counter, nor the jars and packets of brightly coloured goods on the shelves behind the lady that Elizabeth is talking to. She watches Michael pick up a toffee apple, its red shell sticking to the skin of plastic wrapping.

Elizabeth is picking up a small packet with a chicken on the front, while Cate nearby is fingering something unidentifiable in a slim blue package no longer than a pencil.

You can have anything you like, you know.

Pualele nods at Elizabeth, who is looking back at her expectantly. She wanders down the first aisle past cereals and flour and tins of tomatoes and peaches, stopping in front of the biscuits where packets of every conceivable variety confront her. She can have anything she likes. But to choose when there is more choice than she has ever thought possible, well, it is more than she can comprehend. Her eyes flick left to right and back again, and she is no closer to choosing something than when she began at the top of the aisle.

A movement distracts her and she turns her head to see that the girls are already waiting for her outside. Michael is talking to the lady behind the counter, so she quickly chooses the first thing that catches her eye so she can rush outside to the girls before he spots her on her own. She slips out the door to join the two girls, who are chatting happily in the afternoon sun. Pualele looks at the box in her hand. It has a drawing of a white spaceman on a pink planet. She admires the colour of the packet, then carefully opens it and withdraws a white stick with a pink tip and leans against the window like her two friends.

A packet of spaceman cigarettes! You're a funny girl, Pualele!

Elizabeth laughs as she plucks a potato chip from the bag and pops it into her mouth.

Pualele sucks on the end of the cigarette and it immediately crumbles into a sugary paste on her tongue. She closes her eyes as she savours the sticky mass, thinking that her brothers and sisters at home would not believe that she is leaning against the palagi shop with her new friends and with the sweetest taste she's ever known exploding in her mouth. She opens her eyes only when she hears the banging on the window. The lady from behind the counter inside is yelling something at them.

Pualele follows Elizabeth and Cate back into the shop. The lady has come out from behind the counter and as she reaches Pualele she snatches the spaceman cigarettes from her hand. Pualele steps back in horror.

You're not in the bloody Islands now, you know, she screeches. *I'm calling the police.*

The other three are staring at Pualele. Michael seems to be almost enjoying himself, while the girls' mouths are opening and shutting like gawping fish. Pualele presses her fingernails into the palms of her hand, willing herself back in time to her village, not sure what she has done wrong.

You did pay, didn't you?

Elizabeth frowns at her.

Nothing makes sense, and now the happiness she felt a few seconds before has been replaced by fear. She has broken some unwritten rule and she wants to ask what she has done wrong – how she can fix it – but she doesn't want to make things worse.

Have anything, Elizabeth had said to her. She needs Kasi or Father or her mother here. They would know what to do and would take charge of the situation and fix things while she melted into the background. Instead, the lolly in her mouth turns into a sickly glue so that the only thing Pualele can do is to stand mutely before the shopkeeper.

Please Mrs Merrick. She's only new. Please don't call the police.

Listen here! She needs to be taught a lesson. Mrs Merrick's face has taken on an unnatural red blotchiness.

Pualele fixes her stare on a ladder in the woman's stockings as the high-pitched barrage of words blends together in an uncomprehending babble. She has a sudden vision of her mother with one stockinged leg stretched out from under her Sunday skirt, a bottle of clear nail varnish in one hand while in the other she holds a tiny brush that she carefully passes over a snag to stop just such a ladder happening.

Can't just take what you like, girlie.

She was going to pay. She'll pay now. She just forgot, didn't you, Pualele?

Pualele keeps her head down, thinking about the right thing to say as she focusses on the run in Mrs Merrick's stocking. She has to get out of this mess, she has to say something. She licks her lips and tries to swallow the last of the offending sugar stick before speaking, her voice barely more than a whisper as she unglues her tongue from the roof of her mouth.

I don't have any money.

What? What did she say? There's spittle on Mrs Merrick's lips as she looks from Cate to Pualele. *I'll not be having the likes of you playing games with me.*

Here. I'll pay. Cate holds out some silver coins and Mrs Merrick spins round to face her.

It's already stealing, you know. Once you're outside the door and that.

Plee-ease! Cate's voice wobbles as she moves closer to the woman.

Mrs Merrick stands for a moment and everyone is still as they wait for

83

the woman to make her move. Finally she grunts and reaches out, taking the money from Cate before turning back to Pualele. The ladder starts to run up her stockings as her thick legs exert all their pressure on the sheer nylon. Pualele watches the ladder disappear under her too-short smock.

She knows what she's done. Mrs Merrick waggles a finger in her face and Pualele pulls away from her. *Pig ignorant! She can't even look me in the eye – should send them back to the Cook Islands or wherever it is they come from.*

Michael smirks in the background.

And don't let me catch you in this shop again, you hear me? Her voice rises to such a high pitch that Pualele has to stop herself from covering her ears. Mrs Merrick goes back inside with the money and Michael follows her.

On the footpath Pualele wants to explain to Elizabeth and Cate how stupid she feels. She wants to say sorry and start the afternoon over again – without Michael, and shops, and Mrs Merrick.

How could you, Pualele? Elizabeth's bounce has disappeared, and for the first time since Pualele has known her Elizabeth's face is still as she looks at Pualele through watery eyes.

It was just a mistake, Elizabeth. Leave her alone.

Pualele wants to thank Cate, but she's terrified of what Elizabeth might say to her next. She's ashamed of what she's done and she knows that she has embarrassed her new friend. She responds in the only way she knows how.

In between the cars on Ponsonby Road, Pualele runs.

The sounding of horns follows her as she sprints between the vehicles, choking a little as she breathes in the exhaust fumes of the cars. She keeps running back towards her house along Richmond Road, stopping only once she is inside and has slammed the blue-paned door shut behind her. She bends with her hands on knees, panting, her heart beating so loudly in her ears that she is deaf to the approaching feet slapping on the kauri floors.

Where's dinner?

It could never be said that Uncle Sam ever *looked* hungry. But even perceived hunger can do funny things to a man, and his question requires only one answer. Pualele straightens up. She needs some of those packets and tins from the shop. She could just open them up and there would be dinner, ready to eat. Thoughts of the shop make her feel sick and she gulps, trying to settle her queasiness.

Well?

Sorry, Uncle. She moves quickly to squeeze by him. She's almost past when the back of his hand connects with the side of her head. The blow takes her by surprise and she trips, falling to her knees. Uncle Sam hauls her up onto her feet by her arm, pulling her like a doll down the hallway towards the kitchen. She stumbles along and recovers enough to run the last few steps into the kitchen.

She pulls out the tray of sausages and Aunty's leftover chop suey. Uncle Sam stands in the doorway and watches as she lights the gas and sets the pot of chop suey on the stove top to heat. She keeps her eyes on the pan as she picks up the tray of sausages single-handedly, but her wrist gives way and her hand tips forward so that the sausages slip off in a solid semi-defrosted mass onto the floor. *Splat.* She trembles, trying to brace herself against the blow. She keeps her chin tucked in and feet wide apart so that she won't fall over this time.

When nothing happens, Pualele glances towards the door. Uncle Sam has gone. She gathers up the sausages and puts them into the frying pan. As they cook they spit onto her skin, and the kitchen fills with the smells of fried sausage meat and reheated cabbage. She feels the pull of air as the front door opens and listens as it is closed. A heavy bag is thrown on the floor in the hallway.

Smells good! Kasi is standing in the doorway in his muddy blue overalls, grinning. *How was school?*

Pualele tries to smile back but succeeds only in making a grimace. She could tell him how she's neglected her homework, and how for the first time in her life she has stolen and been caught. Or she could explain that she's managed to lose the only friends she has in this place where they want to '*keep cool*' but wear more clothes than most Samoans own. And there is no point in telling him that Uncle has hit her so hard on the side of the head that her ears are still ringing. After all, they've all had a good hiding when they've deserved it, and a girl who neglects her duties and steals from palagi doesn't merit sympathy. Pualele just isn't sure what to say in response to his innocent question, but she swallows and finds her voice.

Good.

Kasi beams at her.

What's for dinner? He leans over Pualele and with two fingers plucks a sausage from the pan.

Oww! Oww! He juggles the sausage before finally grasping it and tearing off a chunk of the barely cooked meat with his teeth. Pualele laughs at her brother and tries to push him out of the kitchen, but Kasi just braces himself against the door as a breeze blows down the hall.

Afakasi! their father calls. Kasi immediately heads for the front door.

Needs more cooking! he whispers back to her as he leaves the kitchen. She makes to chase him and throws a dishcloth that misses him and lands at the feet of Uncle Sam as he steps out of his bedroom. Carefully he bends and picks up the cloth without looking at Pualele, who is paralysed in the kitchen doorway. He walks towards her, stopping only when he is all that she can see. He folds the cloth carefully and holds it out to her. With hands quaking she takes it from him and backs up into the kitchen, where the sausages are now stuck and burning in the pan.

Father's hand lands on his older brother's shoulder, and Uncle Sam turns to face him.

Smell that – Pualele's a good cook! Father's face is grimy with a black smudge across his cheek, but Pualele thinks she has never before seen him so proud.

Uncle Sam grunts.

They're all the same, he says as he turns away.

Cooking is not what she wants to be doing. Nor does she want to live with Uncle Sam and Aunty Sefi or go to school in New Zealand. It makes no sense to her that her uncle and aunty want her here when all she seems to do is disappoint and make them angry. She can't help comparing Uncle Sam to her father – similar in so many ways and yet her uncle's flashes of impatience and anger frighten her. She wonders whether her being here is really just Aunty's idea. Pualele knows her uncle and aunt well enough now to know that what Aunty wants, Aunty gets.

It's an overwhelming thought.

She feels suddenly nauseated, not sure whether it is from the smell of smoky burnt pig fat and reheated cabbage or from the slap to the side of her head. There is room for only one thought in her head – she doesn't want to be in New Zealand.

CHAPTER 10

OLGA'S JOURNAL

The night was abuzz with murmuring as I lay there sleepless next to Pero. I heard snatches of whispered conversations. Father Bilić and Jure spoke with Mama.

. . . we've got him but he's not talking.

. . . they'll come looking for him . . .

There was a growing dread in my belly. I wanted to know who they'd found and who they were looking for. I wanted to know if we were in danger. Perhaps I should have spoken then – it would have been easy to betray myself as a jealous young girl. But other thoughts seemed to justify my silence. In my own defence, if I'd known what was to happen that next day – I would have spoken.

But I didn't.

I kept silent because I wanted to hurt Mila the way she'd hurt me. I hoped that when they found her and Dragan together they would be pilloried for running off together, and then ostracised from the village. In my child's mind, she needed to suffer so that I might heal my broken heart.

꘎

The next morning the mountain was enveloped in the kind of thick fog that dampens your clothes if you stay in it for too long. I was quick with feeding the chickens, and once inside again I joined Pero on the floor where he was playing with his marbles.

Ola. You can help.

Mama pointed with her nose at a pile of darning that she had placed on the table. Socks spilled out from underneath Ivica's trousers and Uncle Jure's shirt. I mouthed a *Sorry* to Pero and sat at the table, starting on the shirt. The fog had eclipsed the sun, so Mama lit an oil lamp.

As I thatched the small hole in the elbow I was startled by a knock at the window. My hand jerked, sending the needle tip into my finger. I sucked on it, tasting the warm blood as Mama opened the window and passed out a covered basket to a pair of disembodied arms in the thick and soupy air. She leaned out of the window and whispered into the mist, shutting the window again and immediately returning to her own stack of mending as if nothing had happened. I watched her and waited.

Keep your eyes on your work, Olga. I don't want to have to wash that shirt again because you've pricked yourself.

I hid my curiosity and went back to pulling the thread through the thick cotton shirt, carefully extending the darning to cover the speck of blood.

Pero had grown bored and was now next to me, rolling his marbles along the grooves in the table. Mama reached out, covering the small balls with her hand, stopping them. Her face relaxed as she spoke to him.

Go and see if we missed any eggs.

Pero slid off the seat and headed for the door. I remember him stretching up to pull the door open, his jersey and undershirt riding up to expose his lower back. I could see his slender waist and his spine pressed hard against his skin.

Mama and I continued sewing without speaking. Eventually she stood up and opened the door, allowing some of the dampness to come inside. She stepped out into the yard, the air so thick that it wrapped around her until she was gone, like a diver disappearing into the sea. I couldn't imagine the villagers finding Dragan or Mila out there in the mist.

The door was wrenched open and I jumped in my seat. Mama stood there, her fog-dampened hair sticking to her face.

Quickly!

What's happening?

Move, Olga. They're searching every house.

I dropped the shirt and needle on the floor and ran towards the door. I heard shots crackling like pine cones in a fire as Mama pulled our coats off the hook behind the door and thrust mine at me. Before I'd buttoned the front she was clutching my wrist and pulling me after her. We headed towards the chicken coop and I suddenly realised that Pero was not with her.

Pero!

She pulled on my arm until we were in the coop. I followed her as we clambered over the wall at the back, and she grasped my hand again as she started up the mountain. I pulled free of her and stopped. A cold sweat was spreading over me now. Mama's hand moved and I thought she was going to strike me.

Mama! Where's Pero?

He's with Father. Come on. She wiped her forearm across her face and turned back up the hill. I had to run to keep pace with her, confused by the confidence of her answer. I wanted to scream at her, but fear kept me silent.

Somewhere deep in the thick fog, I heard men shouting and the splintering of a wooden door being kicked in. I flinched at the sound, quickening my pace so that I was at Mama's heels, glancing back into the grey blanket that shielded whatever was happening below in the village. Mama raced on and once again I found myself having to run to catch up with her. We were both panting heavily as the fog had begun to thin into spectral wisps until finally it disappeared altogether, leaving us exposed above the shrouded village.

Finally we paused to catch our breath and I immediately recognised the place. The mountainside up there was a tableau of rocky outcrops in between clumps of trees. To the right of us was the grazing meadow, and if we'd kept going higher we'd find ourselves at the cave entrance. I looked up at the milky sky and when I looked back, Mama was already moving on, motioning for me to follow across the mountain.

We were headed towards the old village with its overgrown houses when I saw Pero with Father Bilić, my brother's arms wrapped carelessly around the priest's neck. I cannot tell you how relieved I felt seeing him. They were waiting for us outside a crumbled building that was set into the hillside and was partially hidden by a forest of vines. Mama tore Pero from Father Bilić, locking him to her.

In here.

We followed the priest as he lifted back some of the thick growth to reveal a door. We found ourselves in a small space that had once been a room. It smelled earthy and felt cold, and as my eyes adjusted to the light inside I could see weeds and plants encroaching from outside. Rosa and Oliver stepped from the shadows to embrace us. We clung to each other as if to shut out the world. As I disentangled myself from Rosa's arms, I noticed the basket my mother had passed out our window now sat in the corner of the room. Next to it was a pile of blankets and a gun.

You'll be safe here until tonight. We'll move then.

Thank you, Father. My mother kissed the priest on both cheeks. He turned his attention towards me, a sort of smile on his face. I avoided his eyes, focussing instead on his boots.

Don't worry, Olga. You did the right thing. The soldier will talk and we'll find Mila.

His words sank in slowly and my face felt clammy as my mouth opened and closed. It felt as if I had no control over it. I must have looked quite peculiar because Mother and Father Bilić were looking at me as if I was a fish gasping for air. Mama reached for me as my head started to spin. I stepped away from her outstretched hand and took a deep breath, trying to take control of myself.

I . . . I think there's been a mistake.

I felt like I'd swallowed a rock, the words sticking in my throat. Mama's eyebrows drew together, while the priest's lifted towards his receding hairline. I knew I had to go on and stop whatever I'd started. I had to stop the men and the guns.

When I saw Mila the other night . . .

Rosa pushed herself up onto her feet and stepped towards me, her face a tapestry of emotion. I tried again to say what I should have said a dozen times before now.

Mila and . . . My head started to spin again. *She walked off . . . alone.*

My mother exhaled like a burst tyre, slumping against the side of the warped walls of the house as she put her arm around Pero.

What do you mean? Father Bilić growled.

She was with Dragan.

Dragan? What was he doing there? And the German?

I shook my head. *There was no German. Just Mila and Dragan.*

Oliver stood to the side and as I spoke he let out a choking sound.

The priest grunted, lacing his fingers and bringing his hands behind his head. I wanted Father Bilić to believe me and looked around for support. Oliver looked as if he was about to say something, but as he leaned forward towards me, Rosa pulled on his shirt collar, preventing him from moving. He stood there, breathing heavily, his shoulders heaving, but he said nothing as his mother's hand remained at the nape of his neck, silencing him.

I thought about telling Father Bilić that Mila had left on her own accord. She had decided to run away. I turned wildly from Oliver to the priest. *Say something, Oliver.* He avoided my gaze.

The priest released his hands and let them fall to his sides as he stepped away from me. He paused by the door, his hand on the gnarled wood as he considered what he'd just heard. He turned and muttered something to Mama. As she nodded her assent, he left us in the ruins. I was glad the priest had gone. At least, I thought, they knew there was no need for fighting.

The relief I felt at Father Bilić's departure was replaced by a growing fury as I looked at Oliver. I couldn't fathom why he had refused to speak up, say *he'd* got it wrong. He was my friend and he could have told them what I had actually said to him. Then I recalled Mila's words – *There is no us.* It occurred to me that the twins were more alike than I had ever considered before. He was just like her, and bile rose in my throat as I watched him sheltering at his mother's side. I was suddenly as desperate to be away from him as I had been to get away from Mila. I wished the whole family gone.

Can we go home now, Mama?

She stepped forward and involuntarily I shrank back into the corner. I will never know what she thought of me. Her face was closed and tight, and in the end she said nothing as she turned her back on me.

◈

I was thankful that Pero was with us. Without him it would have been a painful silence punctuated with glares from my mother. As the day wore on, I watched the shadows change shape and darken on the ground. The fog had finally dissipated, leaving the winter sun teetering on the mountaintop, ready to fall off and plunge us into darkness.

Mama entertained Pero by telling him stories that I'd heard a thousand times, while I wondered how long we would have to wait in the ruined house. I tried my best to fade into the background amongst the brambles that had pushed their way in through the fractured walls and missing roof tiles. With nothing else to do, I went over and over everything in my mind. I wasn't a liar. I'd told the truth (except the parts that didn't matter to anyone but me). I'd done the right thing by clearing up the misunderstanding.

I was distracted from my thoughts by the sounds of birds searching for food and wind ruffling the trees. I tried to guess what kind of bird I was hearing and in which tree it sat. As I listened, the sound of stones crunching became clear. A small gasp escaped from me before I could catch it. Mama held up her hand and manoeuvred herself so her small body filled the narrow entrance, blocking whatever was out there from the rest of us while Rosa reached for the gun still lying on the floor. As I stared at Mama's back, she moved aside. I could see fingers wrapped around the edge of the door hanging off its hinges. It opened to reveal a solemn looking Uncle Jure with Father Bilić, and for the first time ever, my uncle avoided my eye.

Let's go.

Mama and Rosa were now standing in front of the two men.

Mama opened her mouth to reply, but Jure went on, filling the space where her words should have been.

Olga. Were there any Germans the night you saw Mila?

I shook my head and he let out a hiss as his breath escaped through his teeth. He turned to Father Bilić.

We keep this to ourselves.

The priest moved his head in agreement as Rosa lurched forward.

But Mila?

Let's go. Uncle Jure cut her off.

I won't go without her.

We don't have time for this, Jure growled.

She pushed past Mama until she was centimetres from Jure. She ripped the front of her dress open, buttons popping off onto the ground like confetti. There was just enough light left to see the marks on her chest. Mama sucked in her breath and moved to Rosa's side as Father Bilić crossed himself.

They can do whatever they like to me, but they won't have her.

Jure looked down and took a deep breath. Oliver placed a blanket around his mother's shoulders, wrapping it across her chest.

We leave now. Whether you come or not is up to you.

Jure's businesslike manner left no room for discussion. He turned towards Mama and motioned for her to go ahead of him. She pulled Pero to her side and then looked over her shoulder. I thought she was looking for me, but I quickly realised she was looking at Rosa, willing her to follow. One by one I watched them all leave. I waited for someone to tell me what to do, but it was as if I was invisible. There was a movement behind me and I remembered the priest. Father Bilić looked at me and jerked his head toward the door. I hadn't been forgotten after all.

We soon caught up with the others, and I was shocked to see a rifle slung over Mama's shoulder. She handled it as if she had always carried one. The men had guns too and I was suddenly overcome with a deep, dark shame. It didn't seem real to me that I might have caused all this. I wished that I'd never opened my mouth. I'd so many questions and a desperate need to understand what was going on around me, but I knew the best thing I could do right then was not to say a word.

☙

We continued on up the mountain moving eastwards, leaving behind the old village. We were almost at the caves when a sound like one of Dragan's slingshots hitting a tree trunk made me stop. One missile was closely followed by another, and then an entire volley of shots pitted the ground around us. We took refuge wherever we could find it.

I recognised the spot. It was where I'd once hidden with Mila, only this time I lay behind the boulders with my arms around Pero. A few steps away to our right Mama was sheltering behind a fallen log with Rosa and Oliver. I watched in amazement as Mama cocked the gun, loaded it and fired over the top of the log at a protrusion of rocks ahead of us.

There was a scramble of feet behind me and I saw Jure and another man running towards us. They slid to a halt and crouched next to me as shots hit the ground behind the men, sending little puffs of earth and stones into the air. Jure brought his mouth close to my ear.

I'm not really sure exactly what happened next. Pero was next to me, wide-eyed and unspeaking, as I tried to stop myself from losing control of my bladder. We were pressed together with Jure and the young Partisan to the side of us. I could feel a tremor running through Pero. I found his balled fist and I closed my own hand around it.

Jure shouted *Run*. The young man went first, then I squeezed Pero's hand and we followed him. Time seemed to slow down as we dashed the last few metres. It felt as if we were running through water. I dragged Pero on with me, never doubting that we would make it to Mama and safety.

Suddenly I was suspended in a violent red and orange flash. Debris flew like angry bees in every direction. The horrendous sound that accompanied the flash a second later sent fierce vibrations through my body and I was sure that I was about to shatter into a thousand tiny pieces. Nothing I write can convey the horror I felt at that moment, the sheer terror of feeling trapped and yet exposed at the same time, fearing that we might all be killed.

My next clear memory was of being on my knees, Pero just behind me on his stomach. I clamped onto his wrist and dragged him with me, half-scrambling, half-crawling until we were behind a cairn on the track. Mama was facing us now, thrusting the gun into Rosa's hands and shouting something at me, but all I could hear was a ringing in my ears. As I tried to understand what she was saying, something trickled into my eyes, blinding me momentarily.

In panic I wiped them, and saw that my hand was red. I stared at the blood dripping off my fingers and then down at my dress, which was now speckled with bright red polka dots. Up on my sleeve a shape like the boot of Italy was forming.

Mama was running towards me and I anticipated her warm embrace. She was on her knees, a hand on each of us, dragging us behind the logs. I crawled behind them and sat on the ground, pulling my knees up and leaning back against the hard wood as she placed her hands under Pero and lifted him to her.

A primal sound came out of her as she shook him and then put her head to his chest. There was so much blood that their clothes were turning black, but I couldn't understand how such a small boy could produce so much blood. I lay there unable to speak, feeling as if I had been punched in the throat. I grabbed at one of Pero's arms, but my hand slid off his blood-slicked skin. I begged God to leave my brother. I asked him to take anyone else, even me, but to leave Pero alone.

The blood in my own head pounded against my skull as if trying to burst out. Mama was keening, swaying backwards and forwards, and Pero's arms flopped in time with her rocking. I don't remember how long I was transfixed by my brother's listless arms, but at some point I saw one hand move and his fingers grab her sleeve. I closed my eyes and thanked God that he was alive.

It was at that moment that Jure slapped down beside me, pulling the body of the young Partisan. I couldn't tell you what his face looked like because I could not tear my eyes away from the gaping hole where the right side of his chest had been. His plump heart seemed to be beating against the shattered bones of his rib cage as other viscera and blood spilled out of him onto the ground. I vomited between my legs. Through no choice of his own the Partisan had almost certainly saved our lives by taking the full impact of the explosion.

The gunfire eased, and after some shouting and a few quick bursts of fire, it stopped completely. A call rang out from one of our own and, before daylight vanished, Father Bilić emerged, followed by several other men. They wore the red star of the Partisans on their hats and thick beards on their faces, and they didn't seem to me the kind of men who would have any tolerance for my kind of mistake.

Mama was next to Pero and I sidled over to them. Pero's eyes were fluttering open and I felt a sense of relief. I sat with them as Uncle Jure and the men spoke briefly and I watched my little brother's eyes open. Looking at him, I whispered his name. He didn't smile back, or even seem to see me. I spoke his name more loudly this time, but again there was no response or recognition in his face.

Mama! There was urgency in my voice.

I touched her on the arm and she looked at me. She was exhausted but calm.

Look at him.

She looked into his face and kissed his forehead.

At his eyes, Mama, look at his eyes. She held him at arm's length and looked at him, gently wiping away the young man's blood from Pero's face with her own sleeve.

She couldn't see it; he was conscious and breathing, but he was not there.

As I watched Mama with Pero, Jure came alongside and took him from her, kissing his cheek. Jure only saw a boy who'd cheated death. My mouth was dry and I felt like they had abandoned reality for a more palatable truth. I felt that I was the only person who could see that something terrible had happened to Pero. Or had it? Perhaps I'd got things wrong again? I decided it was best not to say anything else as we moved on.

I considered falling behind and losing myself in the dark, but a twig cracked behind me and there was Father Bilić watching me, herding me like I was a sheep straying from the flock. When we reached the cave I paused. I could be near them in the open air, but the cave, our cave, was a different story altogether.

The priest nudged me gently onwards. *Get inside, Olga.*

Father . . . I'm sorry.

He looked but said nothing. I couldn't read his face in the dark, so I put my head down and entered the cave.

Inside the air was thick with the smell of sweat and gunpowder. My mother was bent over Pero as Jure wrapped him in a blanket and placed him in my mother's arms. I looked away. The dead man's body was brought into the cave by two of the surviving Partisans. The body was wrapped in a sheet and rolled under the ledge where Oliver had found the guns. A sarcophagus of rocks and stones was piled under the ledge. While the priest spoke his words, the Partisans stood at the mouth of the cave, holding an oil lamp that swung like an incense burner.

I took my place along the wall and closed my eyes, thinking that I could hear a scratching from the recesses of the cave. But that could have been my imagination.

☙

That night Mama came to me as I slept. She carried two rucksacks and in her hands she had a pair of boots. *Go quickly*, she whispered in a voice that invited no comment. In the weak light from a candle, she motioned towards the clothes at my feet.

She dropped the boots at my side and then busied herself stuffing one final blanket into one of the packs. I was clumsy in my half-sleep, struggling with arms appearing where my head should be and my toenails catching on heavily darned socks. I picked up the left boot and weighed it in my hand. It had thick soles that were caked in mud and leather uppers that had been scuffed by an unnamed donor. I placed the boot on the ground by my foot. My toes ended a good four centimetres from the tip of the shoe. I looked up at my mother, the unasked question lying between us. She handed me two pairs of thick woollen socks. I stuffed one sock each into the toes of the boots and then pulled on the second pair. The boots were still too big.

Mama put on one rucksack and pushed the other towards me. I followed her to the cave entrance where Oliver and Rosa were already moving off ahead of us. Outside, a half-moon veiled by gossamer clouds hung in the sky above us. Uncle Jure and Pero were already there, waiting.

Won't you change your mind? Mother asked. Her voice was wobbling and I examined her face. Her eyelids were swollen and I felt guilty that while I'd been able to sleep, she had not.

I wasn't sure that he'd heard her. He dropped his head, staring at the ground. My mother grabbed his hand and pressed it to her lips. They stayed like that until I shifted and they remembered I was there.

Jure encircled Mama with his arms and let his lips run over her forehead, the bridge of her nose, her lips. He released her and pushed her gently away, turning towards Pero, who had been standing silently in their moon shadow. Jure slipped a small doll made out of a length of rope into his hand.

To keep you safe.

Pero stared at its raggedy arms and button-eyes. It had loose pants with a drawstring belt and looked like a miniature version of Pero.

He gave a slight shiver as if from the cold, then his body was still once more. He was always desperate for Jure to make him things, harried him endlessly for some toy or trinket, but now he was silent. He twitched again. Mama moved forward as his body began shaking uncontrollably, as loose and pliable as the rope doll.

Pero's fingers let go of the doll and it fell to the ground as Mama wrapped her arms around him, pinning his flailing arms to his sides while his head continued to shake. A small yelp escaped from him, and whatever he saw in that doll I didn't want to know. But I picked it up, clutching its plaited body to my chest. Then as suddenly as the shaking had begun he was still and silent again, clinging to our mother as she turned her back on Jure and me, shielding Pero from the offending gift.

Jure's eyes became glassy. He pulled me to him and I felt his stubble graze my skin as he kissed my cheeks. He squeezed me so hard it hurt, and when he released me, I became afraid. I wanted him to hold me to him and not let go. But instead we stayed where we were, staring at each other.

Can't you come too?

He pulled me back to him. I buried my face into his warm chest. I could feel his heart beat and I did not want to leave this man who had been more of a father to me than my own.

Mama disengaged my knotted fingers from Uncle's jacket. Jure reached for her, but she swatted his hand away. A sob escaped her. She grabbed my hand, and with Pero on her other side we turned and walked away. We'd gone only a few steps when I pulled free of her hand and ran back to where my uncle stood. I wanted to tell him I loved him and that I was sorry and sad and angry, but most of all that I felt totally alone. It's easy now to think clearly about what I wanted to say to him, but when I opened my mouth, *Don't forget to feed Šuša* came out instead.

He squeezed my arm and nodded. I wish I'd hugged him one last time before I ran back to my mother, but I never did. It didn't enter my mind that I would never see him again.

We walked quickly, making our way downhill and skirting the village and the houses that dotted the hillside above the coastline. The buildings were made out of the same blocks of white stone carved from the mountainside. They had been built by hand and each block was cemented to the next by orange clay, giving the houses a mottled appearance. Even in the dull night light we could see the marbling of white stone and ochre cement and I thought I saw curtains waving goodbye in the windows as we passed by.

We kept the track to our left, using it as a guide, shadows flickering from behind every tree and rock. When we reached the steepest part of the mountain track, Mama paused briefly to pick up Pero. He clasped his hands behind her neck and wrapped his legs around her waist. She carried him like that, picking up the pace until we were soon running down the mountainside. She never said a word to me, not even when I stumbled. We passed stands of olive trees and the neglected vegetable patches of those already gone, but she kept her focus on the path that was taking us to the sea.

On the beach, I saw the skiff waiting in knee-deep water. The night air was cool and fresh, and I was thankful at least for that. The moon cast a shimmer of light across the inky water, looking like a path of liquid silver running to where the sky meets the sea.

In the boat there were already five others, including Oliver and Rosa, waiting on a vessel meant for two fishermen and their catch. My mother unwound Pero's arms and legs from around her and pushed him forward towards Rosa. She reached over with another passenger to pull him on board, slopping water over the gunwales into the boat.

You can't bring all that.

Mama hesitated, wobbling on the slimy stones underfoot. She removed the rucksack from her back and reached out to take the one that I had been carrying. She held both the bags in front of her and stood her position in the water. The sea was slowly numbing my legs. My teeth chattered as we stood there. I could see that Mama was also trying to keep from shivering as she waited.

Your choice. You or your bags.

She looked at the others in the boat, but no one would meet her eyes. My mother turned to me. *Come, Olga.*

If you want the three of you on – no bags. We're already overloaded.

I shifted on the stones, making them crunch against each other, reminding me of marching soldiers. Mama stood firm.

We're coming like everyone else. Her hand fixed on the edge of the boat, tipping it in our direction and making the other people on board shift uncomfortably. They sat on the boxes and bags they were taking with them.

For God's sake, Filip, let them on. I recognised Ivica's voice. He was sitting on what seemed to be a crate of chickens but was just a down-filled quilt that was losing its feathery stuffing.

The sea's flat. We'll be fine.

Filip pulled the back of his hand across his forehead, wiping away sea spray. He turned and walked towards me, muttering. Before I could react, he placed one arm across my back and the other under my legs and carried me to the boat. I let out a whimper as I landed in the boat. I saw Oliver sitting next to Rosa, his arm protectively around her shoulders. He glanced over at me and then turned and spat into the water.

Mama.

Shsshhh. It's OK. Ivica pulled Pero and me next to him, humming to us while Filip turned and went back to where Mama was waiting with the rucksacks. They stood in the water, neither moving. It was my mother who shifted first. She held out the rucksacks and they swung in the air before him. The only sound was the tide as it slapped against the wooden boards of the boat. Filip grunted and reached out for the bags. He took them from my mother and nodded for her to get into the boat. Once she was settled, Filip let the bags trail in the water as he walked around to the starboard side of the boat. He lifted the dripping bags, dropping them onto Ivica's lap. *If the wind picks up, throw them over.*

CHAPTER 11

PUALELE

She pauses outside the door. The sound of children inside the classroom buzzes and hisses like the electricity pylon that heaves with unseen power on the street corner. Pualele quietly opens the door and walks in. The noise stops, not instantaneously like turning off a switch, but more slowly, like the time it takes for a light bulb to finally fizzle out and die.

She walks between the desks towards the seat next to Elizabeth that is still vacant, trying not to catch anyone's eye. There is a folded piece of paper on the chair and she picks it up and unfolds it as she sits down.

You better watch out for Pooh-a-lee-lee.
She thinks everything is free.

There is a collective smirking and whispering that floats all around her as big fat drops fall onto the paper and the words begin to swim before her eyes. Her face becomes hot and she crumples the note in her hand, pushing her nails in so hard that they bite into her palms. The physical pain distracts her from the humiliation of the note and the sniggering children, and by the time the door opens again and Sister Margaret comes into the room, Pualele has escaped the classroom and is walking next to Sione on the way to the swimming hole.

As the children filter out into the playground for morning tea, Pualele sits at her desk.

Pualele, Sister Carmel would like to see you.

Pualele nods at Sister Margaret and pushes herself to her feet. A hot pricking sensation starts again behind her eyelids as she moves towards the door. The school is a blur as she rushes towards the principal's office, convinced that the events yesterday have reached Sister Carmel. Snatches of conversation reach her ears along with the sound of laughter as she scuttles along, keeping close to the sides of the buildings. She can't make out what they're saying, but she doesn't care any more. After this, she won't be coming back to school again.

She opens the door and stops. Seated on the bench outside Sister Carmel's office is the Italian girl, Annunzia, and the Vietnamese boy, Lok. They are still gazing at each other, trying to discover what crime they have committed, when Sister Carmel's door opens.

Enter.

The school secretary, Mrs Jones, steps aside as the children file into the office.

Well. We seem to have a problem.

Pualele dares not catch the nun's eye, so she stares at the floor. It is going to be worse than she thought.

Your names . . .

Despite herself, Pualele scratches her nails across her palms.

. . . they're simply not good Catholic names.

She raises her eyes to get a glimpse of the nun.

Things will be much easier for everyone if we use proper English names that everyone can say. A saint's name, for instance.

She wants to tell her that she has three names already. That she is named after her grandmother and her cousin. She is already somebody – she is Pualele Sina Auva'a. There will be another name when it comes time for confirmation, but no one has told her of having to have an English name. She feels herself disappearing. She doesn't want to be anybody else – she just wants to go home to Samoa, where no one wants to make her something she isn't.

Sister Carmel makes eye contact with each child as she speaks.

Luke . . . Anne . . . and . . . well, I suppose Pauline will do.

Pauline! This is surely worse than being expelled. She cannot bear to think what she will tell her parents and Aunty Sefi. Pauline isn't even a real saint's name. And St Paul is a boy not a girl. She wants to cry all over again.

You may all go now.

Pualele is last to leave but just as she touches the handle to close the door behind her, Sister Carmel calls out to her.

And Pauline?

Pualele turns towards her voice, eyes on the floor.

You must look people in the eye when they speak to you.

Slowly Pualele lifts her eyes until she is looking openly at the nun, her face growing hot as she holds her gaze.

Close the door on your way out.

She slips out and heads to the church that dominates the school grounds. Outside there are questions and talking and people everywhere. In the church, a solemn hush washes over her and Pualele melts into the pews without having to be a part of anything else other than her own thoughts.

She admires the Stations of the Cross and the statues that are positioned around the church. They are far more spectacular than anything she has ever seen before. The statues look so real: the serpent around the feet of the Blessed Virgin Mary and the bloody wounds on the crucified Christ.

Pualele is entranced by the dead Jesus on the cross with thorns piercing his temple and nails embedded in his hands and feet. She stares at the gaping red wound in his side that looks like the inside of some overripe fruit. She grips the back of the pew in front of her and snatches her hand away as the head of a nail sinks into the palm of her left hand. As she looks from her bleeding hand back to the wounds on the statue, the line separating what is real from what is imaginary becomes blurred. Everything seems jumbled up together, with black doris plums taking the place of bleeding hearts.

Pain has become something different too. She sits back and presses her nails into the small cut. She winces as her hand begins to throb, the sensation travelling up her arm, her neck and right into her head. Her eyes close and she lets the air hiss out between her teeth as she digs her nails in. Facing the crucifixion, she kneels down. For the first time in weeks, she is at peace.

☙

After school, Pualele runs home, stopping only at the letterbox to collect the mail before springing up the steps to open the stained-glass front door. She leans against the door to catch her breath before going to her room and dropping the mail and her school bag on the floor. She kicks her bag so it spills its contents across the floor before throwing herself down on her bed, burying her face in the pillow while her mind races over the events of the day.

She quickly dismisses the cruel taunts of the children and the note on her chair from her mind, but she finds that she can't stop thinking about her new name. Now that she is safely at home, Pualele can pretend that she doesn't have a new palagi name. No one will know about it if she doesn't tell them, and she no longer has any friends who might call at the house for her. It will be easy – she can be Pauline at school and Pualele at home, and with Aunty Sefi she can be whichever Pualele she wants her to be.

She pushes herself up until she is sitting on the mattress, happy with the plan she has come up with, until she wonders what her mother would think of all this. Pualele begins to feel uneasy. All the Auva'a children know who they are named after and how they are to behave, and here she is taking on new names and plotting how to deceive her family.

Her shoulders sag. As she considers what to do, she spies a light-blue envelope amongst the mail on the floor. She jumps up and plucks the letter from the pile of bills and reads her father's name on the front of the envelope. She is disappointed that there is no separate letter for her, but she hopes there is a letter inside the envelope to save on postage.

In the kitchen she finds the kettle already full of water and when it begins to boil a few minutes later, she waves the envelope over the curl of steam. Her finger eases under the flap until the glue gives way and she is able to withdraw the neatly folded paper. Inside her room she closes the door and lies back on her pillow to read the letter.

My Dear Husband,

It has been many weeks now since you have gone, and we all miss you so. Especially the little ones! We pray every night that you are well and we look forward to your letters.

I thank you for the money that we received today – Banu says he has some chickens for sale and I think that I will buy some. Leti will not like the competition, but she is getting old and I need to plan for a time when you return and we will have a feast in your honour! Besides, I am keeping two of her piglets – the others I have sold. We have never been so rich!

I think I will also use some of the money to take Papavai to the palagi doctor when he comes again. He has been off colour and Mere says that the doctor may be able to help. I suspect his real illness is one of envy. He has been in sour spirits since you left and I know he would like to return to New Zealand – he still thinks himself a young man and sometimes I think he would like to live back there again.

I hope my Afakasi is working hard. I am so proud of him working with you and earning New Zealand money. He is a good boy and I hope he will find a nice Samoan girl in New Zealand.

Is Pualele settling? I worry about her – she is not a strong one like the other children, but it is right that she is with Sefi and Sam. They will give her a good life in New Zealand. Maybe I should tell her about Mama, who raised me and loved me more than anyone and that she always said I was a lucky little girl because she chose me to love. Do you think if I wrote to Pualele and spoke about how happy my life has been that it would be easier for her to settle? I don't know what the right thing to do is – perhaps it would only make things worse.

Tell Afakasi and Pualele I will write to them both on Sunday after church.

I must go. There is much to do these days without you all. I can't wait for your letters to arrive and hope that it won't be long before we can all be together again.

Your loving wife

Olina

Pualele folds the letter and places it back in the envelope. *It is right she is with Sefi and Sam . . . They will give her a good life.* She is despondent at the thought that her mother has given her away. Pualele doesn't think her situation is at all like her Mama's. Olina's mother, the woman who had fed her and raised her and loved her, was in fact, her aunty. Mama never knew the woman who had given birth to her. Papavai had returned from New Zealand with the baby Olina and had given his daughter to his sister to raise. And no one ever knew who Olina's birth mother was. What Pualele knows for sure is that Olina's childhood is nothing like her own. Pualele has only ever known Olina – her one and only true Mama. So how can it be that Mama would be so agreeable to Aunty's desire to have Pualele live with them?

All Pualele wants in the whole world is to be with her mother and father and her brothers and sisters in their village, not here in Auckland where she has to be some other person that she doesn't know. Her eyes come to rest on the prayer card propped up against the wall.

If it hadn't been for the second Pualele Sina Auva'a, she would never have been sent here. She reaches down and picks up a book that has slipped out of her bag and throws it at the picture of the girl. The book misses and hits the corner of the drawers before crashing onto the ground. She rolls onto her belly and pummels the bed with her fists, kicking with her feet until she's panting. Without thinking she curls her fingers into her palm.

The pencil case lies on the floor amongst the rest of the contents of her bag. She reaches for it and rolls onto her back. Inside the case she picks out the compass, fingering the sharp point as she twirls it around in front of her face. She sits up, her back against the wall and then, with an even pressure, she begins to draw ever-smaller circles on her palm until the point settles in the centre of her hand. She contemplates the needle-point resting on her hand for several seconds before pushing the compass into her skin. She sucks in her lower lip as a bead of blood appears where the point has entered.

She releases the compass. It falls onto the floor as she gazes at the blood pooling in her hand, her head throbbing as adrenaline pulses through her body.

Looking away from what she has just done to herself, she brings the palm to her mouth and sucks at the blood. Her eyes finally come to rest on the shrine to her cousin. She thinks about the shrines and statues in the church, calmly standing on their plinths, waiting for the people who will come and pray before them. Later she will consider who she really is, but right now she thinks of nothing as she recites the Hail Mary and digs her fingernails into her flesh.

CHAPTER 12

OLGA'S JOURNAL

Her name is Maureen.

It's a very old-fashioned name for such a young woman. She says it was her grandmother's name. It annoyed me how she'd said:

It WAS my grandmother's name.

Does this mean her grandmother changed her name, gave it up so Maureen could have it? I'm being mean-spirited, but she could've said that she shared her name with her grandmother. Or, better still, that she was named after her grandmother. I'm being overly sensitive I know – I'm a grumpy old woman and I apologise to you both.

You might not think it from what I've just written, but we had a nice conversation today and she told me a little about herself. She's a dancer. She sings too, but she says she's not really good enough, so she gets roles in the chorus of musicals. She told me their names, *Cats, Wicked*. There were others but the only one I knew anything of was *Mary Poppins*. She's worked all over the world – London, Toronto and New York. That's where she discovered the tiny lump in her breast. She'd just finished a US tour and had no health insurance, so she had to come home. I guess that's why she's been so withdrawn; she doesn't really want to be back here in Auckland, even though her family live here. Maureen says the man who comes with her is her brother Eddie, and when I told her that

I'd been worried about her when she was absent those few days, she almost cried.

She was at her cousin's wedding along with a take-home concoction of chemicals that the cousin's future husband to be (a doctor) hooked her up to each day. The wedding was on Waiheke Island. I've never been there, but I've heard that it's nice. Maureen says it was like being in Italy, with the faux-Tuscan venue they'd hired festooned in flowers and silk bunting. The photographs were taken in a tiny formal grove of mandarin trees. Eddie arranged for a jazz band and they played Rat Pack-themed covers. Maureen said she was only sad she hadn't the energy to dance all night.

ଔ

I told her I was once in Italy, but the only islands I ever spent time on were the ones off the coast of Dalmatia. Growing up, I'd heard so much about them. On the island of Hvar they lived much as we did, tending plots of land, raising animals and fishing, but I'd also heard stories that made their lives seem magical when compared to my own.

In summertime, lavender blanketed Hvar in a purple haze, and before the war the harvest festivals transformed the towns and villages with wild flowers and kolo dancers. I'd heard of freshwater bubbling up from the ground and forming streams that fell over cliffs in veils of water. And then there were the tales brought back by their sailors about foreign lands where jungles hid people who wore nothing but coloured paint on their brown skins, and where they ate monkeys' brains and smoked golden pipes.

These legends, that had once captivated me, now abandoned me as we started out across the island. The only thoughts in my head were tormented feelings and images of Oliver's down-turned mouth and Pero's vacant expression. I kept looking to my mother for some kind of acknowledgement, but she walked on silently beside me, straight-backed and steady with never a glance towards me.

Cold droplets fell onto my skin as my pace quickened. I needed to get out of the rain, but more than that I was anxious to get as far away as possible from Oliver and his mother. I didn't care where we were going. I placed one foot in front of the other, falling into a guilty silence as we followed the goat tracks and roads that rolled across the island.

Sometimes I felt gratitude towards the Germans for having forced us to leave. My steps would speed up before I remembered Pero, or I would catch sight of Oliver with a snarl on his lips or Rosa whose tears for Mila were endless. I'd fall back into a shameful shuffle, counting each step until I reached a thousand before starting all over again. I tried to focus on the ground, surveying the pebbles and stones that had lodged themselves in the dirt roads and paths that we followed.

I stayed as close to Mama as I could, wanting her to pull me to her and to have her console me, even though the shame I felt was so overwhelming that I kept thinking the only option I had was to run away and disappear like Mila. Everything that had happened was my fault. I would almost convince myself that things would improve if I left, but I had only to look at my mother to know that I wouldn't run away. We continued on together, as close as two people can be without touching. Sometimes her sleeve would brush against mine, and I would play with the idea of reaching my hand out and threading my fingers through hers. But the gap between us would open up again and I would feel as alone as I'd ever been.

We marched on with the adults taking turns to scout ahead. For two weeks we moved like that, crabbing our way slowly towards the port of Stari Grad, sometimes resting a day when locals provided us with shelter from the winter. The town was nestled into the rock that surrounded the bay, and it was a slight reprieve to be amongst other people again. We were transported by boat to another island and were told later that we had escaped by just one day, the Germans taking the island the day after we'd left. Our luck was holding. Or so they said.

※

How long must we wait? These were the first words I heard Mama speak to anyone since the night we'd left our village.

The young Partisan muttered, *Soon.* He walked away, leaving us mainland refugees staring out onto the bleak harbour of Komiža. There was talk of fishing boats taking us to safety. But all we could see in the harbour were a few ageing skiffs sitting low in the grey water.

As dusk fell over the port I sat on a low stone wall, knees tight together with hands in my lap. I'd taken to slipping away to escape Rosa's detachment and Mama's indifference. But mostly I did it to avoid Oliver.

A cold breeze blew in from the west and a mantle of purple light fell over the bay. On the horizon I could just make out a flotilla of storm-coloured vessels heading towards the island like an army of seafaring beetles. At last, I thought, we're moving on. I hoped and prayed that we would somehow be separated from Oliver and Rosa and that I could finally leave them behind.

☙

In the late hours we set out on a rust-marked British military cargo steamer fitted with barrage balloons to prevent an assault by air. All across Europe, the fat wire cables stretched like spiders' legs into the night sky, tethering the balloons above cities and ports to deter airborne attack. I remember looking up the long legs to the black underbellies hovering above our ship and I imagined that the steamer would lift up off the water and we would all float away.

Our ship was shadowed by two patrol boats that sliced through the water like black metal swans protecting their young. On deck there was total darkness, while below we huddled around the weak light of gas lamps. I crouched down next to Mama, bent forward as my stomach heaved. I lost the contents of the day's rations into a waiting bucket and forgot all about Oliver and Rosa.

The rolling of the vessel mixed with the diesel fumes and the continual shudder of the propellers meant that throughout the night I was joined in vomiting by many others. The earlier positive mood turned to one of fear as we lurched through rough waters towards an unknown destination.

As the night wore on many people fell into semi-consciousness, exhausted from the effort of staying alive and trying to remain upright. My head lolled on my chest but then, as the sea rocked the boat one way and then the other, I was repeatedly jerked awake.

I struggled to my feet and picked my way through the sea of bodies, my head hanging heavy on my shoulders as I made my way up onto the deck. I slumped down and clung to the rails as the fresh air slowly revived me. Out of the corner of my eye I saw someone else on deck. I lifted my leaden head and looked, not believing what I was seeing.

It didn't seem possible that she could have followed us all the way to Komiža and onto the ship without anyone seeing her before now. But there she was, standing at the railings. The wind had whipped her hair into a tangle that made it impossible to see her face clearly in the dark, but I would have known her silhouette anywhere. I tried to moisten my mouth so I could call out to her, but I couldn't loosen my tongue from the roof of my mouth. With great effort I attempted to stand up, but my feet slipped from under me, the deck slick with vomit and sea spray, and I fell back onto the deck. I opened my mouth to call her name, but nothing came out and I realised I couldn't see her any more.

Finally, I pulled myself up and ran along the deck, searching every form and shadow. I kept going until I saw a movement to my left and turning towards it, I collided with Ivica. I tried to push him aside, but I was too weak and gave up the fight, collapsing against his thin body. My heart raced but I allowed him to lead me below deck once again. He asked me no questions, and for that I was grateful.

༄

I awoke in a daze of exhaustion, my head on Mama's knees. I peeled the tongue off the roof of my mouth and gagged as a tang of acid saliva hit my taste buds. Mama passed me some warm water and I gulped down several large mouthfuls. I would have felt much better if the movement of passing the cup between us hadn't stirred up the air and sent a waft of stale vomit towards my nostrils. I belched up a watery stream all over the both of us. She said nothing and I followed her lead. I wasn't sure what or who I had seen the night before, but experience had taught me to keep my thoughts to myself.

We're there! Ivica was smiling and gesturing towards the stairs. From where I sat I followed his gaze. My head was encased in a fog, but as my brain started to clear I could make out the shapes of rushing figures, desperate for the first view of landfall.

༄

Ivica held out his hand to me as I stepped off the gangplank onto Italian soil. Portside was abuzz with activity, and as I set foot on the dock Ivica released my hand and I was swept along in a stream of people. I called his name, but my voice was lost in a cacophony of foreign languages and the whirring and crashing of dockside operations.

There seemed to be men everywhere in khaki and grey uniforms, and the air was heavy with their sweat as they moved with purpose. They surrounded me and I tried frantically to twist around to see if I could spot Mama or Ivica, but the press of bodies made it impossible for me to move and I wasn't tall enough to see further than those that hedged me in. As my head started spinning again, the noise became too much and I became afraid that, if I lost my footing, I would fall to the dock and be trampled. The heaving crowd was moving like a barely controlled wild animal.

As the horde moved away from the dockside I could finally see into the distance. The skyline of the port was outlined against a sharp blue sky, the white spires and buildings nestled in the curve of the harbour. My breathing quickened and I tasted the briny air tinged with the stink of char. I caught sight of some scarred dockyards and the carcass of a battleship lying half submerged in the water, its nose pointing heavenwards out of the oil-slicked harbour. Next to the drowning battleship sat other navy vessels and jammed next to them were fishing boats and cargo ships.

I heard someone call my name and I craned my neck backwards as a hand closed around my forearm. There was a wildness about Oliver's ruddy face as the same dark hair that fell around Mila's shoulders stuck to his face.

Let me go!

Where do you think you're going? Spittle flew from his pink lips as he tightened the grip on my arm. I said nothing in reply and we stood there like that, buffeted by the onshore crowd.

Let me go, I cried as I tried to get away, but his hold tightened. *Help me, someone!* People stepped around us, like water eddying around a rock in a river.

Help, please.

Two soldiers stopped. They said something to me, but I couldn't understand their babble. One of them grabbed Oliver by the hair and pulled him backwards so that he was forced to release his hold on me. The two struggled briefly, the soldier quickly overpowering Oliver and trapping him in a headlock. Oliver swore at him and continued to squirm until the man increased the pressure on Oliver's windpipe and he ceased to fight.

I wanted the soldier to let Oliver go but I was powerless, only able to dab my eyes as they started to fill with tears. When I looked up again, the other soldier was in front of me. He pointed at his chest and shouted his words as if I was deaf.

Shifting position, he held out his hand to me. I caught a whiff of diesel from the dockside and it made my stomach somersault. The soldier had a slightly dishevelled appearance and rings under his eyes. His mouth twisted into a leer and he touched my wrist. I jerked away. His eyebrows rose and he gestured towards me, his voice assaulting me again.

He bent down until his face was centimetres from mine. His stale breath, mingled with the strong fuel smell, reminded me of the German soldier, and the vomit rose up. I didn't think there was anything left inside me, but I began to choke, trying to hold it back. The soldier's smile vanished as his lips curled back in disgust. He jumped back, but it was too late. I spewed a liquidy soup over his boots.

He threw his hands up in the air and started yelling. I lurched backwards, smashing into a passer-by. People were now stopping to see what was happening. Oliver jabbed his elbow into the gut of the soldier holding him and broke free. He flew the last few paces to where I stood and snatched up my hand, yanking me through the gathered crowd. I didn't have time to argue and let myself be pulled along.

The soldiers were roaring at the crowd to stop us, but no one was going to stop a girl reeking of vomit. A whistle blew somewhere in front of us and we kept going until Oliver pulled me into an alley. We collapsed in a disused shop doorway, its front boarded up and slivers of broken glass crunching under our feet. I held my breath as the sound of boots pounding in unison approached. Three uniformed men ran past without a glance in our direction. I looked at Oliver questioningly.

He shrugged.

Do you think they're looking for us?

I don't know. If you hadn't started screaming . . .

You were hurting my arm.

He snorted air out of his nose and kicked the closed door of the shop. I watched him mutely, not wanting to anger him further. What seemed like several minutes passed before he spoke.

Do you ever think about that day after Mila went missing? His voice weary.

Every day.

Me too.

I'm sorry. I didn't mean for any of this to happen. My apology sounded weak even to my own ears, but Oliver nodded in acceptance. We stared at each other for a moment, neither of us knowing how to fix things.

What did we do, Ola?

I swallowed, unable to find any words.

It was my fault, he said.

No! It was me. I should have explained.

I shouldn't have jumped to conclusions. He seemed to understand how the world worked in a way I didn't. If only I'd stopped him that day when the words had come out of me all wrong – maybe it would've been different.

It's my fault Mila's gone . . . and Pero. My voice was barely above a whisper as I circled back in my mind.

It's called WAR, Ola. He sighed, but then he held his head up and looked straight at me. *And don't worry about Mila. She'll be OK. I know it.*

I saw her.

What? He stopped a moment to let his mind catch up. *What did you . . . Where?*

The ship. Last night.

He sniffed and shook his head. I let my gaze fall away too, leaning my back against the wall of the shop. Even when with absolute clarity I told the truth, he didn't believe me. I felt on the point of total collapse and considered following Pero's lead and not speaking at all. The building began to tremble as if an earthquake was shaking its foundations. It took a few seconds for me to realise that it was me who was shaking. Oliver put his arm around my shoulders and led me back towards the boat and our mothers.

༺ ༻

We spent the night on stretchers in a disused warehouse. Mama had found somewhere to wash my outer garments, but they hadn't dried completely in the winter air. The damp clothes chilled me, but I no longer felt the need to hide from Oliver and Rosa.

Soon we were on the move again, piling obediently into several army trucks, squashing in with our few bags and random possessions against the thick canvas sides. As we rumbled off towards the south, the whispering started. *Where are they taking us? What are we doing in Italy?* Six months before, the Italians had been looting our homes and fighting our people. And yet here we were, seeking shelter amongst those who had sought to crush us.

We passed by farmers working on small holdings much like our own. An old farmer stopped his donkey and silently watched us trundle by. He had the same weather-lined face and wiry body as a dozen older men in our convoy. His clothes hung off his thin frame, but in a reedy voice he called out to us.

Vivo il Partigiano.

The convoy erupted into a chorus.

Partizani, Partizani. We passed other people working the land or walking the roads. They looked starved and beaten by the war, simple people who had no interest in other men's politics but who were part of it all the same. We had much in common with them, and I wondered if it would be the same if we were travelling through America.

Or Germany.

We were transferred onto a train, the first train that I'd ever been on. I could smell the oil and I started to feel queasy, remembering the cargo steamer. Looking at the hulking black engine, I gagged on the fumes that swirled in the air. Pero sat quietly staring into the middle distance, and I felt guilty at my reaction when he seemed incapable of showing any emotion.

I rested my chin on the window ledge of the train and welcomed the air that came rushing onto my face as we hurtled though the Italian countryside. The towns were make-believe. All white and perfect with orange tiled roofs. The names flicked past me – Mola, Brindisi, Otranto. They may as well have been Berlin, St Louis or Auckland. The names meant nothing to me. All I knew was that with every clickety-clack of the train we were moving further away from Dalmatia.

We alighted from the train, feeling disoriented. The town we had stopped in seemed like a paradise. While the winds sang of loneliness, we were led with our battered suitcases and travel-worn clothes to abandoned villas. The entrance to the house we found ourselves in was large enough to envelop our entire house. Marbled floors led to a staircase that rose up to a second level and bedrooms that were adorned with polished tables and chairs and beds big enough for three people to sleep in.

I followed Mama and Pero into the room that was to be ours. A chair stood by the bed covered in an ornate red brocade fabric. I ran my finger over the material, felt its bumps and traced the fleur de lis pattern over the stuffed seat. The bedcovering was similarly ornate in heavy red and gold damask. It was like what I imagined Mila's sister would have in her American house. The tight little fist reappeared and gripped my gut once again. Then I remembered what Oliver had said. *She'll be OK.*

☙

A few days later we marched to a camp. It was crowded and dirty and there wasn't enough food. The hunger was gnawing at everyone, making people irritable and impatient. But I didn't complain, I barely had enough energy to raise myself off the stretchers we slept on.

I don't remember much of the camp, other than persistent chills and a rash that marched its way across my body and along my limbs as I succumbed to camp fever. I ached all over. The fever showed no signs of easing, my mother bathing me in an effort to keep my temperature down. I wish I'd been aware at the time of how she'd tended to me and saved me from typhus, because surely then I would have seen how she loved me, how she would do anything to save me.

When I finally opened my eyes, I saw her tenderly washing my body in the oily glow of a kerosene lamp. The lighting made her appear younger, smoothing out the lines on her face and making her seem almost ghostly. She sat up abruptly, looking almost embarrassed when she saw that I was conscious.

Have I been asleep long? She shook her head and reorganised herself, moving away from me. I watched her when I thought she couldn't see me, waiting in the hope that she might invite me in. But her face set into a hardened mask and there was no way to get through to her as she turned to where Pero sat on the floor, twirling a stick in his hands.

In my naivety I thought about finding some stairs to throw myself down, or getting a knife to cut myself to gain her attention. But I couldn't bring myself to do it. Mama remained locked behind her shield, and I became resigned to the fact that this was how it would be.

By the time I was able to feed myself and walk without assistance, we were on the move once more. We boarded a converted cruise liner, where I leant on the railings and watched Italy disappearing in our wake. I closed my eyes and let the winter sunshine kiss my face, waiting for new memories to fill my mind and wash away the old ones. When I looked again, I caught sight of Mt Etna, its white peaks starkly outlined against a sky that was the deepest blue.

There were hundreds of refugees on board, but unlike our other boat journeys I wasn't seasick. Still, as the days sailed by, nobody seemed to know where we were going.

Every day I watched the horizon, hoping this would be the day that we would find our new resting place. Then one morning, as the air warmed itself before the growing sun, it appeared. Over the bow towards the southeast I noticed a smudge where the sea met the sky. As I focussed, it blossomed into a lumpy mass, and then into mountains. The ship sailed parallel to the coast as the ship's decks became flooded with people, and Oliver, Rosa and I joined them.

Alexandria!

It sat on the edge of the sea, our very own Heaven on Earth. Its buff-coloured minarets and buildings stood proudly erect under the North African sky. We reached Port Said at the head of the Suez Canal, not really sure what we were seeing. The port shimmered as heat rose off the desert sand, like a reflection in water rippled by a pebble.

We followed the calls to leave the ship, and as we alighted onto the dock Arabs in long robes and wearing fezzes appeared carrying wares in giant wicker baskets or tied in flamboyant fabric knapsacks.

It's Jesus! A child was pointing towards the dock to a man with camel-coloured robes and a black beard that billowed over his round belly. His fez had been knocked off in the commotion, but he stood there fanning himself with a palm leaf while all around him other traders swarmed, jostling and bumping in order to get at the newcomers to sell their wares.

Come away. Mama was pulling me with one hand as she held onto Pero with the other.

But, Mama . . . I waved my hands towards the baskets of fruit and food that a small group of women brought towards the ship. The baskets overflowed with dates and oranges and red fruits that I had never seen before.

I pleaded with her to buy some.

She ignored me: we had no money.

We lingered by the boat with our bags, penniless and without the exotic foods and trinkets that were available on the wharf. As the sun started to slip beneath the western horizon, a loud crackling and piercing squeal made me cover my ears. The loudspeakers kicked into action.

I watched Pero hide himself amongst Mama's skirts as we covered our ears against the rush of words. The buzz of the afternoon dissipated as people looked at the loudspeakers spewing out their message, while others stared into the desert, lost in their own worlds far away from the boat as we waited for someone to translate the foreign words.

On the other side of the wharf sat several empty rail wagons that I hadn't noticed up until that point. Without ever hearing anyone say it, I knew we were leaving the boat behind. Mama and Pero and I walked with Rosa, Oliver and Ivica towards the windowless wagons. The rectangular shape and wood gave them the appearance of cheap coffins. The inside of the rail cars was no better than the exterior. There were no seats, no toilets, no information. Ivica stood in front of us, his arms limp at his sides as he gazed at our surroundings: the wooden slats, the sliding side doors, the disenchanted people. He squatted on the floor as a breeze slipped in and stirred up the faint odour of animals. He cupped his face in his hands, and then crumpled into the side of the wagon. Mama reached over and squeezed his hand.

Later, when I learned of the people put on trains that ended forever in the extermination camps, I thought of that African train. The coffin-like carriages should've sent us running, but we boarded like cattle, meekly following one after another. I wondered what it had been like for those jews and gypsies packed into boxcars that were destined for places from which they would never leave. They knew nothing about what really lay in wait for them at the end of the line and perhaps they too locked away their fears and simply ushered their children ahead of them. Or perhaps they went mad with fear of the unknown and hit their heads against the walls of the boxcars until they lost consciousness and no longer thought of anything. Or maybe they clung to hope and believed they were destined for a better place. I can't remember what I thought, I know only that I was tired and that I submissively did what I was told.

Word came eventually about our destination. People shuffled uncomfortably.

A camp.

In a desert.

I could hear the low whispering between the adults. How were we going to survive in a desert? The train slowly moved off to the south, the doors half open to the Arabian night where palm trees flashed by along the Suez Canal. The train finally rocked me to asleep as its wheels sang their African lullaby.

A-fri-ka, A-fri-ka, A-fri-ka . . .

༄

I was woken the next morning by the Egyptian sun seeking out the insides of the wagon through the gaps, teasing me awake. I sat up, rubbing my eyes as I unwound my body after sleeping the night partly curled onto my rucksack and partly on the wooden floor where Pero lay at my feet. I inhaled deeply and tried to stretch, but the air was stale with the stench of too many bodies, and my arms hit a shelf that ran along one side of the wagon. I gave up and placed my feet flat on the floor, pulled up my knees and wrapped my arms around them.

The train seemed to be slowing as Oliver and another man slid the door all the way open until we were flooded with light. It took several seconds for my eyes to adjust and, by that time, the train had almost stopped. People started to tip out of the train onto the sand, and Mama held onto Pero as she pushed me forward. I tried to lean back against her hand, revelling in the contact, but she pulled her hand away so that I almost fell backwards. A second later the crush of people had moved me to the edge of the wagon and out onto the ground. I focussed on a sign poking out of the desert sand:

El Shatt

There, in that train station of sorts, I gazed out at the kilometres of desert stretching in every direction. It wasn't a place. It wasn't even a real town. It was nowhere.

I was afraid of how far we'd come. I'd run from our village, but the reality of the Sinai desert, with its washed-out landscape and a sky so big that it almost swallowed up the earth beneath it, was enough to make me regret leaving. I yearned for the smell of the Adriatic – fresh and salty and alive. I longed to feel the mountains, the smooth ancient rock beneath my feet, and the pale green shoots that sprang up from the awakening earth in spring. I would have loved to feel the ochre and yellow leaves of autumn cracking into a thousand pieces in my hands, and I dreamed of plucking ripe figs and letting the juices from their ruby hearts run down my chin.

I turned my head to the east and let a dry wind lift the hair from my forehead. I could make out the canal a few kilometres away, and at the edge of my vision I could see something else. I put my hand up, shielding my eyes from the sun, but I wasn't prepared for the row upon row of military-issue tents that were lined up on the sands. British soldiers, clapboards in hands, started organising us, marshalling us into groups that set off towards the camp.

One of the soldiers threw his arm out, a crooked smile on his face.

Welcome to El-Shit! It was many months before Oliver finally told me that this was not how to pronounce the name of the camp.

From the station we walked with our sacks and backpacks and battered suitcases, a collection of broken people and children come to live in an uninhabitable land. There was a sound of engines firing up to the west as we trudged along. We watched as a fighter plane climbed into the air over our heads. A few people dropped to the ground and some started to run before understanding that they were Allied planes. The soldiers must have thought us an odd bunch diving down onto the sand like that. We were hardly worth bombing. With our tattered clothes and rag-tag-collection of rucksacks and bags, anyone would think we were a band of gypsies.

The camp was dominated by a khaki neatness. There were hundreds of tents in rows, broken up here and there by more substantial buildings that had real walls and corrugated iron roofs that housed the military storage depots, workshops and administration buildings. The thing I recall most about those buildings is that they didn't flap in the dry breeze like the tents we had to live in.

As we waited in a queue, I longed to wash myself. I had no idea what we were waiting in line for and I became impatient and agitated in the suffocating air. In contrast, all the fight and strength seemed to have drained from Mama. She waited without speaking to any of the other refugees, and only shuffled forward when the queue started to move, her hands resting on Pero's shoulders as she guided him onwards.

Once at the front we were confronted by a soldier sitting behind a fold-out table, screeds of papers and a stamp pad and cards lying in front of him.

Name?

When no response was forthcoming, the soldier looked up, a frown on his face. He sighed loudly and tapped his pen distractedly against the ink pot. Just as I was about to reply, Mama stepped in.

Ana Mastrović, she said, and pointing to my brother, *Pero Mastrović*. And then almost as an afterthought, *Olga Mastrović*.

He issued us with stamped identity discs, and assigned us to a tent before we set out with Oliver, Rosa and Ivica for our new home. Outside the administration block was a laundry building where we would later take our clothes to be disinfected. There was a sharp smell. It tickled my nose, but it was a relief from the stench of human sweat and excrement.

We followed the instructions carefully. Row number 45, tent 0602. Oliver led the way, but I was soon disorientated. The housing units were all identical. And there were hundreds of them, housing thousands of people. They were made up of two tents placed end to end and joined together.

I stepped inside tent 0602 and gazed up at the ceiling. Several linings meant to keep out the cold night billowed down above us. It was like a folk tale Uncle Jure had told me, of Ciganin and their travelling tents. The sides were held up by thin poles. I reached out and touched one, letting my hand slide down the bamboo reed. It was covered in a soft, sock-like fabric that felt luxurious to the touch after weeks of living in the same coarse clothes.

The others had already found their camp beds at the back of the tent. The beds were low to the ground, sacking stretched over wooden frames. Mine was directly across from Mama and Pero. Ivica, Oliver and Rosa were just next to us. In all, there were fifteen people including our small group living there.

I couldn't imagine how we would survive. There were no sweet animal aromas or fresh sea breezes, and there was a complete lack of colour. The dryness was insufferable. It robbed us of every last bead of sweat from our faces and arms. Our dehydrated skin cracked. Even at night time, when the temperature dropped and we pulled our coats around us, our skin was taut and dry. I never got used to the way the Sinai sucked the moisture from my eyes, so that it hurt to blink, and tears never came.

My stomach rebelled against any food I put into it. Dry bread and the mealy weevil-laden slop that was served up to us came up as soon as it had settled in my belly. If by chance it settled in my stomach for any length of time, I soon found myself racing for the stinking latrines as my bowels loosened almost as quickly as the vomit rose in my throat. I became thin and I swam in my clothes. I had to knot my underwear so that they wouldn't fall off me, my waist now little bigger than Pero's.

It seemed to me that Pero didn't fare much better than I did. In fact he seemed not to grow at all. He remained in his silent world and soon the silence spilled out to engulf my mother. The camp, in contrast, had its own life. The sound of children playing and adults talking and singing and praying spread throughout. Those sounds became a proxy for my mother's voice. I knew what the silence cloaked, and I had no desire for that cloak to be lifted.

☙

Living in those huge desert tents you could never physically be alone. I created my own world, a make-believe America where our family was reunited on streets of gold and where we carried no memories of the past; there was only the imaginary present. During the day I went to the camp school and started to learn English, but I couldn't wait until classes were over and I could retreat into my own world again.

While others around me felt lost and abandoned, unable to go back, powerless to move forward, I'd found a way to feel content in our displacement. Here I could pretend that no one knew what I'd done and I could resolutely live my new life, just like a man dying of thirst believes in the mirage on the horizon.

Night time was different. As I burrowed under my blankets, the tents spoke to me. Some nights it was a mournful speech of loss that made me feel sad, but I nevertheless managed to shut it out with images of St Louis steamers and invented sounds of American music. But if the wind rose up across the desert and sandblasted the tents, our tent spoke to me of condemnation and it was Mila I heard. Nothing could drown out her gravelly voice – not the snoring or crying or the lovemaking that was to be heard almost every night in the tents of El Shatt. Her voice was relentless, and no matter how hard I tried to conjure up a future and erase my past she kept on going and I was damned to listen to her.

Thereisnous, thereisnous . . .

All through this time Mama kept me at a distance. She too became thinner as time went on, the Sinai shrivelling her to a permanent walnut brown, and on the inside her heart hardened against me.

One night I crept over to her bedside to watch her as she slept. Pero lay like a doll in between her and the tent wall, his eyes open, staring at the ceiling. Mama was motionless except for the rise and fall of her chest. As I wriggled on the ground by her, she rolled on to her side to face me, flinging one arm over the side of the bed, where it dangled like a vine. It was at night time that I most missed the Pero that was, and I longed to feel his warm body next to mine. But Mama held him close and there was nothing left over for anyone else. She used to hug us – Pero, Jure and even me – and as I remembered how she had been, I reached up and touched her. Her fingers were cold. I held my breath as I took her hand in mine and felt the rough patches on her palms and the tips of her fingers. I scanned her face, noticing the pale spider marks at the corners of her eyes. Without thinking, I squeezed her hand and felt the welt on her knuckles where a louse had bitten her and she had scratched it raw. Her eyes remained closed as she tugged her hand away and rolled onto her other side, her arm falling possessively across my brother. Her breathing continued in a perfect rhythm as I scuttled back to my bed.

CHAPTER 13

PUALELE

As the weeks pass, St Mary's becomes Pualele's refuge. Whenever she enters the church she immediately curls her fingers into her palms and then, as she recites the prayers and songs she knows by rote, she loses herself for a time as a calmness rushes through her veins. She looks forward to Sundays, not just because of Mass but because there is no school.

She feels proud to see the flower arrangements on the altar that she has helped Aunty to arrange. Twice a week Sefi strides into the church with armfuls of flowers. Pualele stands by the altar and passes each stem and branch of foliage to her aunt to place in the vases. Pualele looks on in sheer wonderment as the displays emerge from a ragtag of shoots and flowers. The giant hydrangea heads are her favourite. They are more like pink and purple pom-poms than flowers, and sometimes, when no one is watching, she holds the stems and circles them in front of her, smiling as she revels in a moment of pure freedom.

In contrast, Sefi's face creases in concentration as she places each stem carefully into the green oasis that will hold the arrangement in position. She fusses and adjusts the flowers until they are just so, then she turns with a broad smile lighting up her face, nodding with satisfaction at Pualele, who grins back.

Although Aunty Sefi loves being in charge of the church flowers, she loves playing bingo more. The flowers are her duty, but it is bingo at St Mary's Parish Hall, first Tuesday of every month, that she lives for.

The first time Aunty wins the bingo jackpot she goes straight out and buys herself a brand new pair of shoes. They are black patent-leather with a rounded toe and a silver buckle that fastens to the outside of the foot. It is of no matter that her feet are so big that they spill over the top of the shiny leather; she wears them every day.

Come. We go see Mrs Magasiva.

Mrs Magasiva knows *everything*. She is the undisputed Samoan matriarch of Rich Man Road. Behind her back they all call her 'the Queen' – although everyone knows that *she* knows they call her 'the Queen'. Mrs Magasiva holds court every Sunday after Mass in the church hall, where the Samoan community gathers to exchange gossip and news from Samoa, to ask after children and jobs, and sometimes to commiserate over problems or losses. At other times it's to celebrate each other's successes.

Pualele suspects that it is Mrs Magasiva who has somehow heard about her misdemeanour in the Four Square and has shared it with the world. She is also certain that the Queen has a direct line to Mama in Samoa, and she is afraid that she will find out about her palagi name and tell Mama. Pualele carefully avoids Mrs Magasiva at every opportunity, and the thought of going to her house fills her with terror. She doesn't understand why Aunty doesn't wait and talk to her after Mass on Sunday.

Still, Pualele obediently follows Aunty, scraping her roman sandals on the gravel as they head for the Magasivas' house. She knows something strange is going on when Sefi, who normally crosses the road directly in front of their house, walks an extra fifty metres along the road to the zebra crossing, her shoes crunching the loose red metal all the way. Each step is precisely placed. Pualele becomes impatient and runs ahead, kicking the tiny stones as she goes. Aunty doesn't scold her for scuffing her sandals or running ahead, so intent is she on her own careful progress.

At the Magasiva house, Aunty stops on the steps leading to the front door and taps her shoes on the railing as if she were a man removing mud from a pair of work boots. A sprinkle of red gravel falls off the leather soles, and while Pualele removes her roman sandals without needing to be told, Aunty leaves her new shoes on.

Sefi hammers on the door with her balled fist and the Queen is at the door immediately, almost ripping it off its hinges as she readies herself to launch into a tirade.

Sefi! Her forehead wrinkles as she looks Aunty over from head to toe, her gaze lingering on the patent-leather shoes.

Oh! Beautiful! She signals for us to come in, making a clicking sound that shows her delight. Aunty stands fast where she is and clears her throat before delivering her news.

We won't come in, Merita. I have only come to tell you that you won't be seeing us after church this Sunday.

The older woman's mouth falls open.

We will take Pualele to St Heliers.

On Sunday?

With working it is the only day. We might go for a walk.

Aunty Sefi slyly looks down at her shoes, blushing at her audacity before the Queen. They both arrived in New Zealand many years before, but it has been the Magasivas who have flourished, with jobs and their own house and more than a half dozen children, and all with, what seems to Sefi, to have been very little effort. But maybe, just maybe, things are changing.

The Queen stares at the shiny black shoes, a frown forming on her face.

Pride, Sefi, is an ugly thing.

Aunty doesn't flinch. *See you at Mass, Merita.*

Aunty ushers Pualele off the veranda, taking tiny clacking steps across the wooden boards as the door slams shut behind them. She stops at the top of the stairs, the toes of her shoes hanging over the lip of the veranda as she takes a moment to enjoy the view. Pualele looks on from the footpath, not really following what has just happened but understanding that Aunty is happy. As Aunty leaves the Magasiva property, Pualele skips across to the curb. She holds her arms out as she balances on the edging away from the biting red pebbles and places one foot in front of the other, mimicking a tightrope walker. Aunty smiles at her, before spotting Pualele's bare feet and pursing her lips.

Ach, Pualele – your sandals.

☙

On Sunday the heels on her new shoes, coupled with her bravado, make Sefi appear taller. In contrast to her aunt Pualele never wants anyone to notice her. Amongst the swarm of parishioners at St Mary's on Sunday she tries to appear as small as possible. She swivels and slips out of the way of families hurrying for the door of the church, women clutching babies and men shepherding snot-nosed children toward salvation.

The flush of a winner's purse has Aunty proudly surveying all before her and, after Mass, clutching a large bag, she announces loudly to anyone within shouting distance, *We take the bus to St Heliers.*

The Queen looks on. Her lips pull tight and her nostrils flare as she glares at Sefi's sheer nerve. But for once she holds no sway over this family and she can do no more than watch as the Auva'as walk away.

CR

In all the months she has been in Auckland, Pualele has never been to the seaside. Admittedly she's glimpsed the harbour waters sparkling like Christmas tinsel in the distance, and she has smelt its briny fragrance on the wind gusts that sweep up from the harbour, but there's never been the opportunity to go near it until now. Pualele has always loved the sea and she wonders what creatures are to be found in the waters of Auckland harbour.

She squeezes into a seat next to Father and Kasi, while Aunty Sefi and Uncle Sam sit in front of them. They sit on the seaward side of the bus and Pualele's legs jiggle in anticipation as they are bounced over road works as the bus winds its way around the waterfront.

Someone has written in thick felt pen on the back of the seat: *Lisa 4 Eva. Lisa for Eva.* Who these girls Lisa and Eva are, she doesn't know, but the graffiti reminds her of the *Reefer* and the messages that she'd read carved into the side of the cabin. She shakes her head as if to dislodge the memory of that terrible voyage.

The first sight of water is disappointing. To Pualele's eye, the sea is a cloudy grey-green colour and not the twinkling blue she has seen from afar. At a bay around a bend in the road several boats tug on their moorings as the tide tries to pull them out to sea, while a man plays fetch with a dog in the shallow water. The bus continues on, in and out of bays, until Aunty announces that they are finally at their destination.

Pualele smiles as she inhales the sea air. It makes her nose tingle, reminding her of home. Between her and the sea lies a flat park, where some people picnic while others kick balls over their heads. On the far side the men are already on the slim strip of sand, removing their shoes. Pualele watches as they walk into the water, which thankfully now looks more the colour of the sea she is used to. The men stand in the water, waves gently breaking into a white foam around their legs. She spots a dinghy anchored just off the beach, rising and falling with the gently rolling waves, and she heads out across the park to join the men.

Come. We have a picnic. Sefi's hand closes around Pualele's wrist like a manacle, pulling her firmly away to a patch of grass where Aunty has laid a lime and purple lavalava. Pualele busies herself laying out the contents of the bag – fried chicken, containers of chop suey and a banana cake with coconut icing. She helps her aunt without a word, wishing she was laughing with the men at the water's edge.

People walk by in their Sunday best, many of the children carrying ice cream towers of every colour. Pink and chocolate, white and blue, some even with chocolate sticks poking out of them or concealed under a thick layer of candied sprinkles. Pualele stares and swallows hard. Just when she believes that she might die if she doesn't get an ice cream too, Sefi stands, purse in hand, and motions for Pualele to follow.

The ice cream comes from a truck. The side of the vehicle that faces the pavement is open to form a kind of raised counter top and below this counter on a glass panel, a myriad of ice creams and drinks are on display. It's like a sumptuous dream, and Pualele's mouth waters as she licks her lips and looks at the possibilities before her.

The man serving in the truck looks like a grotesque white marshmallow. His soft body is squeezed into a blue polyester smock that strains the buttons so they look as if they might pop right off should he move too quickly. The Marshmallow Man adeptly pulls levers and fusses with cones and clear plastic dishes as a machine spews out soft swirling snowy ice cream.

Pualele steps forward and places her fingers on the clear glass that forms part of the counter top, pulling herself up on tiptoes. She watches as the man sprinkles hundreds and thousands and plants two chocolate sticks into an ice cream island. A second dish of snowy peaks he smothers in strawberry sauce before he delivers them over the edge of the counter into eager hands. In all her life Pualele has never seen such creations. She licks her lips in anticipation, jigging up and down on the spot as she waits her turn.

Aunty looks straight at the Marshmallow Man. She puts her hand in her pocket and pulls out the last of her 'legs 11' winnings, placing the $2 note on the counter and not breaking her stare. The man moves uncomfortably.

What can I get you?

Aunty is still while the Marshmallow Man breaks out in a blotchy crimson colour and picks up the ice cream scoop. Pualele imprints the image in her mind. Not of the Marshmallow Man nor even of the ice cream sundae that she hopes will soon appear before her eyes, but of Aunty Sefi. Her poise and confidence has Pualele in awe and she can't take her eyes off her. The man clears his throat and starts to tap the end of the scoop on the counter, but Sefi continues to contemplate the offerings, her head bobbing as her finger slides down the list of offerings.

Finally, Sefi pokes her finger at the picture of the sundae and Pualele's face cracks into a grin wide enough to fit in the entire sundae boat!

Marshmallow Man places the ice cream island – with its chocolate flake poking up like a stake in the ground – onto the counter before Pualele's eyes. She spies the pink wafer and decides to save it until later but quickly stuffs the flake into her mouth.

Ach! Pualele! How many times I told you?

Pualele stops and thinks hard, wrinkling her nose as she tries to remember what exactly she's been told.

Careful not to dirty your Sunday clothes.

Pualele nods and with her free hand brushes away a piece of stray chocolate from her chin. They walk on in the sunshine, and as a sticky trail of ice cream runs from a clear plastic spoon down onto Pualele's fingers, she licks furiously at it before Sefi notices.

She's never had an ice cream like this before, but she understands Sefi's concern. Pualele smiles and lets Sefi take her hand and they cross the road to the park and the waves breaking on the beach.

Hey! Kasi is waving from the sand. Aunty's grip tightens on her hand and she looks up at Sefi as the woman's face clouds over.

Kasi is in front of them in a few bounds.

Can I have some?

No. No. Sefi's voice is uncompromising.

Pualele and Kasi wait for an explanation.

Germs.

Pualele looks from Aunty to her brother. Doesn't Aunty know that they always share food? Hands in the same bowls scooping out rice, slurping sweet warm drink from the same coconut shell? The ice cream is melting down onto her hand again and trickles onto her wrist. She watches the chocolate trail heading for the white cuff of her shirt.

I won't let it happen again, Aunty is talking to herself. Although Pualele hears the words, she is distracted by the dark stain on her blouse that is spreading like ink on blotting paper. She is sure Aunty is saying something important, but she's just not sure what. Adults often make no sense at all, and right at that moment Pualele couldn't care less what Sefi is talking about.

Aaah! Aunty squeals. *Your shirt!* She grabs Pualele's wrist and the ice cream tumbles out of the container onto the ground at their feet. Pualele continues to hold the spoon and container while looking back at the melting heap as Aunty drags her towards the sea. Uncle and Father watch in astonishment as Aunty strides into the water and plunges Pualele's arm, container and all, into the salt water, rubbing the white rayon between her fingers.

They stand in the ankle-deep water, the bottom of their lavalavas soaked, as Sefi makes a *tsk tsk* sound and shakes her head at the stained cuff. Pualele looks down at the silver buckles that sit like gilded shells on Aunty's shoes. The breaking waves momentarily obscure the shoes, before the water settles and they appear again like shiny black maisu.

The scream, when it comes, is one of utter despair. It is so loud and piercing that Pualele drops the plastic ice cream boat into the sea and claps her hands over her ears. She closes her eyes and waits for the terrible wailing to stop. Within seconds Father and Uncle are in the water. They take Sefi under each arm and help her over the sand to a bench on the grass, every squelching step oozing seawater out of the patent-leather shoes. Aunty sits doubled over sobbing as she gapes at her entombed feet. Uncle whispers to her, his arm across her back patting her gently, as Father walks towards Pualele.

Pualele wipes the last of the ice cream off her face with a dripping hand. She can see her own worn shoes in the ankle-deep water, but she can't move.

Look what you've done, Father hisses. *Everything she does for you, and look what you've done.*

She can see Father's hands hanging in tight balls at his sides. She braces herself and waits. But Father turns and walks away, leaving her in the shallows as a seagull swoops down and snatches the pink wafer out of the water. She isn't sure how long she stands there, her own briny tears mingling with the sea, but it seems like hours. She wants Mama's arms around her and then, as if she has willed them into being, she feels them wrap around her shoulders.

Don't worry. They were too small for her anyway. Kasi turns her around to face him. His mouth is serious, but his green eyes are full of mischief as he looks at her.

Come on. He takes her by the elbow and leads her along the beach away from the others. Under a pohutukawa tree he signals for her to take off her shoes and plonks down next to her.

In his hand he holds a pale tennis ball. It is heavy from having been in the water and is balding from where a dog has gnawed it. Kasi throws it up in air and Pualele instinctively lunges for it. She tosses it back and soon they are volleying the ball back and forth. She giggles as Kasi dives to stop the ball from hitting the sand, until she notices her sleeve with the stain on it flapping in the breeze and her laughter stops. But her brother isn't one to let her slip into self pity and he flicks sand at her, making her squeal and jump in the air.

What did she mean, Kasi?

He looks at her, one eyebrow raised higher than the other.

About the germs?

He sucks in his lower lip, chewing something over before speaking.

The other Pualele. She got a bug – meningitis. That's how she ... y'know.

Pualele tries to swallow but the ice cream turns to a sour-stickiness in her mouth, and she can't. It reminds her of the Four Square and Mrs Merrick. There are so many conversations and situations that she doesn't understand, and now there are germs to worry about too. She considers whether she should even try to understand New Zealand, because when she does finally comprehend something she quickly wishes she could forget it.

Kasi and Pualele see the waving arms, but without discussing it they decide to ignore them. Soon the voices reach them on the breeze. Kasi gestures towards the adults and she nods in acknowledgement. He picks up the ball and gives her one of his full smiles that show his perfect white teeth and make his cheeks bunch up around his eyes. Kasi is her anchor in this strange new world and she doesn't know what she would ever do without him here.

The voices are louder. Kasi takes the ball in his hand and flicks his wrist so that it flies cannonball-like out past the breaking waves before hitting the water. He turns and takes Pualele's hand and, like that, they walk back to the others.

CHAPTER 14

OLGA'S JOURNAL

Maureen's not told her parents about the cancer.

She's afraid that they wouldn't cope with the news that their perfect daughter with the international career might not be around long enough to make good on her promise to have children and always be there for them. You see, the family has had its fair share of heartache.

First she told me about her oldest brother, Ian. He'd been a representative rugby player. Big and strong and smart. One of the players in the safer positions – you know, the ones who run around at the back directing the game with a kick. He wanted to take over the farm eventually, maybe go to university too and become a veterinarian, but anyone who knew him said he'd be an All Black first. But before his life got going he played in a club final. It was back in the day when you took a few knocks and got right back up and carried on with the game; nothing that had happened had caused any concern. Ian finished the game with a dull headache. Thought he might feel better after a lie down. Only he never really felt better again. The hospital said he'd had a brain bleed and that the damage was irreparable. Maureen's parents still care for him on the farm, but although he is still good with animals he's not so good with people any more.

Then there was Maureen's twin sister, Shona. She was born first (by two minutes, thirty-five seconds) and by the sound of things was equally as lovely as Maureen. She'd won a scholarship to Oxford University and the whole family (including Ian) had visited her there in those hallowed halls where great minds honed themselves before bursting out into the world in every discipline one could imagine. But Shona was knocked off her bicycle and killed on the day that Maureen won her first role playing Cassandra in *Cats*.

So that leaves Maureen and Eddie. Eddie's an accountant and lives with his partner Mike in Auckland. Maureen says her Mum and Dad took a long time to come to terms with Eddie's choice of partner, and on some level she knows they are disappointed with him. For all these reasons she doesn't think her parents could cope if they knew she was sick – just the thought of losing Maureen would tip her mother over the edge, of this Maureen is certain. I want to comfort her, not just because she has cancer but because I understand how she feels – so much heartache levelled at one family and so much responsibility heaped upon one child's shoulders.

Perhaps that is why God has placed us here side by side. I could be making too much of things of course, and I can't pretend to be any sort of expert on families who've gone through trauma, but I feel her pain as if it were my own.

I'm not meaning to compare myself to her, Pualele – well, I guess I am but if ever there were a reason for telling you my story, it lies here with Maureen. I feel I must help her. And you. Life can turn so quickly that we find ourselves on roads not of our own choosing when we could so easily have ended up on a different path and avoided the speed bumps and stop lights of life.

It scares me to think how random life can be. If I'd never gone up the mountain that day; if I hadn't searched for Mila that night; if my father had never gone to New Zealand; if my mother had married Jure and not my father. You never know what impact a choice has on your life until you are looking in the rear view mirror with life reflected back at you. It is only then that you see how a decision as simple as walking outside your front door can change everything.

༺༻

When Mama wasn't about, I looked through the few treasures she had brought with her from home. I used the kauri gum like a worry stone and would massage it until it became hot to the touch. I examined the photo of my brother and father in Awanui for clues as to who they were; and I smoothed out the few clothes she had packed, sniffing the fabric as if to capture the essence of her and make it a part of me.

One day I lifted a silk slip to my cheeks, rubbing its smoothness against my skin, and saw a cotton handkerchief fall from its folds. I pocketed the square of cotton and repacked Mama's things. I'd seen the women in the camp embroidering and sewing clothes from the lining of the tents, and I thought I might do something with the handkerchief.

Women from our tent carefully peeled off the fabric from the bamboo poles that held up the tents. I had watched as they unravelled the cloth until there were hundreds of fine threads spread out on the ground. Out of a hip pocket a spindle would be produced and the threads would be transformed into a kind of yarn in front of my eyes. In our own tent, a woman called Berta was known as the best knitter in El Shatt, and she would happily knit jumpers with the spun thread using needles fashioned from the bamboo reeds for anyone who asked.

I watched the women making fine thread for embroidery, taking the lining from the tents to make dresses and shirts, or making intricate collars to freshen an old coat. Very soon I had almost everything I required. I'd bargained for a needle from a woman who wanted a letter written, and I had carefully pulled off some fabric from the poles when no one was watching.

You'll need one of these. Oliver held a wooden spindle in his hand.
Where did you get it from?
I made it from offcuts from the church.

I was touched. I hadn't realised anyone had noticed me stripping cloth to make into thread.

I better go. Told the priest I'd help before Mass.
I didn't realise you were so religious, I teased.
I didn't realise you weren't. Church isn't so bad, Ola. Maybe you should listen more when you go instead of day-dreaming.

I glowed under his words. It irritated me that he could see through me, but I thought that maybe there was something in what he said – that I should listen and absorb and somehow allow the word of God to get under my skin. There seemed little point in listening more closely to the priest, who took the best of everything at the camp while his flock survived on the basics. I could not imagine that by listening more closely to his words I would transform into a good person and a better daughter more deserving of her mother's love. Whatever the reality, I resolved to take Oliver's advice and listen more carefully at Mass. Then I quickly went about spinning just the right thickness of thread to embroider with.

For several evenings after that I took out the cotton square from under my pillow and sat on the floor of our tent, staring at the cloth. I threaded the needle with my El Shatt twine, waiting to be inspired.

What are you making, Olga? The voice was quiet but confident and belonged to a girl I had seen about the camp. Her name was Kata, and I remembered her name only because of a patch of pock-marked skin on her left cheek that disturbed her otherwise unremarkable features.

I don't know, I replied.

Perhaps, you could put your initials on it – then you wouldn't lose it.

My fingers started to move as my mind wandered. I craved to be back in our village before the German soldiers came, when Mila had sought me out and been my friend, before she had said the words that haunted me still – *There is no us.* In my dreams she came to me, promising me things that a waking Mila never could. She took my hand and we ran together, through a meadow towards a golden gateway. She was a beautiful ghost in those dreams.

But at other times Pero and I would be running away from her. I tried to conjure up her happy face with her full lips, framed by dark locks – but the image always clouded over just as I thought I could see her clearly. And then the night winds would come and she would haunt me with her tent-speak so I couldn't sleep at all.

I looked at the handkerchief and there was a perfect 'M'.

The next night I sat down and saw Mama watching me from her bed. Her features were partly shadowed but I could see that her lips were parted, as if she might say something. She sat with her hands loosely resting on her thighs, and there right in front of me I could see the proof of all that she had suffered. Her look stilled me for a minute and I felt a twinge of embarrassment, my face growing hot. I pulled the needle through the cotton and turned myself away from her eyes.

It had been a long time since I'd seen her looking straight at me. Normally her eyes passed over me like a torch beam searching the darkness. I looked back, but I'd already missed her. She was lying down, with Pero tucked in at her side. I kept working on the sampler until I'd finished two more 'MM's, knowing that Mama would never love me the way she loved my little brother.

༶

The first correspondence arrived via the Red Cross a few months after we had settled in El Shatt. I marvelled at how Father's letter had found us when even I really didn't know where we were. If I had known what was in the letter, I would never have been so desperate to open it. But I was excited when Mama asked me to read Papa's beautifully drawn script to her, a warm glow spreading through me as her dry scaly hands brushed against my arm.

Dear Ana,

I'm so happy to know that you and the children are safe, but I'll never forgive myself for letting you stay when we all could've been safe in New Zealand.

I could barely get the words out and I dared not look at her. I stumbled on.

And I have bad news – but maybe you know it already? Jure's been killed.

The words didn't seem real. They were wrong! I read on like an automaton.

Mate Jugić received news from his sister. The Germans came looking for Partisans in the village after you left and Jure and your cousin's boy Dragan were killed.

Jure couldn't be dead. Neither could Dragan – and where exactly had he been? Can you imagine it, Pualele? I couldn't believe my beloved uncle and Dragan were dead, and worst of all I knew it was somehow my fault. I peeked at Mama from under my eyebrows. Her face was still.

Did you hear, Mama?

She didn't move.

Did you hear what I said? I screamed at her. The Partisan dying was one thing, but this was a shocking reality that was too much for me to take in. *They're dead!* I roared. *Dragan and Jure – they're dead.*

I was on my back on the ground before I knew what had hit me. I saw the flap of the tent fall back into place as Mama ran outside. It took me a moment until I got my breath back, and by that time she was nowhere to be found.

ଔ

Outside the tent, I held the letter in my hand, turning one way and then another, trying to decide which way to run but not going anywhere.

Olga! What's happened?

Ivica!

I crumpled at the knees and he rushed to me.

What is it?

I thrust the letter in his face and he read the words. He helped me to my bed and the tears came at last. The desert breeze could not stop them this time and I felt as if a hot knife was twisting in my belly. It hurt so badly that I thought I might die. I know that I wanted to.

I don't know how long it was, but I finally stopped weeping and realised that Ivica had gone and that standing in his place was Pero, looking at me curiously. I couldn't deal with him right then, so I acted as if he wasn't there and picked up the letter and reread the words, just to see if I hadn't made a mistake. But there they were on the page in my father's tidy handwriting. I couldn't deny them. I read on.

The Red Cross tell me that you are safe with the British (and I hope that this is true) and that when the War is over, they will want you to return to Yugoslavia. Don't worry – I'll book a passage for you and when the time comes you, Olga and Pero will come to New Zealand. Ivan and I are in Auckland now and we've saved some money – not enough to buy land, but enough to buy a fishmonger's shop, so you'll never have to break your back toiling on the mountain again. We will be city people, and one day I will be a rich man!

It will be our new home above the shop – for all of us. Write me if you get this letter so I know that you're truly safe.

Your loving husband,

Ivan

As I finished the rest of the letter, the tent flap was pulled back and Ivica guided Mama to her bed. She lay down and curled up like a small animal, cradling her head in her hands. I got up to go to her, but Ivica stopped me.

She needs to rest.

I left the tent and went to find Oliver. He was now honing his carpentry skills as part of an organised group of builders, and I spotted him helping to erect another storehouse for the camp. His back was to me as he hoisted a beam above his head and passed it up to a man balancing on the upper rung of a ladder. I moved closer and stood in the lee of a tent across from him, watching the muscles moving under his skin. He turned his head as he wiped his face with the back of his arm, catching sight of me watching him.

He walked across to me, his forehead oily with sweat and his cheeks red from the effort of lifting wooden beams into place. A look of concern grew on his face as he looked at me.

What is it, Olga?

I gave the letter to him to read and watched as the colour faded from his face. He bunched his hand around the paper and shook his head. *I'm sorry about your uncle.*

I nodded, trying to get my emotions under control. *I can't believe Jure's gone. I just can't. And Dragan – poor Dragan, I was so mean to him . . .* The tears started to flow down my cheeks.

Oliver sighed and began towards me as if he were going to comfort me.

You'll think I'm stupid when I say this, but . . . well, I thought that Dragan might have known where Mila was. Oliver stopped moving towards me and made a face of disbelief. *I mean, I know I said I saw her on the boat, but maybe . . . you know, maybe I was wrong and they had got together somehow. They could have . . .*

Shut up, Ola. He said as his face twisted into a snarl *Shut your stupid mouth.* He threw the crumpled letter onto the ground and strode off along the tented rows, disappearing towards the east where the camp gave way to the Sinai.

It's not your fault.

I turned to find the scarred-face girl, Kata, looking at me.

They all want someone to blame.

What do you know?

She shrugged her shoulders. *They get angry 'cause none of it makes sense.*

You don't know what happened, I yelled at her. *You don't know.*

She shrugged again and started to leave. I watched her walking towards the tents. Her back was straight and I detected a certain strength in those shoulders; a self-assuredness that was intriguing.

Wait. I ran up to her, not knowing what I wanted to say.

We started walking and before I knew it we were climbing up a small mountain of sand that gave us a view over the whole camp. I was puffing by the time we reached the top and we lay on our backs side by side staring at the sky.

Maybe I did something too, Kata said. She turned her face towards mine so that she was so close I could see the freckles across the bridge of her nose. She wasn't beautiful, but she had a warmth to her that drew me in. In profile, I could see her high forehead and the way her nose turned up slightly at the end and the purple pox scars that peppered her smooth cheek.

It can't have been as bad as me, I replied.

Maybe, but you don't know anything about me.

She had a point and she was so open that it was easy for me to ask.

What happened?

Kata was from a village on the coast like me. We could have seen each other's villages if we'd looked, and although she was older than me we had lived similar lives mere kilometres apart.

I was at school when the Germans came. They were looking for a local Partisan leader and when they couldn't find him, they came to the schoolhouse and lined us up against a wall and opened fire. The teacher and all the children died. Except for me.

She stopped talking and I thought she might be crying, but she went on.

I was standing by my sister and she moved forward as they started shooting, and I lived. I pulled her body on top of me and lay there, even while they forced villagers at gunpoint to dig a trench to put us in. They pushed our bodies into the pit and spread lime over us. Night fell; otherwise they would have buried me alive.

But that's not bad, I said. *They should be happy you lived. What about your parents? At least they must be happy?*

You don't understand. It was my father they were looking for. My mother they shot before they came to the school. My being alive reminds everyone. It's because of my family that the others died.

I reached out and touched the scars, letting my finger slide down to her lips and onto her chin. Large brown eyes stared back at me and she leaned forward and kissed the tip of my nose. As I went to pull away from her she reached out and pulled me back towards her. She kissed me, tentatively at first, and then her hand rested against my cheek as her tongue parted my lips. She tasted salty and sweet at the same time and my whole body tensed. Kata pulled away, looking at me with a slightly bemused look on her face.

You want me to stop.

I stared at her stupidly.

It's OK, she said and I nodded, wanting to please her while at the same time wanting to run.

If you want to stop, you just have to say so. She was on her side looking at me as I lay on my back, staring up at the sky. I stretched my arms up over my head not sure what to say. Her narrow hand with its strong fingers came to rest on my hip where it seemed to steady me.

But I didn't leave and nor did she. We stayed on the hill until the Egyptian sun had started to slip below the horizon, then we headed back to the camp, both of us happier than we'd been in a long time.

ೞ

Oliver arrived back the next night, long after everyone else was in bed. He glanced my way as he passed by me, but I avoided catching his eye. My lips moved and I almost called out to him. I wanted to tell him not to worry, that Mila was alright. But I stayed silent. I got up and went to Mama. She didn't move. I tried to speak to her, but there was no response. Her eyes were shut and I stroked her hair. With a new-found confidence, I became the mother, softly singing childhood songs to her and Pero as the world changed around us.

Mama had lost the protective arms that we all have around us. They had loosened from her when her own parents had left her an orphan, and now with Jure's death she had finally been set adrift, alone and unprotected in the world until we could be reunited with my father. The only sound that came from her was the in-and-out of steady breathing, but I stayed with her, hoping that I could love her back into the world.

ೞ

The next day Mama stirred early. Lifting her head from the pillow she briefly looked around, a puzzled look on her face. Her gaze momentarily rested on me before she lay down again, placing her head gently on the pillow and closing her eyes to the world. I thought about what she would do if it were me lying there slowly slipping away from the world. Someone brought some warm porridge into the tent for her. The porridge was runny and grey and in it floated the bodies of tiny weevils that seemed to be present in every bowl of food in the camp. I'd long since stopped seeing the bugs and simply tipped the spoon onto Mama's lips, trying to tempt her with the food. But her mouth remained closed and a lumpy grey thread trickled down her chin.

I wiped her face and her head turned towards the tent wall as I felt tears spilling down my cheeks. I didn't know what else to do. What would *she* do? I thought. How would she soothe her own soul and make it so she would come alive again?

※

She has typhus, said the doctor, *we'll get her a proper bed when one's free.*

Mama was the first person in our tent to be struck by camp fever. She lay listless on a makeshift stretcher on the floor of the hospital, her body on fire. El Shatt was riddled with the disease. Many people, mostly children, lay there as the molten sun dripped down on the hospital, giving them no relief from the fevers that raced through their aching bodies. I gripped my arms, feeling suddenly cold. *How long will she be here?*

The doctor, a thin man with dark semicircles under deep-set eyes, shrugged. *It's likely you'll all get it,* he said as if offering me comfort or reassurance.

I wanted to tell him that I'd had typhus and that my mother had looked after me, but there appeared to be little point.

Will she be OK? I asked.

He didn't answer me but instead turned his hands upwards and walked away towards the next person lying on the ground waiting to be seen.

The El Shatt air had left gritty sand in my eyes that grazed and scratched at me until I felt a dull ache in my eyeballs. I didn't want to be in this camp with lousy bed linen and weevils in our food. I wanted to find Kata and run all the way back to Dalmatia, away from the desert and the sun that beat us down.

But the resignation in the doctor's voice and the sight of Mama lying motionless made me want to fight. I didn't want to be beaten and for Mama to die here amongst the sick on their camp stretchers and the foul latrines that stunk so bad you had to hold your breath when you used them. I wanted to survive and not be buried in a place where the sands shifted constantly. I wanted to get back to our land where mountains rose up and held us safely in their valleys. If Mama was going to die, it should be there where our dead lay.

I wouldn't leave her. I would do what she had done for me and we would get through this, and together we'd return home when the war was over.

◦ℜ

As the camp fever receded from her body, Mama changed little. She lay in delirium on the stretcher and spoke little. During the day she slept, while at night she lay awake, not speaking. We were all encouraged by the improvement in her – she wasn't going to die. But I couldn't understand why they didn't see that she was still sick. Each day she descended further into herself, while at the same time the doctors expressed their delight in her progress.

Kata came every few days to bring food and to sit with me. The rest of the time I was alone by Mama's side, bathing her as she had bathed me. Pero was looked after by Ivica, and it frightened me how alike Mama and Pero had become.

I knew that she needed a different kind of medicine, but the doctors could not be persuaded that this bag of bones with dull hair and flat eyes wasn't my mother. My mother would have got up off the stretcher and gone about the business of getting on with life. Although her physical symptoms had improved enough for her to return to our tent, this woman was dying.

◦ℜ

Whatever friendship I thought I had with Oliver was gone. I waited for an opportunity to get through, but he refused to let me in. Finally I couldn't stand it any longer. I couldn't bear him not being my friend, so one day I decided to do something and marched up to him as he worked on the storehouse.

He caught sight of me and stopped for a moment, then turned back to hammering nails into the frame of the building. I cleared my throat, planting my feet in the sand, preparing myself.

You can't just ignore me.

He swung harder, lifting his arm back and smashing the nail head until there were large indentations in the wood. He took another nail from his mouth and placed it on the frame and swung again. This time the hammer glanced off the nail head, hitting his knuckles.

He swore loudly as he dropped the hammer onto his foot and let out another yowl. I couldn't help the giggle that bubbled up from inside me and escaped from my lips before I could catch it. Soon it was a full-blown unstoppable belly laugh.

Oliver glared at me as I held my hand up to my face, trying to control myself. Then a flicker of a smile crossed his face as he shook his injured hand, followed by a nervous laugh. Suddenly he was laughing as hard as I was. We stepped towards each other and his arms went around me. I rested my head on his shoulder as the laughter turned to weeping.

I sniffed the last tears away as Oliver looked intently at me. I knew what was going to happen and I closed my eyes. The thrill of his lips on mine was more than physical. I let him move his chafed lips over my face, my eyelids, let him kiss my chin, and I thought of Kata. When he finally lifted his mouth away from me I felt cheated.

I pushed him away.

I'm sorry . . .

Stop apologising, Ola.

I just want . . . us to be friends again.

I shouldn't have done that.

I liked it when he kissed me. It was just that . . . I couldn't tell him that I liked kissing Kata too. He looked like a dog tempted with a treat and then kicked for accepting it. I felt confused and my bottom lip began to wobble and I sniffled involuntarily. I heard him curse himself and step close to me again, placing a hand on my shoulder.

I'd like to kiss you a thousand times over, Ola. He let his hand fall away. *You're so young.*

I'm not.

His eyes locked on mine, searching inside me. I wanted us to never argue. Maybe I just needed to get used to his touch and I should let him kiss me again.

Look, we're friends and . . .

But that's all . . . He chipped in quickly.

Then why did you yell at me if that's how you feel?

You must've known how I'd react when you said about Dragan maybe knowing what had happened to Mila? He reprimanded me as if I was no more than a child and I indeed felt very young next to him. He stepped forward and placed his hand on my shoulder.

Listen Olga, I admit that when I read the letter about Dragan and Jure being killed, I thought along the same lines as you – that Dragan and Mila . . . Well, anyway, that Dragan might have known what happened to her. So when you said what I'd been thinking. I don't know. It just made me angry that we'll probably never know.

I'm sorry, I said to him once more.

He took my hand and gripped it in his, turning it over and tracing a figure eight on my palm. Without taking his eyes off my hand, he went on.

I just believed – wanted to believe – they were together. He raised his eyes to mine, and I knew what he said to be true. *Now it's just us, Ola.*

I let the words settle in me and an understanding travelled between us that can exist only when two people have known each other for a very long time. The weight of his hand in mine told me I belonged, that there *was* an 'us', and I knew then I had finally found someone that would always be there for me.

CHAPTER 15

PUALELE

That evening it is Pualele who cooks and serves dinner. Aunty refuses to go to the Orange Dance Hall with Uncle Sam and instead takes to her bed. A melancholic veil falls over the house. Even Kasi is morose, not even bothering to shoot Pualele a smile or give a quick wink.

As soon as she finishes with the dishes she goes to her room and closes the door. She squints against the failing light, making her way over to the dresser and the candle. The flame flickers wildly on the brand-new wick that stands above the protective glass surround. She jumps back to avoid its flicking yellow tongue.

She turns and sits on her bed, wishing that she had never been so desperate to have an ice cream. It was selfish and greedy. Mama would be mortified to know how badly she had behaved since arriving in New Zealand. She should write and tell her that she'd never meant to do anything bad; she'd just wanted an ice cream like the other kids. Aunty had offered. And it was Aunty who had marched them into the water.

The flame catches her eye then and she watches it, mesmerised as it dances in front of her cousin's picture. She catches a glimpse of cousin Pualele smiling back at her. She wonders how she'd caught a germ when she hadn't a brother or sister to share with. She tries to feel sympathy for the poor dead girl in the picture, but instead all she feels is intense hatred.

Pualele hasn't felt this kind of anger towards her dead cousin since the day she threw a book at her picture and missed. Her face glows hot as she chews on her lip. She is sick of seeing the stupid smiling face on the wall, and she knows that because of this cousin that she never met she is living in Auckland and not home in the village with her family.

Without thinking, Pualele goes to the dresser and the frame that displays the card with the girl trapped in time staring out at her. Her fingernails graze her palms, and then as she glowers at the photo she reaches out and seizes the picture frame. She rips the Sellotape off the back, disinterring the card from its resting place.

Her eyebrows draw together as she reaches for the candle, and with a steady hand she holds the other Pualele over the licking flame. She watches in fascination as the card starts to darken and warp from the heat, the girl's face puckering before finally bursting into a blue-tinged fire.

As the flame spreads, Pualele searches for somewhere to drop the burning card. She rushes towards the window, wrenching the sash upwards with one hand as the heat in her other hand becomes intolerable.

The curtain whips up in the evening breeze, touching the flame. She lets out a squeal and jumps back into the room, the curtain now billowing out towards her, trying to wrap itself around the burning Pualele. Her free hand shoots out and grabs the curtain, thrusting it aside long enough for her to drop the blazing photo out of the window.

She leans out and watches as the paper floats downwards, tiny pieces of blackened card falling away while other shreds of paper hang in the air, flaming red and orange in the breeze before finally burning out to nothing.

She rests her head on the windowsill, her relief coming in small tears that trickle onto the painted wood. She is glad the prayer card has gone, but she feels sick when she thinks about what will happen when Sefi finds the photo missing. She lifts her head, straining to see if she can catch a glimpse of the church's steeple. Maybe she should jump out the window and go there, away from the house and the people in it. A quiet sanctuary in which to pray and calm herself is just what she needs.

Pualele's nose twitches and she sniffs the air. She spins around. The varnish on the dresser is bubbling where the tipped-over candle continues to burn. She throws herself across the room, arms outstretched ready to snatch the candle from its resting place, but she can only watch in horror as the cotton curtain comes to rest over the top of the candle holder just as it becomes a sheet of fire.

The open window fans the flames and they jump onto a lavalava lying on the floor. Pualele grabs a nearby book and bats at the flames, but they seem to run away from her, racing across the walls, gobbling up the fleur de lis as they go. Pualele throws her book on the ground and runs screaming for the door.

Fire! Fire!

Father and Kasi burst out of their room, followed by Uncle and Aunty from the kitchen a few moments later. Father pushes Aunty and Pualele towards the front door while Uncle shouts at Kasi to get water from the kitchen.

Aunty and Pualele stand in the street, and Aunty's wailing brings the neighbours out of their homes to see what is happening. As others keep watch from their porches and behind hedges and around corners, Mrs Magasiva materialises by their side. She ushers them across the road and onto her veranda before either of them have a chance to speak.

Someone calls the fire brigade and an engine arrives with flashing lights and siren blaring. Orange and red flames are now rising from the back corner of the house. Three firemen run inside with a giant hose and pick-axes while others connect the other end to the hydrant. The fire crackles and spits and a thick blanket of smoke rises into the air, blacking out the lights from the street behind. To Pualele it looks as if some evil spirit is escaping into the night, and she shudders. She loses track of time and what may be minutes or hours pass by as she prays and continues to stare at the house, willing her father, uncle and Kasi to appear. Her fingernails play at her palms. Just when she believes that the men are gone forever, one by one they emerge from the thinning smoke.

The firemen follow behind them and Pualele leaps to her feet at the same time as a police car arrives. She begins to call out to the men, but the Queen claps a hand over Pualele's mouth, pulling her backwards towards the front door.

Quickly. Inside. The Queen is insistent, pushing Aunty and Pualele into her front room where Ben is looking out through the curtains.

You can stay here tonight. I'll send Ben to get the others.

The police, Merita.

Don't worry. They only come to see what's happened.

Aunty sits down, chin on her chest, dejected and out of fight. A low keening is coming from somewhere deep inside her: *aie, aie, aie* . . .

Ben steps forward. *She's right, Mama. We should talk to Willi. He'll find somewhere for* . . .

Aunty's head snaps up and she is shouting, *Keep Willi and his people out of this. If it wasn't for that man we'd own our own house by now.*

But he'll find somewhere safe until . . .

Enough. Mrs Magasiva holds her hand up at Ben. Pualele thinks she looks just like a policeman and she wonders who this Willi is.

Do you know how it started? The Queen tilts her head towards Pualele, but she stares at a spot on the floor, her heart racing. Her bottom lip trembles and she shakes her head, squeezing her hands as hard as she can. Mrs Magasiva says something that Pualele doesn't catch and then the Queen is in front of her scooping her up into her arms. She makes soothing sounds and presses Pualele's face into the soft buttery flesh of her bosom as she carries her into a room where the other Magasiva children are pretending to be asleep. The Queen lays her down next to one of the girls and then sits next to her, making slow circles on Pualele's back until the girl finally slips into a fitful sleep haunted by spectral curtains and crackling flames.

∞

When Pualele awakes she finds herself alone and the room already filled with light. She looks at the unfamiliar mattresses and tapa-covered walls. In a moment of confusion she does not know where she is. It is only when she breathes deeply and smells the smoke in the air that the events of the night before come rushing back to her.

Her head throbs, and soon the thumping is echoed by footsteps in the hallway. They pause outside the door to the room and she closes her eyes again and lies as still as she can. The door opens and someone steps in. She hears them move across to where she lies and feels a familiar hand rest on her shoulder.

Come. We go home.

Pualele gets to her feet and waits for her head to stop pounding. As she looks at her father, she feels a pang of guilt as she takes in his bloodshot eyes and the dark circles that lie under them. She does not speak but tentatively follows her father out of the Magasivas' house. There is a fear growing inside her, but as they step onto the Magasivas' porch she is relieved to see the Auva'a house still standing, with taro leaves peeking up over the fence and the blue-paned front door exactly where it should be.

Father takes her hand and she walks tall next to him, across the empty road and down towards their waiting home. As they approach the house an acrid dampness envelopes them, and Pualele's confidence disappears. Up the steps and in through the front door the sharp smell of burnt paint and timber are unbearable, and she chokes a little as it catches in her throat.

Aunty and Uncle are in the front room waiting for them. Kasi is nowhere to be seen. Father ushers Pualele into the room and she jumps at the sound of the click of the door as Father shuts it behind them.

Sit down, Pualele. Uncle indicates a spot on the floor with his eyes.

She sinks down onto her knees and places her hands on her lap, the fingers on top curling over the hand below. Aunty immediately starts crying, the sad keening cry: *aie, aie, aie.*

Have we not been good to you, Pualele?

She nods.

And have we not been generous, given you clothes and food?

She nods again.

And we say nothing when people say you steal from the shop.

She gulps and glances at the three adults sitting in a line in front of her: judge, jury and executioner.

Then why is it you play with fire and try and burn our house down?

No.

Uncle rises to his feet.

You dare say different. He was now standing over her. *The firemen. They see what you did. The police. They come and they see what you did.*

His large paw shoots out and grasps her collar, pulling her to her feet.

The landlord says we pay for all damage. We lucky he doesn't make us find a new house. You think it easy to find a new house when you try and burn one down?

Pualele squirms and rises onto her toes as she tries to stop from choking. She shakes her head. *No.* He releases her so that she stumbles, almost falling over.

And do you think we ever get back Pualele's picture? Uncle's voice is very quiet and his words wobble at the end.

Then it is Father grabbing her, stopping her from falling over. He stands in front of her and slaps her twice. The hot sting spreads across her cheeks and she feels the skin puffing up around her left eye.

You very lucky, Pualele. I should beat you, but I'm not a violent man. Sefi and Sam give you one more chance. Any more problems, you go back to Samoa.

The physical pain is nothing compared to the humiliation she feels at her father's words. All she thinks about is going home to Mama and the other children, but not as a disappointment. She can cope with the taunts of the children at St Mary's, the critical eye of the shopkeepers and the nuns who want to rebrand her, but although the one thing that she longs for is to go home to Samoa she can't face the shame of returning to the village a failure.

You sleep in our room and next pay day I buy you a new uniform. Pualele makes fists with her hands and digs her nails in.

You come to work with me until your father gets a new uniform. We don't want palagi thinking we can't afford one. Uncle Sam starts to walk away before he stops and turns back towards her.

And Pualele – last chance.

She feels grateful for his restraint and wishes she could be what he wants her to be. At school Pualele is desperate to be friends with the girls and to please the nuns, but she knows she will only achieve this if she leaves her Samoan self at the school gates. In the house on Richmond Road, she wants to be nine-year-old Pualele, daughter of Iosefo and Olina Auva'a, but even her own parents seem complicit in her rebirth as someone else's child.

It is beyond her ability to understand what people want from her and why. There is only one thing that is certain: Pualele Sina Auva'a no longer knows who she is.

☙

That day everyone except Kasi stays home to clean up and wait for the fire chief. Pualele's bedroom is a gaping blackened hole in the side of the house. She has lost everything – if it hasn't been burnt, it is drowning in pools of rank water left by the firemen. The rest of the house has escaped the flames, although there is the lingering smell of smoke throughout. They all know they are lucky that the local fire station is only minutes away.

The chief arrives later in the morning with Mr Hanson, the landlord, at about the exact time that Pualele's left eye finally swells shut. The fire chief is a trim man whose skin sticks to his frame as if he is vacuum-packed into his body. His shoulder blades are visible through his shirt. Pualele feels that he might pierce the pocked skin of his jawline if he keeps on thrusting his pointed chin forward as he looks at the damage to the house. Mr Hanson stands next to him, a self-important man who is as wide as the chief is narrow. The landlord grinds his teeth as he lingers by the official's side, waiting for his opportunity to pounce on the feckless tenants. Both men wear patent-leather shoes.

Just a few questions for our investigation. The chief holds a pad in one hand and, in the other, his pen hovers over the paper as he continues. *Whose room is this?*

My daughter's. Uncle Sam's voice is quiet but firm.

You're very lucky no one was hurt. Pualele blushes violently as she stands unseen behind the door.

Who else was home at the time?

Sefi steps forward in front of Father and Uncle, her arms waving like the wings of a bird in distress. *My family. We've been here ten years. Never any trouble.*

No trouble? Mr Hanson mutters.

The chief shoots him a warning look and Mr Hanson says nothing more.

Of course this is just routine, continues the chief.

Aye – routine. Aunty Sefi's head is bobbing up and down, her hands now clasped in front of her. Sam glares at the landlord and wraps his arm around Sefi's shoulders. *Well . . . me, my wife . . . brother . . . nephew . . .*

The landlord sounds as if he is choking at the words and he is unable to contain himself any longer. *Overcrowding – see I told you, Roger. And illegal. I never agreed to half the Islands moving in, and . . .*

Many times I ask you to repair things and you say 'no'. I do it. And how many times we ask you to buy the house and you say 'no'.

Please. The fire chief cuts Uncle Sam off. *I'll take it from here, Malcolm. Why don't you wait outside and we can inspect the outside after I'm done.*

Mr Hanson mumbles as the chief takes his elbow and motions towards the door to the hallway. *Alright, Roger. You be careful – these niggers are tricky.*

The chief doesn't flinch at the words and merely returns to pointing his chin at Uncle Sam and Aunty Sefi.

And your daughter?

Yes, yes, of course. From her hiding place, Pualele looks at Uncle Sam and then to her father, who is looking passively at the floor. She cannot believe what she is hearing and seeing. Why won't her father say that *he* is her father and not Uncle Sam? The question pulses in her head and in this instant she knows that he is leaving her.

I think my men got your names last night. He flicks back through the pad and trails the pen down the side of the page. *Yes, I think we have everything for now. I'll just take a look at the outside with the landlord and that will be all.*

A sigh of relief escapes from Aunty's lips and she breaks into an appreciative smile. *Thank you, sir. Thank you very much.*

CHAPTER 16

OLGA'S JOURNAL

You will think me heartless for what I am about to tell you, but I cast off Kata as easily as our friendship had begun. Oh the thrill of being with her, the excitement of it all, gave me such joy, which was a rare thing in those days. But somehow none of it could compete with Oliver and everything his love represented. He was my past, my present and my future.

Kata and I were still in that honeymoon period when you make a friend or find a match and nothing the other does can be wrong. But we didn't really know the depth of the other person, only what we knew of our histories. We had connected because of the shame we felt surrounding our departures from our villages, and sometimes that is how a friendship might start. A shared pain. But you need more than that and it is easy for such a relationship to fizzle out because there is nothing more than that one commonality to carry it on.

Callous as it may seem, I avoided her, and if truthful to myself (although I'm not sure I can say what the truth is any more) I simply avoided her because I didn't know how to tell her that she could be my friend but that my future lay with another. And how conceited was I to even think that I had a future with Oliver when all he'd done was kiss me once and hold my hand. Again I plead the innocence of youth and of a girl who was searching for love she could rely on and who thought that she had found it in a boy the image of her adored Mila.

There are some memories that we try to hold on to so we can recall them when we are old like I am now, and so we can remember how once we were loved. For right now, the only people to touch me are the nurses and doctors and of course you, Pualele, when you lend me your arm. Then there are memories that arrive uninvited into our present and refuse to leave us be. I will never forget the night the war stole Pero's soul away, nor the day that Kata confronted me, for both haunt me in their own terrible way.

She knew immediately that something was awry. I did not go to the school or by her tent or anywhere we would have easily run into each other. When she asked people, I had always just left, or had just been seen, or they didn't know where I was. I was like a phantom that people had heard of but not seen, always just out of sight.

But she was persistent. On a day when I ranged far from our tent to the southern-most point of the camp and sat there in the open with Pero, the sun turning our skins African, Kata found me. I wasn't aware of her approach until a shadow fell across Pero, and I looked up to find her eyeing me warily.

You're hard to find, she said in a tone that suggested she knew my game.

I couldn't look at her, but you have to understand that I didn't know how to say what should've been said. I didn't have the words or the examples or any of the things that a young woman these days might. But she was strong, Kata. And she wouldn't let me get away with ignoring her even though she knew what it all meant.

I've been wanting to talk to you, she said.

Oh God, I thought, leave it alone, leave me be.

Or maybe, she challenged me, *you've got something you want to say to me, Olga?*

The tone of her voice raised my heckles and I felt suddenly righteous.

What do you want from me? I said to her in my coldest voice.

She laughed at me, knowing how painful this exchange was for me. It was funny to think that only a week before we had been the best of friends in our closeted world and now I could not bear to have her near me.

What is it you want? I said again.

You tell me, she countered, far cleverer than I ever was then or now. Although she baited me that day, I cannot fault her for it because I was the cruel one.

I took up the family trait of silence and looked away from her to where Pero played on in the sand. The sun was directly above us and so hot that I began to feel dizzy under its heat. I momentarily saw a dark night and heard Mila's words again. I shivered.

I know what you've been up to, Olga. She was in a conciliatory mood. *I'm sad you couldn't tell me.*

I didn't want to be forgiven or to be friends or to talk about anything with her. It felt like déjà vu even though the roles were reversed and the landscape could be no more different.

I never made any promises! I said fiercely.

Oh, but you did, Olga, you did.

I looked up at her and saw she was utterly devastated. The colour drained from her face and as the scars became darker against her washed-out skin, she dry-retched there in front of Pero and me. It was only at that point Pero looked at her with fright, as if he'd been unaware that there had been anyone else with us.

She glanced at us guardedly when she had finished. I should've been comforting this girl who had been such a good friend, but I was perhaps more like my mother than I realised. I staunchly stared back at her, offering no words of remorse or comfort until she turned and walked away.

CR

We left Egypt when I was sixteen. In all those years Mama treated me politely but never spoke to me as a mother does with her daughter. I lived in my own self-contained world, attending the camp school and embroidering and making clothes, but apart from time with Oliver I stayed away from people. When I could, I climbed the sand hills that loomed at the edge of the camp. I would lie there with Oliver where Kata had first taken me and he and I would talk about the future as I had once done with his sister. We would watch nameless people in the camp moving about like tiny insects on the desert floor, and when it was time to return for dinner we would slip quietly back into the camp.

CR

Almost everyone from our village returned to Dalmatia, including Ivica. But my father was true to his word. A Red Cross package arrived with passage secured on a boat that would take us, Rosa and Oliver to New Zealand.

The rumours about Rosa and the Germans had reached El Shatt. She had been shunned by many of the women in the camp, and she knew the kind of welcome she would receive if she returned home. Rosa had tried to get to America where her daughter Edita lived, but she was unable to get visas for herself and Oliver. New Zealand had thankfully become their only option. I told myself that fate was keeping us together.

༄

We left Port Said on a converted soldier transport ship called the *Victory*. We travelled for five weeks. More seasickness. I have a vivid memory of retching over the railings on deck, thankful that I was alone, when a familiar voice intruded.

I brought you a towel and some water.

I lifted my head and Oliver gently wiped my mouth with the corner of a moist towel. I tried to smile, but stopped. I was afraid of being sick over him. He chuckled at me.

You're beautiful. Even when you're sick.

The pitching waves set me off again and I ran for the railings once more.

Was it something I said? He laughed.

I couldn't speak and Oliver thankfully stopped talking too, but he stayed with me until I was exhausted. He helped me off the deck down into the open hold of the ship where the bunks were packed tightly, one next to the other like kernels on a cob of corn.

Whenever the seas picked up he would come and find me. Sometimes when it wasn't so bad we would just sit and talk. Other times he held my hand or rubbed my back, and perhaps it was tenuous but I felt a happiness that kept the past locked away.

I convinced myself that I had nothing to be ashamed of in the way that I'd treated Kata. After our last encounter I only ever saw her in the distance at the camp. She'd become invisible to everyone once again and I had no idea how or where she spent her time, though I suspect she knew my movements well. It was as if my rejection of our friendship had once again left her alone and adrift in El Shatt. When we left I thought to ask after her, but in the end I hadn't the courage to put voice to my curiosity.

CHAPTER 17

PUALELE

Uncle Sam is a mechanic by trade, but for ten years he has worked for Davison and Davison Funeral Directors as a general maintenance man. Uncle Sam can fix anything – including the Lincoln Continental. Occasionally he helps in the embalming room or the crematorium, but mostly he keeps the fleet of four vehicles in top condition.

Hello, Sammy! Sorry to hear about the fire – everything alright?

Hello, Mr Davison. Yes, we're OK.

Terrible thing, fires. Mr Davison gazes past Uncle to where Pualele stands. *And who have we here?*

The funeral director moistens his lips, looking Pualele over as he rubs his hands together. She moves uncomfortably on the spot, wishing he'd turn his attention to something else. She pretends she's not looking at him while peeking with her good eye, fascinated by the light that reflects off his bald head. As if to make up for his lack of hair, he has cultivated lamb-chop sideburns and has a pair of eyebrows that look so much like exotic fuzzy caterpillars that Pualele gapes openly.

This is my niece, Pualele. She comes to help until she goes back to school.

Oh, Pualele. The caterpillars jump skyward as the man's ruddy skin pales and she wonders if it is because his paisley tie is pulled too tight around his neck. *Well . . . errr . . . as long as she's no bother. We can always do with an extra pair of hands.* He clears his throat like a man does before saying something important.

Well, then. Mrs Davison needs some help cleaning up the embalming room. Hope you're as good as the other little one.

Pualele's face burns with shame as she thinks about her dead cousin. If only both her eyes had swollen shut then she wouldn't have to see Uncle's face twist momentarily before he catches himself.

Don't worry, Mr Davison. She'll do as she's told. Mr Davison smiles at the words and looks directly into Pualele's one functioning eye. There's something about his look, the rubbery lips and wild sideburns, that makes Pualele flinch involuntarily.

ଘ

The embalming room is an assault on her senses. Her nasal passageways burn with the chemical smell – they are already sensitive from the fire. The light is extra bright, leaving no nook or cranny unexposed. She screws up her face.

You'll get used to it, love. Mrs Davison is as hirsute as her husband is bald. Her thick blonde hair is pulled back into a chignon, the centre part showing her dark roots. The light from the window catches her side profile and Pualele can see the light fuzz on her chin and cheeks.

We've had a few through yesterday and Tom's got another one to do this morning.

Pualele chews her lip and waits.

Get yourself a broom from the cupboard over there and you can sweep the floor for me. There's a good girl.

Mrs Davison leans over a bench top as her arms draw vigorous circles with a cloth. Pualele wanders towards the wall, searching for the cupboard. She finds a series of silver handles and pulls on the middle one.

The door is heavy and she closes her good eye as she gives it an extra tug to get it to move. A cool rush of air washes over her as she opens her eye. Through the partly opened door she sees a pair of long bony feet with yellowing toenails pointing at her. On the big toe of one foot is a brown tag attached by a string. Pualele's jaw drops, and even her closed eye opens a sliver in fright. She hears Mrs Davison behind her, clicking her tongue against her teeth.

This is Mr James, she says as she reaches around Pualele and pushes the door closed. *Tom's to do him later.*

She turns towards the other wall. *The door you want's over here.*

She pulls out a red-handled broom and thrusts it in Pualele's direction. *It's alright, love. Mr James won't hurt you,* she says, stretching over and giving her a squeeze on the arm. *Dead men can't hurt you.* And then almost as an aside she says, *Least not the way the living ones do.*

She touches her finger to Pualele's cheek, and before Pualele can stop herself, a tear forms and travels towards Mrs Davison's hand.

I tell you what. Why don't we leave this 'til later and we'll go make a cuppa for the boys?

Pualele gulps and nods. She isn't crying because of poor dead Mr James. It is because in a funny way that she doesn't understand, she feels happy.

❦

That night there is a light tapping on the Auva'as' front door. Uncle Sam goes to see who it is and returns a few minutes later leading a tall palagi woman dressed in a fuschia house coat and teetering on eight-centimetre colour-matching patent-leather wedges.

Hello. I'm Edith Davis. I've brought some things over for Pauline. I'm Catherine and Michael's mother. She holds up a paper shopping bag stuffed with clothes.

Please, please. Sit down. Aunty Sefi is on her feet.

No, no. I can't stop. Edith Davis clears her throat, her mouth opening and then shutting as if she's lost the thread of what she wants to say. *My Cate says Paulin . . . Pu-A-Lee-Lee is a very good netballer.*

Yes, and very bright girl.

The two women smile and move their heads in agreement with each other as the men shift uncomfortably in their seats. There is a pause in the conversation that stretches out a little too long before Mrs Davis fills the space as Aunty's eyes grow larger. She is staring at the other woman's shoes.

Father is standing now next to Uncle Sam and Mrs Davis smiles at him and steps back a little.

I'm Pualele's father. This is Afakasi, her brother.

165

Pleased to meet you, she replies, looking from Kasi to Pualele and back again. *What beautiful eyes.* Her hand flies up to her face as she blushes violently at her own words. The truth is that Kasi is used to women looking at him like this. His lighter-toned skin and striking green eyes are thanks to some palagi forefather, and he knows that they are characteristics the female population finds attractive. He merely smiles back politely, knowing what the woman is thinking.

Sorry. I didn't mean . . . I must go, the children are home on – you never know what they might get up to . . . ummm . . . Oh dear. Mrs Davis looks in danger of completely losing control before she quickly clears her throat and recovers.

There are some school clothes for Pu-A-Lee-Lee. In the bag.

Oh. Aunty Sefi shifts awkwardly between gratefulness and embarrassment. *You are very kind,* she offers with a smile.

Mrs Davis wobbles on her patent shoes and Sefi looks down at them again, her smile fading.

Well. Goodbye then.

Sefi shows her out and returns to the room just as Father speaks to the space left by the woman.

We will give thanks for the good fortune we have received this day.

Uncle and Aunty kneel on the floor and nod sagely as Kasi and Pualele mutely follow their lead and slide to the floor next to them.

Our Father, who art in Heaven . . .

Pualele closes her eyes and sways gently to the incantations as she curls her fingers. She can't help thinking that things are on the up. She now has new clothes, can go back to school and, best of all, Cate Davis has said that she is a good netballer. There's been some bad luck, for sure, but even Pualele knows that sometimes you have to suffer a little to make it to Heaven. And that's what this life is all about. Everyone says so – *Suffer the little children to come unto me.*

She moves her lips in time with the others and hopes her suffering is over, for tomorrow is Saturday and Kasi will be home to play with her and he has promised to take her to the park. She peeks at her father, afraid that he might know that she is not following the prayers, but his eyes are closed and she hears that they are drawing to a conclusion. She says the final words aloud, happy in the knowledge that tomorrow everything will be better.

‖

The sound of smashing glass shatters her dream about butterflies. Men are shouting as Father and Kasi struggle to their feet. Kasi almost falls on top of her as he balances on one foot, trying to put his other one into a trouser leg. Someone kicks the door to the room and it smashes open, rebounding off the wall. Uniformed men push the door back and once inside the room they grab her father and brother by the arms. Kasi yells unimaginable things at the men in Samoan while Father murmurs what might be prayers or curses as he resists the men who are dragging them out into the hall.

Pualele can't get enough air into her lungs and her shoulders heave as she pulls the covers around her. But another man enters the room and pulls her out of the bed by her hair as she finally collects enough oxygen in her lungs to let out a scream. Aunty Sefi appears behind him, hitting the man with a broom.

Leave her alone.

The man turns towards Aunty to ward off the blows before another man arrives and wrestles the household weapon from her grasp. He engulfs her in a bear hug, pinioning her arms to her sides. She grunts and continues to struggle as the first man pulls the blankets off the bed, exposing Pualele who is wearing one of father's old T-shirts and is curled in a foetal position facing the wall.

She's mine. She's mine. Aunty Sefi sounds more and more unhinged as she screeches at the men, who are focussing on the young girl attempting to hide her underwear and bare legs under T-shirt.

Prove it, one of the men says laconically.

The fire. Aunty Sefi stumbles over her words before she manages to arrange them in order. *Everything in her room . . . was burned.*

The first man looks from the girl curled up on the floor to the older woman.

Please. She pleads desperately, *I show you photos.*

The men say nothing initially and Sefi clenches her hands together to stop them from shaking.

You go with her, one of the men barks at the other. *I'll stay with the girl.* The second man nods, takes Sefi by the arm and marches her out of the room.

Pualele lies still, willing herself to vanish.

What's your name? The man nudges her with the toe of his shoe.

A little wave of panic ripples through her. What a question! Does she give the palagi answer, or the Samoan one? And if the Samoan one, does she go into an explanation about her ancestry and the fact that she is the third Pualele Sina Auva'a? The man waits.

Pualele, she mumbles.

Speak up.

She clears the lump from her throat and tries again.

Pualele Sina Auva'a. The man sniffs and walks across the room to some of Father's clothes piled on top of a trunk. He starts rifling through things: a quick inspection of a shirt, a pair of workman's overalls, and then the man lobs them onto the floor. As he tosses a pair of pants on top of the heap, a letter falls from the pocket and silently skids across the floor, settling at Pualele's feet. She keeps her eye on the man as he continues looking through the pile of clothes while she slowly stretches out her foot, sliding the envelope back until it contacts with the edge of the mattress. She is fairly certain that the man shouldn't be going through her father's things, but she remains silent and concentrates on wedging the letter between the kapok bedding and the floor before the man turns around.

A defeated Aunty, her head hanging loosely between her shoulders, re-enters the room with the other man.

He holds out photographs and the other man takes them. There is one of a baby in a white christening gown, the child's name clearly written on the back. The man grunts.

There's a bunch of baby pictures and stuff.

Birth certificate? Passport?

The fire. Aunty pleads with the man.

The man searches her face, his jaw moving as he mulls over his options. Aunty looks away. He clears his throat and turns to his colleague.

This one, the kid, he pauses and gives a dismissive nod towards Aunty, *and her husband are legal. The other two are overstayers, like the fire chief said.*

No, Aunty Sefi squeals as she claws at the man's arm. He shoves her hands away and holds his head high as he goes on.

Your relatives are being deported under the Immigration Act 1975. He sneers. *When are you coconuts gonna learn you can't come in here and take our jobs?*

Aunty's shoulders droop forward and she begins the low keening *aie aie aie* as the man with the photos holds them out for her to take. She reaches for them, but he lets them go before she can grasp them properly and they fall to the floor. Aunty yelps like a kicked dog as the other man chortles.

Pualele doesn't comprehend what's happening. She's mortified that she is semi-naked. She can't follow what these men are saying to Aunty. She wants to know where Father and Kasi are and to ask what the man means when he says that they are taking jobs and are overstayers.

Uncle appears at the door with yet another uniformed man. Sefi throws herself into his arms, sobbing as the man looks on impassively.

You're lucky we don't prosecute you for hiding them, y'know.

Uncle holds the man's stare, his breathing heavy, like he's been running a long way. He stands there like that as the men turn on their heels, walking over the photos as they leave the house, the front door left swinging wide open behind them.

CHAPTER 18

OLGA'S JOURNAL

My first sight of Auckland as we sailed into her harbour was of the patchwork houses on the hills that ringed the harbour. Behind some of the houses, cows dotted the hillside like miniature black and white toys in a children's play farm. I surveyed the land for vines and olives and the stone walls that held the soil from falling into the ocean – but there were none. The city revealed itself in oyster colours, buildings jutting up into the sky, some more than five or six floors high – a modern city.

It was exciting to be landing in a place such as this, but I didn't show it. I'd learned from my mother to keep my emotions tucked away from the world. I stood on the deck of the ship in Auckland Harbour in a state of anticipation, for now my life could finally start. We were all lined up at the railing like a set of matryoshka dolls, from the biggest to the smallest. And although we never spoke of Mila, she was there too, her presence next to us that day on the deck of the *Victory*.

Gazing at Auckland, with its buildings and proper roads, I marvelled that we were as far away from our village as we could go without falling off the earth. It was our own South Pacific *Gateway to the West*. Mama was her new self – drawn and composed. I wanted to shake her until she smiled – but it didn't seem right when Pero was similarly po-faced at her side.

☙

I hadn't seen my father or brother in several years and only had the vaguest idea of who to keep an eye out for. As we carried our things down the gangway toward the waiting crowds on the dock, Mama went first. People pressed in close to me as they jostled to get past. I was reminded of what had happened at the Italian docks and my pulse quickened. Mama kept up her steady unhurried pace and I fell in behind with Pero.

Ana!

His slicked-back hair was black and shiny and sat like a helmet above his scrubbed face. He picked up my mother and spun her around as she clung onto him, a look of detachment on her face. Someone touched my elbow.

You've grown, little sister.

I threw myself at him and he stumbled backwards from the impact. *Ivan.*

They call me Joe here.

A lock of hair fell across Joe's face and I could see what Pero would look like in the future.

Olga.

My father's voice. He placed his hands on my waist and turned me to face him. I felt his calloused palm through my thin dress, and knew then that the suits he and Joe wore weren't their normal outfits.

You are beautiful, moja mala. His brown eyes warmed me as he left one hand at my waist while his other held Pero up on his hip. Pero stared in confusion at the man who held him so casually, but as always Pero said nothing. Father was a picture of happiness and he laughed easily as he surveyed his small family together once again. As an afterthought, he looked around until he found Rosa and Oliver standing off to the side.

Rosa. She came up to us and Father kissed her on both cheeks. *Who's this?* Father stepped towards the young man to her right.

This is my Oliver.

Well, you've grown. You'll do well here. He grabbed Oliver's hand, pumping his arm, grinning madly at him in excitement while Pero clung furiously to Papa's suit jacket.

You'll come with us, Rosa. No need for the boarding house – we have plenty of room in Richmond Road while you sort things out.

We don't want to be any trouble, Ivan.
No trouble.
Just until we can get our visas for America.
As long as it takes.

A thought flashed through my mind. Would Oliver and I stay in New Zealand or go to America? But just as quickly as it had come, the thought was gone and I was back standing on the wharf in Auckland.

Papa had a Ford flatbed truck, and he loaded our meagre belongings onto the back. Mama, Pero and Rosa squeezed in beside him in the front. Joe, Oliver and I sat on the open back of the truck, leaning against the cab with the bags at our feet as we headed for our new home.

With every gear change, the truck slowed and lurched. I felt as flimsy as the rag doll in my bag as my body was thrown backwards and forwards. Everything was moving too fast for me. I worried what my father would say once he realised his youngest son was mute and his wife couldn't stand to be around his only daughter. His almost compulsive sunny personality seemed to be a direct counterbalance to those of us who had arrived from El Shatt. He had no idea what sort of people he had unloaded from the *Victory*. I needed to lie down, close my eyes and not open them until everything was still and quiet and made sense again.

I barely noticed the streets and buildings we passed by. Then we turned into a road lined with plane trees. Their spiky branches were nude, leaves swirling on the ground as they were chased around by a cheeky breeze.

The road started to descend and the jerky gear changes stopped for a moment as we coasted down the hill.

This is it, sister, Joe shouted over the engine, *Richmond Road.*

Through the trees I spied house after wooden house. Their rooftops were covered with corrugated iron and they were mostly painted a dirty white that seemed responsible for holding the buildings together. Some houses had grand verandas while others were fronted by modest porches. There were walls that bulged out from the buildings, with different coloured glass patterned into the windows. I was horrified. There was not a solid stone house to be seen.

Father hit a pothole and I was lifted into the air, landing hard on the truck. I could feel the bruises before they were even there, and as we hiccupped along the road, I began to feel as if we would never make it to our destination alive. Oliver's hand landed on my thigh where it lingered for several seconds. I smiled at him and he gave me a nod before he looked away, letting his hand slip down between us so that his fingers touched mine on the wooden slats of the truck.

Here we are.

I had forgotten about Ivan/Joe for a second, and was startled by his voice as the truck turned down a side street and then quickly into an alleyway beside a block of shops. We stopped in front of some wooden steps leading up to a dark-green door. The building was grey, but it was solid. Concrete and brick – only the window frames were wooden, so that at least was something familiar. It was a plain building compared to the nearby houses with all their cornices and fretwork, but the simplicity of the architecture of the block was resonant of our own Dalmatian buildings, and I was comforted by this. A fresh easterly had come up off the harbour and whipped up the plate-sized plane leaves in the alley. The gust mingled with the smell of old fish and I wrinkled my nose as I stepped off the truck onto the loose metal driveway. The alley was lined with corrugated iron fencing that was rusting where the rivets had shot through and allowed the rain to eat away at the greyness of it. I moved my feet and listened to the metal crunch as I swivelled around. There was no garden and no sign of vegetation except for small clumps of weeds that flourished along the fence line. I wanted to be quickly inside, away from the ugliness of the yard.

Welcome to Richmond Road Fisheries. Father swung his arm expansively, laughing and smiling, and I wondered now if he wasn't quite mad. The hair that had been so carefully moulded under the pomade was now lifting up from his scalp in the breeze. He beamed at Mama, who managed a thin smile back. I was so unaccustomed to such displays of lightness and cheer that I couldn't believe it to be real.

Rosa, there's a room upstairs you can have. Oliver and Joe can share. My eyes followed his up-stretched arm pointing towards windows high up on the building. I didn't think to ask where Pero or I would be sleeping.

The outhouse is behind you.

I turned to look at the iron shed that was wired together into an improbable building that leaned like the tower in Pisa.

Mama stared at the iron shack. She stood stock still for several moments before she spoke.

Who lives there? She gestured towards the other windows on the first floor of the building.

No one. They're used for storage for the butcher and greengrocer. They have their own houses. He fixed us all with a look of excitement. *Work hard 'n we'll be rich enough to buy our own house too. Come. Let's go in. I want to show you something.*

His reply seemed to lift the mood. The women became more animated, and their faces relaxed so much that if you didn't know her, you would have believed my mother was happy.

I walked up the steps and followed Father. As my eyes adjusted to the light inside, my spirits dipped. We stood in the sparsely furnished interior of the dining-come-kitchen. The bench space hadn't been cleaned in a while and I could see a frying pan wedged into the sink where a green ribbon had stained the vitreous china basin. On the kitchen table lay an empty plate, the fork and knife crossed in the middle marking where the food had once been.

Come on, Pero. My father held out a long cord that hung from the ceiling in front of my brother, a cork dangling at the end. I imagined the cord swinging under the weight of a bottle of wine, the cork tight in the neck of it. You will laugh at me, but I thought how strange that these New Zealanders hung their wine from the ceiling like that!

Pull the cord, Pero, come on. Pero obediently tugged on the cord and a loud click later, a light snapped into life. Pero pulled again and it went off and then again, on, off, on, off as my brother grinned at the magic. You mightn't think there's anything special about an electric light being switched on, but for my father, a man from the village, this invention hanging in our New Zealand house was clearly a source of immense pride. *Light,* he marvelled out loud as if he was Nikola Tesla himself.

Light, Pero said, repeating the English word.

It was the first decipherable word he had said in three years and if the light had been something to be impressed by, my mother's reaction on hearing Pero's spoken word was one of pure astonishment. I have no idea what my father knew about his son. I don't know if Mama had told him that Pero hadn't spoken in years, or that he refused to engage with anyone at all, but Father was impressed with Pero for a different reason.

So clever, he laughed, *just arrived and already fluent in English.*

ଔ

Joe (we were using his new name already) was a lean young man with quick eyes and an easy manner like Papa.

Come on Olga, I'll show you your room. I started after him but couldn't help looking to where Oliver stood in the kitchen. He was openly staring at me, and I stumbled. Joe peered over his shoulder and caught the look that went between us. He smiled at us and extended one hand towards me. I blushed under his gaze, following him to the staircase that marched upwards and let him lead me up to my new home.

My heart was thumping in my ears. I didn't want to share my feelings for Oliver with him; I wanted to keep what we had to ourselves. And I don't know why, but there on those stairs, before we had ever settled into our new country, I had a sudden premonition of Oliver leaving me. I must've looked funny because Joe gave me a queer look and asked if I was alright. I kept my vision to myself and indicated with a nod that I was fine. But inwardly I felt as if somehow life was about to be torn asunder yet again.

CR

Everything echoed in our new home. Every step and dropped enamel mug, every whisper and creak of my parents' bed, could be heard in the upstairs flat. Even the building itself seemed to speak to us. The wind sought out the cracks between the windows and the building, invading constantly so that I thought of our first home in New Zealand as the whistling house. My room was more of a large storage cupboard, with no windows. Papa removed the door and we hung a blanket across the front of it for privacy. I soon got used to my 'cell'. After the years of communal living, it was luxury to have a space that was all my own, but I never slept a whole night through without being woken by the recurring dream.

The dream had left me for a while, but on arriving in New Zealand a version of it had found me once again. Each night I tried to stay awake as long as I could, always feeling as if someone was watching me. When I did finally fall asleep, I found myself back on the mountain with Pero. We would be running, scrambling through the undergrowth as I felt a breath on my neck. In the new dream, I was in a tug-of-war with the faceless nameless thing that pursued us. I pulled Pero by one arm while whatever chased us pulled him away from me, like gravity sucking him down into the darkness, laughing at me. I always woke groping in the dark, as the laughter turned to gypsy music and my brother slipped into the night. If Pero hadn't been sleeping safely on a mattress in my parents' bedroom, I am certain that I would never have been able to sleep at all.

Each morning, Papa rose early with Joe and Oliver and headed for the fish markets on the wharves for the daily catch. Not long after they left in the mornings the poultry man would be at the kitchen door with his delivery of fresh chickens. Sometimes there were even rabbits with their fur still on. Mama and Rosa would skin them and place them on hooks ready to display in the shop window.

At eight-thirty I would walk Pero to school at St Mary's Convent. He was lucky that there were two other Dalmatian families whose children were also at St Mary's. Pero still wouldn't speak Croatian and knew only a few words of English, but the Nola and Ravlich children were kind enough to translate the nun's instructions so that he was able to follow what was going on in the classroom. Every day he learnt a little more and I could see this once silent and terrified child changing in front of me. As soon as I had delivered Pero into his classroom, I would head back to the shop, ready to serve customers with my own broken English when it opened at nine.

Papa did all the shopping for us from the markets. He bought our fresh vegetables and fruit from Turners & Growers, but from the upstairs windows that looked out onto the alleyway, I could see into the yards of the houses at the back and the neighbours' vegetable plots, brimming with winter harvests, and that made me envious. There were apple and plum trees, and I marvelled at the lawns that the people clipped on Saturdays. I felt trapped in our upstairs house and thought that this must be how Šuša felt when we locked her in her pen. Then I would feel sad, wondering what had happened to my dear Šuša.

◯₰

I sound ungrateful, but I took every opportunity to escape the flat and the shop. I found where we lived and worked as stifling as the desert. I spent a lot of time imagining a new life with Oliver. Sometimes, it was in St Louis, and others, I would see us back in our village living in a substantial house of Italian marble and luxurious furnishings.

It was the regular customers with their peculiarities and complaints who provided some respite from feeling trapped. Most were good people who treated the Mastrović fish shop with respect, with the exception perhaps of Mr Skinner who once a week would enter the shop with a *There's something fishy going on in here.* He would buy one side of a smoked snapper for his wife to warm for him in a white sauce. I could never tell whether she got to eat any of it, but he always left the shop with a *Cheerio then, CATCH you next week.* You could hear him guffawing at his own joke as he stepped out onto the street. Mother never acknowledged his humour one way or the other, she simply took his money and ignored his boorish jokes like any good shopkeeper.

So desperate was I to be away from all of it that I even looked forward to church on Sundays. It was the only time I left the house except to go to the Yugoslav Club. The congregation at Mass was a mix of Dalmatians, Irish, Maori and Polynesian.

Without ever saying why, my mother stopped attending Mass altogether. I wondered at the time if this meant she had finally thrown Catholicism out in order to become a full-blown Communist. As had become the way in our family, one week she went to Mass and the next week she did not and no one ever discussed or mentioned it, everyone carrying on as if it had always been that way. My father went to Mass each Sunday with us, and I thought about asking him why Mama no longer went to church, but I didn't really know how to start the conversation. There was a lot not said in our family.

For me, in this new world where we didn't know many people and where, even more importantly, no one really knew me, the church became a community I could be part of and where few questions were asked of me. I suppose I have to add that it gave me perverse pleasure knowing that my mother couldn't bear to go near the church. At best I was still indifferent to Catholicism, but I admit to finding something comforting about its familiar customs. I was grateful that inside the church no vila chased me and no demons came to harangue me as I prayed. Oliver had been right when he'd once said to me, *Church isn't so bad.*

By then Pero was thriving at the convent school of St Mary's and I happily accompanied him to Mass each Sunday. I suspect that the reason he was always so keen to go to Mass was the enjoyment he seemed to get from listening to the English that was spoken by the parishioners outside the church. He steadfastly refused to speak Croatian, but he was becoming fluent in English at such a rapid rate that it put the rest of us to shame.

I have told Maureen all about this. I'd already told her vague details about the war, but I wanted her to know about Mama abandoning her faith and how I was spurred on to go to church, not by any love of God, but by spite and because I thought it did me no harm. When I said this to her I expected her to be disappointed in me, but her reaction to all this was accepting and non-judgemental. Imagine. A nun who went to church because she thought it a barb in her mother's side. Or the even more egregious reason, that it wasn't so bad a way to pass the time – which is hardly good grounding for taking Orders. But there you have it, I've told both of you who I am, and I've made no secret of my vindictiveness. All Maureen could do was look at me with sympathetic eyes as if I'd had every right to behave as I did.

I've seen it before in laypeople, Pualele. You see, sometimes when they meet you they form a deferential view, as if all nuns are saints. I couldn't bear her to think that she was in the presence of sanctity and virtue when I know what I really am.

But that wasn't the end of it. Today she came into the hospital bearing a *Scientific American* magazine which had an article about post-traumatic stress disorder. I'm not sure if she gave me this magazine because those soldiers had lost their minds in the deserts of the Middle East, or just that she presumed to know the strangeness of my mother. But then she said the most unbelievable thing: that my mother was probably suffering from this PTSD condition – and Pero and me too. At first I was irritated with her, for I don't believe it. Perhaps Pero suffered in this way when he wouldn't speak and was lost within himself. But my mother and I were different.

Maureen has the wrong idea of who we were and even though she is only trying to help me, she doesn't know that what little I have told her was not the half of what happened between my mother and me. Now I feel I have to tell her things that I never intended to, just so she doesn't think me something I am not. It is another responsibility. I never asked for any of this, I never did.

℘

Sometimes after Mass, Oliver and I would walk home together. Joe was the only one who really knew about us, and without having spoken of it he was complicit in my need to keep our relationship quiet.

Spending time together was further complicated by Oliver's relationship with Rosa. He was a dutiful son with a doting mother, and he was a constant companion to her whenever she needed him.

Why do you always have to go with her? I asked one day.

She's had a hard life. And she's all alone.

What about me? I whined, feeling myself getting angry. I had no understanding then of why he would feel this way about his mother. I had no ability to see that relationship through any other lens than my own warped view.

Oliver stroked my hair and planted a firm kiss on my mouth.

Don't worry. Soon we'll have all the time in the world. He smiled reassuringly and I forgot to be cross. Within those casual words was a tacit proposal. He said no more than that and he'd never asked me outright, but somehow he'd posed the question and I'd said yes and we both understood that this is how it would be.

CHAPTER 19

PUALELE

Pualele is inconsolable. For a week she lies there while Aunty Sefi paces up and down, sighing as she tries to tempt Pualele first with hot food and then with cold food. Sefi cannot understand why Pualele has withdrawn so completely, curled on her father's mattress, facing the wall, eyes firmly shut to the world. She is at a loss at how to break through to her niece, who seems unable to stand or talk or even move.

The officers hadn't just taken her brother and father away, they had removed the last hope Pualele had of holding onto herself. Without Kasi and Father, there was no one who knew who she really was. It would have been easier if they had all been stolen away that early morning. Instead she was left on her own to live the life that she had been cast into, and to forget who it was that she had once been. All anyone said to her was how lucky she was that she was in Auckland and not back in Samoa. What an opportunity, they had said. But they were wrong.

Pualele. You must eat. Aunty Sefi uses the soft, low voice she reserves for priests and nuns and others of importance. It is deferential in tone. Pualele sniffs and keeps her eyes closed, willing Aunty to give up and go away.

Pualele. Hot koko Samoa.

The sweet smell of the hot cocoa and sugar makes her nose twitch. Her mother made the best koko Samoa in the world. On special occasions she would roast the beans before making a thick chocolate paste. She would pour hot water over the paste and sugar to make the drink, adding a little coconut cream – her own special touch. Just for a moment Pualele turns her head and lets her eyes follow her nose. She thinks she sees her mother standing over her, a steaming cup in her hand. She smiles at Pualele and motions for her to take the cup and drink from it. Mama has come to take her home.

Aaah. Koko always makes people feel better!

As her mother speaks, her features dissolve into those of Aunty Sefi. Pualele can't hide her disappointment, but she sits up and takes the cup from her aunty before taking a long drink, savouring the sweet sensation in her mouth and letting the drink burn its way into her. She wraps her hands around the cup. Aunty is right – she does feel better. But she isn't ready to move just yet. Finishing the cup, she places it on the floor next to the mattress and slides back down onto the bed, turning her back on Aunty Sefi and closing her eyes, blocking out everything and everyone.

ೀ

Pualele.

She doesn't move.

Pualele.

Go away, she thinks.

Pualele, you must get up. Sister Margaret is here to see you.

She squeezes her eyes shut as the blankets are pulled off her.

You must hurry. Can't keep Sister waiting.

The nun stands in the kitchen, her gaze running over the ordered open shelves and shining floor. She nods, as if in appreciation of Aunty Sefi's housekeeping. Pualele feels as if she is walking through water, each step slow and deliberate until she comes to a stop just inside the kitchen door.

Well. Good to see you up, Pauline. Her voice is so soft that Pualele has to lean in to catch her words. She remains still as she waits for the nun to go on.

I understand your father and brother have returned home to Samoa? You must be sad.

A single tear escapes and rolls down Pualele's cheek.

Now, now. Sister Margaret reaches out and wipes the tear away. *You must be strong, because you have been given a great gift, Pauline. Your parents have sent you here, into this good home . . . to our school. You are a lucky girl, Pauline.*

Lucky? LUCKY? She wants to yell at Sister Margaret that it's not so – there's nothing lucky about *Pauline Ow-var.*

Your aunt and uncle are very worried about you, Pauline. And I'm sure your family in Samoa would be very sad to think that you are not . . . well. Such an opportunity. The nun tries to sound jolly, but Pualele is unmoved.

Suddenly the nun's voice rises and Pualele flinches at her words. *There's to be no more of this. You must come back to school tomorrow – no more lying in bed.* As if stunned by her own boldness, Sister Margaret blushes.

Pualele stares blankly at the floor, concentrating on pushing her fingernails into her hands. She knows that she has no say in what happens to her. She is Pauline and Grey Lynn is her home now; she may as well forget about Samoa and Pualele.

Now, the nun's voice soft and cajoling once more, *I hope we understand each other, Pauline.*

There is a pause as the two women stare expectantly at Pualele, her eyes fixed on a spot on the wall. She wants to run away and contemplates escaping out the kitchen door and heading to the police station. She is fairly certain that if she asks them, they will send her home too.

The problem is clear to Pualele – none of the adults in her life realise that she doesn't belong in Auckland. She belongs in a fale with her mother and father and Kasi and the younger children and Leti. But instead of being with her family, she is trapped here. She hopes that with her father and brother back in Samoa, her parents will see the error they have made and will send word that she should come home too. But, but, but. Pualele cannot forget what she knows to be true. Mama has given her away and doesn't want her back. They are saying she is *lucky* – but even her own mother doesn't want her.

But she doesn't say any of this. The women are waiting for a different answer so, finally, she bobs her head in acknowledgement and the two woman let out a collective breath.

Good, says Sister Margaret in no more than a whisper. *And I expect that we'll have no more of this.* She waves her hand aimlessly and Pualele tries to decipher what she means. The nun leaves, turning sideways to fit her girth through the door. Aunty follows her down the hall, opening the door and thanking her for coming. Pualele hears Sefi return to the room.

You do what Sister says, but don't say anything at school about the police and your father and brother. Aunty is by her side, holding her elbow. *Stay out of trouble*, she hisses.

Pualele stands there immobile, trying to think. Don't say anything. Don't get into trouble. Don't be a bother. There is always a list of what *not* to do. But she knows what she does want. She wants her mother – wants her to come and take her away from this place.

Understand?

Pualele nods mutely. She understands perfectly.

Say nothing.

Do nothing.

Be nothing.

☙

The next day Pualele gets to school in time for the bell and shuffles into class. She slides into her seat and makes sure that she does just enough to get by without anyone calling on her to do anything. She tries to remember back to when they had arrived in New Zealand and how she'd been excited, even if a little scared. It is a place of richness and potential that she hasn't ever grasped. She should be excited and grateful to be here, but all she has ended up feeling is a great sense of isolation, knowing that being in Auckland is something that she will have to endure until she can go home.

The letter to Mama sits in her pocket waiting to be posted. Her hand rests on it and she thinks of the words that she has written there beneath her uniform. Mama and Father will read the letter and see how much she wants to come home, and then they will send for her.

But how can she ever go home, she asks herself? With Kasi and Father gone, there will be no more money arriving in Samoa from New Zealand and life there will be a struggle once again, no thanks to Pualele. Then there is the great debt she feels she owes to Uncle Sam and Auntie Sefi. They have given her everything and she has rewarded them with endless trouble. She has to make amends and as she considers what to do, she becomes resolute.

Her hand slips into her pocket and her fingers curl around the envelope, crumpling the letter. She is going to be the best Pualele Sina Auva'a anyone has ever met. She won't speak unless spoken to and she will do only what is asked of her, without question. No more talking out of turn, no more asking for things and never again will she bring shame on the family. She's been a slow learner in the past, but she now knows her place. As soon as the bell rings again for morning tea Pauline will go straight to the church. She will pray that God will forgive her for being reckless and that He will help her find the strength to carry on.

ೞ

A few nights later she lies on her bed staring at the ceiling. At first she can't be sure that what she hears is a knock on the door. Then it comes again, a tapping, as if the someone on the other side is unable to knock any harder. She pulls up her knees under the blankets and hugs them to her. The door opens slowly and Uncle steps into the room holding a large towel under one arm. He stands in the doorway, shifting uncomfortably from one foot to another as if the floor were burning underneath. Pualele shrinks further back against the wall, pressing her spine against it.

Finally he moves forward and she hears a mewling sound. There in the crook of his arm emerges a small black face with a white stripe down its forehead. The kitten's eyes are too large for its face. As it looks at Pualele it cries again and sinks its claws into Uncle Sam's arm.

Yeoww! Uncle Sam throws his arms open and the kitten escapes onto the bed, where it cowers against the wall by Pualele's feet, hissing and spitting. Very slowly Pualele slides down the wall and edges towards the kitten. It shuffles backwards on its haunches, puffing into a heckled ball of growling fur.

Uncle Sam steps outside the door for a moment, reappearing with a saucer of milk which he places on the floor. The kitten puts its nose in the air and creeps across the bed before jumping down onto the floor and skulking over to the saucer. It dips its face into the full cream and jumps back shaking its head. Pualele giggles and Uncle Sam smiles.

Can I keep him? she whispers.

Sam nods.

She hugs herself again and examines the little ball of fur that is now slurping greedily at the milk until it is almost all gone. He has three white feet and a white ring around his tail. She will look after him and love him more than anyone. Here is something she can write to Mama about. She can tell her all about her new friend. What name should she give him? Koko. She will call him Koko. He isn't brown, but he is warm and comforting – and Pualele hopes that he will learn to love her too.

She keeps Koko in her room, leaving the window open slightly so he can escape outside when he needs to. He comes to her when she calls him now, and she often finds him asleep on her bed when she comes home from school. In a few short weeks his rib cage is well hidden under a layer of fat – she steals small pieces of meat for him at every opportunity, as if feeding him will keep him safe.

༄

Pualele lies on her bed thinking about the letter she still hasn't written to her parents about Koko, while the kitten sits on the windowsill, his tail swishing slowly back and forth. She doesn't notice that he has jumped down into the garden, but she is at the window in seconds when she hears cats fighting. She throws the window wide open and leans out and shouts in fear. *Koko!*

She makes out a snarl of cats on the grass. She swiftly grabs one of her school library books off the table and hurls it, sending the cats fleeing in opposite directions. Her eyes scan the yard trying to pick her Koko out of the fleeing melee, her voice now more desperate. *Koko?*

She clambers out of the window and runs to the fence on the left, peering over. *Koko?* There is no sign of him. She runs to the opposite side of the property. She places one foot on the wooden cross battens of the corrugated iron fence, rattling the iron as she clutches the top of it. She looks down into the neighbour's backyard and sees what looks like a large cat barrelling towards her. As it gets closer it yaps and launches itself up at her, bounding halfway up the fence and giving her such a fright that she topples backwards onto the grass. The Jack Russell stands his ground and barks hysterically at the iron wall, while Pualele lies winded on the ground on the other side of the fence.

She struggles to her feet as the back porch of the neighbour's house is suddenly illuminated by a single hanging light bulb. Knocked by the neighbour, it swings an arc of light across the yard as he rushes outside, yelling at the dog to stop barking. The man throws something at the dog, sending it scurrying away from the fence with a yelp. *Bloody cats*, the man says to no one.

Pualele lies still on the grass for a several seconds before jumping up. She runs quietly on bare feet down the side of her own house towards the street. *Koko?* she whispers.

Something runs under a hedge across the road and she follows it. She keeps whispering the cat's name and listening, following the random movements of night animals until she finds herself on the street outside the Magasivas' house.

The front door rasps on its hinges and Pualele looks up to see a woman leaving the house. She steps back behind the fence and watches. The figure makes no sound as she crosses the porch and descends the stairs. A pair of sequined platform shoes are hooked over her fingers, and as the light from the lamp post bounces off them, it seems to Pualele that the air is alive with exploding stars. She leans back against the fence and curls over, making herself as small as possible.

You should be in bed, Pualele.

Ben Magasiva stands before her, his coat agape revealing a silk top and gold lamé hotpants that pull tight across thighs that are thick as a rugby player's.

She stares mutely back at him, not knowing what to do or say. He looks like a carnival clown with his tangerine-painted lips, cheekbones shimmering with glitter and pale-blue shadow above his dark-brown eyes. She wants to run away, but at the same time she wants to ask him why he is dressed like this and where on earth he could be going.

I'll walk you home. You shouldn't be out here at night.

Koko's run away.

Aaaah, Koko, he says, slowly turning her so that they are both facing the Auva'as' house. *Sefi tells everyone you feed him too much.*

They walk towards the crossing, Ben's big hand on her shoulder guiding her firmly back across the street towards home.

Ben? Pualele stops at the crossing under the street lamp and looks up at him. *Why are you dressed like that?* She thinks he looks sad at her question, as if he hasn't noticed he is wearing these clothes – but that now he has seen them he is displeased with himself.

You're too young, Pualele.

I'm almost ten!

He pauses then and looks at her with a slightly mocking smile and laughs.

Well, didn't realise you were almost ten. His tone is congratulatory and enthusiastic. It makes Pualele feel as if he is about to break into song. But then his smile slackens. When he speaks again he is serious. *If you're ten, then you'll understand that sometimes fa'afafine are . . . different. But you won't tell anyone that you've seen me, will you?*

Pualele shakes her head. No.

Good, says Ben. *Because if you do . . .* he clicks his fingers in front of her nose, *Poof. All the magic will be gone and I'll disappear.* He pirouettes in front of her and she knows that what he says is true.

She is tired of having people disappear, and she likes Ben. She won't say a word to anyone about this, and even though she is desperate to ask him where he is going, she decides against it. She doesn't want to be responsible for Ben vanishing into the night like Kasi and Papa. She can only imagine what the Queen would say to her mother and Aunty if Ben disappeared. The ladies of the neighbourhood often meet together at the Queen's, and Ben is there just as if he is one of them. Men are never allowed, but Ben is fa'afafine. This sets him apart from the other boys and men, and for Pualele this only confirms that he possesses special powers.

In her girlish dreams, Ben is a Samoan Tinkerbell who dresses in tulle and lace that are as light as air, allowing him to float through the world leaving little trails of magic dust wherever he goes. She wishes she could be fa'afafine too. This would be something worth changing her name for; then she could go home to Mama and never have to leave her again. She could clean and cook and look after the babies and then at night she would don her enchanted outfit of glitter and sprinkle her magic all over their village.

But right now there is no way she is going to lose Ben and anger the Queen, so she allows herself to be shepherded back home, where she finds Koko asleep on her pillow. She lies down, tucking the kitten between her neck and shoulder as the questions swarm in her head like curious bees around a hibiscus flower.

༄

Pualele begins concocting reasons why she needs to go to bed early so that she can slip out and spy on Ben at night. Soon she learns that he goes out twice a week, on Thursday and Sunday nights, always dressed in his cabaret clothes. She is careful not to be seen by anyone and is too afraid to follow him further than the top of the road, allowing him to disappear into the night before she runs all the way back home. She feels anxious when she approaches the corner of Ponsonby and Richmond Roads, so she keeps out of trouble by never straying any further. Once she is back safe in her bed she imagines what he is doing out there in the dark night in his women's clothing and make-up; and she feels afraid for him.

CHAPTER 20

OLGA'S JOURNAL

One day around the end of that first summer, when I was seventeen, I watched Oliver with my father standing at the edge of the congregation. Oliver with his hands behind his back as he spoke, my father nodding at him, saying nothing. I saw him rest a hand on Oliver's shoulder before Mama called me to follow her and I walked away.

That evening, Father sat in front of me at the table.

You get on well with Oliver.

Yes, Papa.

I like the boy. He works hard. He cleared his throat and went on. *Oliver has asked me for your hand in marriage.*

A delicious tingling excitement coursed through me, a realisation of years of longing.

But, there's a problem, Olga.

I jumped at his words and held my breath. Papa had a sober look on his face, his palms flat on the table.

I'll miss you, he whispered.

I breathed again and let out a squeal. Papa stood up, pulling me to him.

Come, let's call him and tell him the good news.

We burst out the door and I ran down the steps.

Oliver.

He was standing with Joe, hands pushed deep into his pockets, feet shuffling nervously on the ground. I ran to him and he opened his arms to me. He lifted me off the ground and we spun around several times, laughing while Joe shouted his congratulations.

Oliver put me down, my head spinning.

Steady. Oliver put his arm around my waist, stopping me from tumbling over.

What's going on? Rosa appeared on the steps behind us. She was unsmiling and her arms were folded across her chest. Papa turned towards her.

Wonderful news, Rosa. You should be very proud of our children.

What are you talking about?

Oliver and Olga. Oliver told me he spoke with you. They're getting married!

No. This ends here. Her voice was sharp, piercing my joy as she shook her head violently. I felt Oliver's arms wrap around me as I leaned back into him.

Rosa? Oliver spoke to me today – he told me you knew?

He said he wanted to marry – yes. Wanted it to be a surprise for me – but, Olga? No!

My mother appeared behind her and Rosa moved to make way for Mama on the steps.

She's a good girl. You should be happy they want to marry.

Rosa glowered back at him.

You weren't there, Ivan. It's because of her that we're here without Mila.

You can't blame her for that. And we've helped you when no one else would.

And I appreciate your help. But I will never forgive her for what she did. Our visas are coming and Oliver and I will go to America.

I know what happened. We all make mistakes.

We all make mistakes, yes! But her mistake . . .

For God's sake, Rosa, he cut her off. *Listen to yourself. She was a child, there was a war. I lost my brother – you don't think I feel . . .*

At least you know where he lies.

Rosa, I'm sorry. But why punish your son too?

She will never marry my son. She glared at me with open animosity. *We will move to the boarding house tomorrow.*

Rosa!

She spun round, pushing past my mother and went back inside the building.

Ana, you talk to her.

I saw a nerve twitch along Mama's jaw line and stared at her as she tilted her head, looking Papa in the eye.

We will do nothing. I expected him to argue with her, to put his foot down and act like the man of the house. That is not what happened. Unbelievably, the two of them stood there looking at one another and some silent conversation took place which ended in my father sighing and my mother following Rosa inside. Whatever madness my mother suffered from seemed to have engulfed my cheery father and left him in a kind of gloomy malaise.

Papa?

It's OK, Oliver said, taking me by the shoulders. *I'll talk to her. She'll get used to the idea.*

Oliver left to find his mother and Papa turned to me then.

You and I need to talk.

I could see the look of resignation in his face. There was nothing he or Oliver could do to change the women's minds.

ଓ

You two are so alike.

I frowned at him. She was cruel and had a vicious tongue; I wasn't like her at all. We sat at the kitchen table and he took my hands in his and stared at them as he talked.

A long time ago, there were two brothers. The oldest brother was a man with big ambitions about travelling and making his fortune. The younger brother loved village life and wanted only what his father had had before him – to tend the land and to have the girl he loved as his wife. The girl wasn't the prettiest, or the smartest, but she was from a good family. This brother was still young. His head was full of passion and fight, but he needed time to grow and have the wildness knocked out of him. So even though the girl loved him, it wasn't the right time for them to be together. But the older brother was ready. He was a man already and needed a wife, and so the mother of the girl decided she should marry the older brother.

She wasn't happy at first, but she listened to her family and did the right thing.

I was struck again by how treacherous the world could be. One minute you have something in the palm of your hand and the next it is snatched away.

And we are happy, my father said. *You must listen to her Olga. Sometimes you don't know what is right for you – but your mother does.*

No. You were happy about Oliver and me and now you've changed your mind. You're afraid of her – that she'll leave you.

I will forget that you said that. He spoke very quietly so that I had to lean forward to catch the words.

You owe her this – we both do.

I tore out of there, wild with anger, clear snot streaming from my nose as I ran. I didn't really know where I was going. The road twisted its way down the hill and up again, my feet hitting the road in time to the little mantra running through my head: *Thereisnous, thereisnous.*

☙

They left early the next morning for the boarding house. I watched out the window as Oliver carried their bags and placed them on the back of the truck. Joe sat in the cab, ready to drive them away. Oliver didn't look over at our house. I don't know if he knew it was hopeless or what he thought, but I thought I would never speak to him again. In ten years, when he became a rich man with a company that built houses all over Missouri, he would send cheques to Joe for him to pass onto me. The world is a different place now, but in those days, in our families, it wasn't our way to disobey our parents.

☙

Every Sunday after that, when I prayed for Mila, Dragan and Jure, I added Oliver too. He and Rosa were absent from church, as if they had already boarded the ship that would take them to America, but he had got word to me through Joe that he would get his mother settled with Edita and then he would be back. I just had to wait.

Mama had other ideas.

Olga. We need to make some crostoli. We have an important visitor.

The visitor was a middle-aged man that my father had known on the gum fields. I heard the rap of knuckles on the door and kept tying the crostoli into perfect pastry bows ready for deep frying.

Hurry, Olga. Go and wash your hands and change into the dress on your bed.

I listened to Mama, even though I knew that I didn't have another dress. As I climbed the stairs I heard the visitor speaking to my parents and hoped that he wouldn't be staying long.

I stood at the foot of my bed, incredulous. Laid out in front of me was a cornflower print dress. I held it up and smoothed my hands over the cotton fabric. It had a full skirt that fell below the knee with a square neck and capped sleeves. I changed into the frock and snuck into my parents' room. In front of the full-length mirror that stood in the corner of their room, I looked over my shoulder as I spun in a circle, admiring the perfect swirl of the skirt as it wrapped around my legs.

As I did one final pirouette I lost my balance, falling against the bed, my foot connecting with something beneath it. I crouched down and edged out a wooden box, careful not to scrape it on the wooden floorboards. Slowly I opened the box. In it lay the things that my mother held precious to her – the letters, the grainy pictures and the winged insect trapped in kauri gum. I took the lump of golden gum out and held it up to the light.

My father's voice travelled up from below and for a moment I held my breath as I heard him start up the stairs.

Coming, I called. He stopped. Then the steps retreated and I exhaled as I manoeuvred the box back to where I had found it, but not before letting the kauri gum fall into the deep pockets of my dress. I arranged the folds of the dress so that the pocket was close to my thigh and carefully descended the stairs, allowing my hand to rest over the lump.

༺༻

Mr Papić was a neatly dressed man of no great height. He was not unpleasant to look at, but I felt uncomfortable as he examined me over the top of his bifocals.

Please, he said, *call me Mijo.*

I stared back, horrified, until my mother poked me hard in the back. I managed a muttered greeting as I focussed on the toes of his shoes.

My father stepped forward and I had the impression that I was in a play but no one had thought to give me the script. *Mijo,* my father said, slapping Mr Papić on the shoulder, *so glad you could come.*

I wanted to shout C*ome for what?* But the conversation had already rolled on and they were talking about me as if I weren't there.

She's a tall girl, said Mr Papić, straightening himself in the chair.

Ah, Mijo, said my father brushing his comment away with a laugh. *You want a dwarf?*

Oh, I didn't mean anything. Mr Papić was already blushing. *I mean she's a strong-looking girl.*

Enough, my mother said, clapping her hands together. *Let's eat something. Olga?*

I don't mean to describe everything in a negative way, for Mr Papić tried his best to give a good impression of himself and to be kind to me. It was clear why he was there at our kitchen table, and if he said anything inappropriate it was my parents who should have been embarrassed for arranging the whole terrible afternoon.

When it came time for him to leave, my mother said overly loudly, *Olga, you show Mijo out.*

My stomach sank as I dragged my feet under me and stood, wondering how I could escape. Mr Papić seemed to sense my reluctance and was on his feet and halfway to the door before I could move.

No, no, leave the girl, she's done enough running around this afternoon. He cleared his throat and addressed me directly. *Perhaps I could call again next Saturday?*

I stopped myself from groaning aloud and wondered why he would want a repeat of such an excruciating afternoon. The whole room was waiting for me I realised. But I couldn't think what to say.

Oh, I said.

Of course, my mother said, *why don't you come for lunch? We would love for you to come. For lunch.*

Well, that would be very nice. He smiled warmly at me. *See you next Saturday.* And then just to me. *Goodbye Olga.*

I stepped back as he held out his hand briefly towards mine. When it became obvious I wasn't going to take it, he let his arm fall back awkwardly to his side.

Goodbye Mr Papić.

CR

He took to calling every week, arriving on a new red bicycle.

Ding, ding. His bell would announce his arrival in the alleyway and my stomach would turn in knots. I spied on him as he rested the bike gently against the back of the building. He would spend some time removing the trouser clips from around his ankles before smoothing his hair. I learned to dread his knock – a hesitant tap-tap-tap. Mama made me dress carefully, and I'd serve tea and sit at the table while Mr Papić gnawed on his knuckles, glancing my way when he thought I wouldn't notice.

Mr Papić wanted to take me to the picture theatre and walk with me in the early evening. Mama looked on and I saw in her face her wish to have me go with this man. But I took pleasure in turning her smiles into frowns by coming up with one excuse after another: a sore throat, a twisted ankle, a headache so debilitating I couldn't leave my tiny bedroom cupboard.

ය

I found Joe and begged him, *Please help me. Find Oliver and ask him to find a way for me to go to America now.*

I'd felt hopeless thinking I would never see Oliver again, but now I was suddenly desperate – and desperation can make us bold.

I'll try Olga, but he's in a tricky position.

ය

A few weeks later Joe joined me on the way to Mass.

Keep walking, he said to me, taking Pero's hand in his and looking up the road.

I saw him there on the bend, leaning against a wooden lamp post as casually as anything. When I glanced back to where Joe had been so I could thank him, he was already halfway up the path with Pero on the way to church.

Oliver grabbed my hand and we almost ran until I found we were at the reserve. We had nothing to say in the beginning it seemed, lying there on our backs looking up at the sky as we had in the desert. He stroked my thigh, and I let him. I think it is what I wanted. For him to touch me and make me feel like his vague promises were real. But he stopped and rolled onto his back again, and I thought that I shouldn't have let him touch me like that. Of course I shouldn't have. We lay there a good while before I had the courage to speak.

I know people here sponsor their fiancées. Why don't we do that for America? Mama is trying to marry me off, and I'm afraid I won't be able to stop it. Please, we have to be quick. We can't wait for Edita to take your mother off your hands.

Oliver looked at me with an apologetic, heart-breaking look.

Olga, I . . . he shook his head. What did it mean? I didn't want to know. This was not what I had imagined. *It's not that easy,* he managed in the end.

I don't know how I was able to, but I got myself up on my feet and tried to regain my dignity by standing over him and appearing righteous.

Things will take their own course, we should wait and see what happens, he said.

That's why we need to act – before my mother sets the course.

I'll try, he replied, trying to placate me like someone trying to settle a small child on the verge of tears. He was stalling so he could get away from me. I saw that as plain as can be.

I need to go, he said, and it sounded like a goodbye. *I'm sorry, but I can't walk you back. You understand.*

I did, only too well.

ଔ

They left, of course, on a morning sailing out of Auckland for San Francisco. And there was no one there to see them off.

CHAPTER 21

PUALELE

One Thursday night Koko runs away. He jumps up onto the windowsill and Pualele sees that he is hurt from some skirmish with another local tom cat.

Koko!

Pualele reaches for the cat but he shrinks away from her and disappears from the windowsill into the night. She jumps out of the window and follows him to the front of the house and eventually along Richmond Road. She runs barefoot after him, calling his name as she goes. Koko streaks away towards Karangahape Road and Pualele runs on, oblivious to her own whereabouts, her sole focus the injured cat. At the next intersection she hesitates. She knows that left will take her up towards Symonds Street. The right will lead her down Great North Road and to the Surrey Crescent shops. But which way did Koko go?

A figure walks across the road. In a panic she turns in the opposite direction and sprints left past the 'Closed' signs hanging in the shop windows on K'Road. At the next corner several women hover, as if none of them can decide whether to cross the road or not. One of them drags on a cigarette and blows out a series of lifesaver-shaped puffs of smoke. Others stand in twos or threes talking and laughing, occasionally moving towards the curbside when a car slows, and often yelling at those cars that accelerate away.

Pualele slows, unsure what to do now as she realises how far she is from home. One woman turns and sees Pualele, looking her up and down. The woman sways a little and then her head cranes forward as she scrutinises Pualele's feet.

Hey. The woman's voice is shrill. *Where are your shoes?* She collapses in laughter as she points, and her friends join her, holding onto to each other in a swaying hysterical gaggle.

Pualele runs past the women towards Symonds Street. The cemetery lies beside the road and she stops outside it as cars cruise past behind her. She glances over her shoulder and for a split second she believes she sees the Queen sitting in the back of a car, but it is only a group of young Polynesians slowing down to look at her. She vaults over the wall into the cemetery, looking out over the headstones that disappear down into the gully. She shivers. She wants to find Koko and then run home, but he is nowhere in sight. She scrambles back over the wall and turns up the road towards the ladies on the street corner. She wishes she could avoid them, annoyed with herself that she's run off without her New Zealand shoes. Her feet are cold, and she isn't sure how to get back home without anyone seeing her and noticing her bare feet.

As she stands there thinking, a Lincoln slows as it goes by. A few metres past her, the brake lights come on and the car reverses back until it is stationary in front of Pualele, its engine running. She watches as the driver leans over and winds down the window of the passenger's door. Pualele looks at the man and then down at the gutter as she hears him unlock the door. She instantly recognises him, it's Mr Davison, the funeral director. He says, *You better get in.*

☙

He puts the car into gear and turns it around. She knows that she is going to be in a lot of trouble with her aunt and uncle, but she is thankful that she is off the street and Mr Davison is taking her home. As the car passes Ponsonby Road, she wants to tell him to turn there, that her home is in Richmond Road, but she is unable to do or say anything.

Mr Davison holds open the door for her and takes her arm, leading her in through the rear door into the funeral parlour. He shows her into his office and to a leather couch where bereaved family come to talk about arrangements or to pay for their loved one's funeral. The only light source in the room comes from the street lamps outside. Pualele is scared and wants him to fill the room with bright light and to not be so close. She wishes she hadn't got into the car and had instead run home in her bare feet. But it is too late now.

Mr Davison closes the door and goes to a side cabinet where she hears the rattle of glasses and a bottle being unscrewed. She can make out his shape in the half light and she begins to panic as he crosses back to stand in front of her. He places a large tumbler in her hand.

Bottom's up.

She sniffs the liquid and feels it burn her nostrils, but she puts the glass to her lips. She takes a generous mouthful of the whisky and immediately spits it out, breaking into a coughing fit. He grunts in displeasure as she wipes her sleeve across her mouth and tongue trying to erase the taste. When she lets her arm drop from her face, he is directly in front of her.

K'Road's not really a place for a good girl, is it? He is close enough for her to smell the alcohol and smoke on his breath. He reaches out and tilts her chin up towards his, her eyes level with his mouth. A sliver of light shines through the partially open venetian blinds across the lower half of his face. She sees right into his open mouth. Between thin tight lips she can make out the nicotine stains on his small even teeth until a thick tongue darts out to lick his lips, and she recoils in disgust.

Changed your mind, have ya?

He pushes his face into hers, his tongue parting her lips and pushing into her mouth. She bites down on his tongue and he shoves her away as he cries out. *Ungrateful little bitch.*

He tries to slap her but she is quick and turns away so that his hand hits the side of her head above her ear, sending her falling back onto the couch. She puts her hands up to protect herself from further blows, but he has already grabbed her shoulders. She tries to squirm away, but he is much stronger and he easily pins her to the couch. She turns her face away but feels his hand move under her dress and hears him unzip his trousers. She bites her lip, tasting the blood in her mouth. The elastic in her panties snaps as he pulls them down to her knees. She can barely breathe as he presses her face against the leather, the bitter taste of tannin now replacing the blood and alcohol in her mouth. A lump of bile rises up in her throat and she vomits over the couch.

For God's sake. He pushes her roughly and she rolls onto the floor. She lies prone, her face on the soft carpet, wishing her heart would stop thumping so loudly.

Disgusting, he spits at her as he zips his pants up. She refuses to look at him.

He strides quickly towards the door but comes to an abrupt halt with his hand on the door knob as if something has just occurred to him. *You say anything to anyone and it won't be good for you or your uncle. I'll have you all kicked out of this country. Mark my words.*

She does not want to be the person responsible for the rest of them being expelled from New Zealand, nor does she want anyone to be hurt. Without being aware of it, she digs her nails into the scars that scallop her palms. As he turns he waves his hand over the soiled couch and says, *You can clean this up before you go.*

The door shuts behind him.

Pualele wants to move, but she feels bruised all over. She places her hand on the couch to help herself up but quickly withdraws it as she feels the slipperiness of the surface. Sliding back down onto the carpet, she cries and is grateful now that the light isn't on. But she cannot summon the energy to move again. She closes her eyes and her body begins to shudder uncontrollably. She will stay here until someone comes to find her.

Then a car engine idles somewhere outside. She listens, suddenly alert.

He is coming back.

A surge of adrenaline courses through her and she heaves herself up off the floor, removing her panties that no longer stay up. She scrunches the underwear into her hand and stumbles to the door.

☙

Outside, the night sky has turned. Pualele is worried that if she doesn't run fast enough the sun will push up into the heavens and Aunty Sefi and Uncle Sam will rise and find her gone. The physical pain is minimal compared to how she feels inside, but she pushes herself onwards.

A dog barks from a porch and starts running towards her as she passes by. Instinctively she leaps off the footpath away from the rushing animal, ready to sprint across the road. The dog comes to a sudden stop as the chain yanks it back and it lets out a small yelp. She has a fleeting thought about Koko, hoping he's avoided the dogs that wander the streets at night and aren't on chains.

She is caught in headlights and holds her hand up to block out the light. Someone yells at her and she jumps back onto the footpath in time to see a street cleaner swerve his vehicle out into the middle of the road, the circular sweepers on the truck just missing her. Adrenaline again rushes through her and she shoots off like a bowman's arrow along the streets towards Richmond Road, slowing briefly only to drop her ruined panties into a rubbish bin.

She climbs in the window of her room as the predawn glow filters into the house. Koko is asleep on her bed and she tries to pull him under the blankets with her, but he struggles free, biting her hand and stalking off to the corner of the room, his tail flicking back and forth in irritation. She sighs and slides in between the cool sheets alone. She listens to the cat cleaning himself. Eventually Koko sneaks back to the bed and crawls under the sheets to lie across her cold feet.

Pualele is still awake when Sefi taps on her door. She pretends not to hear.

Pualele?

She doesn't move. Feet shuffle across the room and Sefi sits on the edge of the bed, gently shaking her.

I feel sick.

Sefi pulls back the covers.

Shoo. Ah, that cat. The cat make you sick. Koko runs from the room, avoiding Sefi's swinging hand. She turns back to Pualele, taking her chin between her forefinger and thumb. She searches Pualele's face and half-open eyes.

You're pale as Kasi. You stay here. I bring you something to eat.

No. My stomach. I can't eat.

Sefi's eyebrows draw together and as she mulls over this statement, she lets her hand fall away from Pualele's chin.

You stay in bed. Sam can take you to the doctor.

No, Aunty.

But you can't eat. You must eat. We need a doctor if you can't eat – this very bad.

I can eat. I can eat. I just . . . I'll eat.

Sefi smiles uncertainly. *OK*. And she leaves to fetch some food, looking back over her shoulder as if she doesn't quite understand what has just gone on.

Pualele sighs in relief and lets her eyes close once again. She cannot move from her bed. She's not sure how she's going to stomach any food, and she desperately wants to wash and scrub until the night before has been erased from her body, but she is completely incapable of moving. If her mother was here with her Pualele would ask her to bathe her with frangipani oil and then everything that had happened would disappear.

Sefi returns with some warmed rice and stands and waits until Pualele has placed a spoon of the food into her mouth. Pualele swallows and is surprised that the rice doesn't come straight back up. She manages a neutral face and doesn't vomit, and Sefi is satisfied.

You stay here today, Sefi proclaims, remaining by the side of the bed. Pualele worries that Sefi intends to stand there all day watching her, at least while she finishes the breakfast.

I'm OK, Aunty. I'll finish this a little later, she forces a smile. Sefi places the bowl of rice next to her bed.

Hhhhmm, Aunty is clearly uneasy. So many things could go wrong while Pualele is alone in the house.

I be home early, she finally says. *You stay in bed.*

Pualele keeps the smile plastered on her face until Sefi leaves the room. She hears the door click behind Sam and Sefi and is thankful they have left her in peace. She lies in bed somewhere between sleep and awake. She is in the funeral parlour on the couch, legs crossed at the ankles, hands in her lap. Her mother asks her if she would like the mahogany with the burgundy polish and fine grain or the pine coffin, its lid a honey-blonde colour with dark knots in the wood. Pualele doesn't understand why her mother is asking her to choose.

She opens her eyes and looks around the room, reminding herself that she is in her own house, in her own bed. But alone in the silence left by her uncle and aunt's departure, her heart quickens. She sees Mr Davison at the front door of their house. The door is unlocked and he opens it and walks down the hallway until he pushes open the door to her room, finding her alone in her bed. She is petrified, not sure if her thoughts are real or imagined.

༄

She wakes with a start. There are footsteps in the hallway.

She burrows down into the bed and wishes she had risen earlier to empty her bladder.

Pualele. The unmistakeable voice of Uncle Sam reaches her.

She pokes her head out from under the sheets.

You eaten? He looks down and grunts as he spies the untouched rice.

Sefi won't like it. You better come with me. You can wash and dress while I have lunch. If you no better when I finish work we go to the hospital.

Uncle leaves her and she starts to hyperventilate. *You better come with me.* The words haunt her in the bathroom as she tries to clean herself, and she thinks about Mr Davison's words, *It won't be good for you or your uncle.* She can never tell Uncle why she can't go to the Davisons to work again. She can't explain, so how can she disobey him? How can this be happening to her? It feels like a kind of nightmare that gets more wicked with every turn, and she prays that she will wake up very soon.

Somehow she dresses and is ready to go with Sam when it is time to leave.

☙

They arrive at the funeral parlour and Pualale is unable to contain the terror she feels. She follows close behind Sam as the small bell above the door tinkles. She expects to see Mr Davison standing there in his morning suit and is relieved to find the entrance parlour empty.

You better wait here, Pualele, Sam says to her. He searches her face, clearly assessing whether he can safely leave her alone. His work is piling up in the workshop and with Pualele looking better now that she is up on her feet, he thinks she will be fine on her own for a while. *I'll be back soon,* he says as the door shuts behind him.

Pualele looks apprehensively around the room, searching for signs of Mr Davison and noticing that someone has cleaned up the vomit from the night before. With the door and windows closed, there is no air in the office and she begins to sweat in the stuffy room. Suddenly the door opens again and Pualele springs backwards. The backs of her legs hit the couch and she falls onto it.

Sorry. Didn't mean to give you a fright. Just needed to fetch something for cleaning the couch. My poor Tom's been sick, working late like he does. Pualele swallows and stands up to let Mrs Davison get to the couch. She is embarrassed that Mrs Davison has been cleaning up. She gets a faint whiff of the stale vomit and gags.

You're looking a bit peaky, Pualele. Mrs Davison reaches out and tilts her chin in the same way as her husband had. *Still, I expect you'll be fine by tomorrow. If you feel like it, I could do with a hand?*

She looks down, avoiding Mrs Davison's gaze.

Mr Davison's not coming in. So I've got a bit to do. Pualele catches her eye. *I think there's something going around and you've both picked it up.*

Mrs Davison starts on the couch and says to Pualele, *Well, you know where the cleaning things are . . .*

Pualele's shoulders sag in relief to hear Mr Davison isn't at work. Though her mind is a jumble trying to process what has happened, she sets to working like she's never worked before, blocking out the physical pain that burns every time she moves. Scrubbing the floors on her hands and knees, she violently rakes the brush over the tiles. She moves onto polishing and shining the mounted fittings that are fixed to the walls for customers to view. In the back of her mind she knows that she must find another part-time job; she cannot keep working here. How she will find another job she can't imagine, but if it paid more than this one then no one would complain. She decides to start looking as soon as possible.

Aunty and Uncle will want to know why she wants to leave the Davisons when they've been such good employers. And Mrs Davison. She will want to counsel her and convince her otherwise. But Pualele is terrified of merely seeing Mr Davison again, let alone working for him – this new shame is too great. She could run away, but running away would mean Mama's letters would never find her. The full horror of what has happened to her makes her palms itch. She turns over her hands that are red from cleaning and looks at the scars and the grime that has settled into the creases of her palms. She picks up the scrubbing brush and flicks away some of the dirt, then rubs a little harder and then harder still until her hands are red-raw.

What's happened? When Mrs Davison sees Pualele's hands she sucks in the air and pulls the girl to her feet. She takes her to the kitchen where she opens a first-aid box and cleans the girl's hands, gently wrapping them in cotton bandages. *That's enough for today.* She looks at Pualele guardedly before tentatively moving a lock of hair that falls across

Pualele's cheek and tucking it behind her ear, which still smarts from last night's slap.

It is easy to let Mrs Davison take charge of her because then she doesn't have to think. Mrs Davison is about the only person she feels will help her if she needs it, but even she can't help with this problem, for Pualele can never tell her.

CHAPTER 22

OLGA'S JOURNAL

My memories of Joe are always precisely imagined. I can close my eyes now and draw him in my mind: the tall spareness of him. He was handsome in an easy way, whether dressed in his loose-fitting jacket and looking like a city slicker, or in a work shirt and sturdy trousers ready for a day working for my father. He wore his soft brown hair slicked back, but always a lock escaped to give him a foppish look. Others were drawn to him and he used this charm to his advantage all through his life. None more so than at the racecourse.

Joe loved the gallops and betting on the races, and he treated betting like a job. He kept a notebook full of notes on individual horses' results, jockeys' form and turf conditions, grids drawn up of winnings and losses and the names and numbers of men listed at the back. At least half the time he made a few bob, which made him more successful than most of the men he knew.

Joe loved numbers and could calculate the profit on a basket of fish to be sold in the shop before he'd loaded it onto Papa's truck. It was the same with horse races. I heard him tell my father once: *It's easy if you just look at the percentages. You see, the top ten per cent of riders win ninety per cent of the races. But only twenty-five per cent of the favourites picked actually win. The only trick is to place the right bet on the right race.*

My father wasn't a betting man, although he loved his card games and would regularly settle into a long night playing Brškula with other Dalmatian men while my mother hid in their upstairs room. I never knew what he thought of Joe and his horse racing, but I knew by then he would never try and stop Joe from anything he wanted to do.

Racing held no interest for me, but Joe spent much of his spare time at the racetrack, talking to trainers and trying to get an insider's view on which horses and riders were doing well on what surfaces and over which distances. It was on one of these fact-finding missions that he met Vaiuli.

Vaiuli was a cleaner and Joe knew if anyone had an ear to the ground it was the cleaner, who could access all areas without being noticed.

The way Joe told it, he was trying to check on a horse that he hadn't heard of from the Waikato. Trainers and jockeys were readying their mounts and preparing to take to the track. A trainer looked at Joe and yelled at him. *You better get outta here.* Then pointing right at him, *He's a fixer.*

Now I'm not saying my brother never took a tip from a match fixer, but he wasn't ever the man who fixed those races up. He was honest, Joe.

The trainer came at him and Joe ran for it. Soon there were other men on his tail. But for Vaiuli's quick thinking in pushing him into a broom cupboard, I'd say Joe would've been beaten up.

CR

Vaiuli lived not far from Richmond Road. He and Joe found common ground in their foreignness. I'd never seen a Samoan man up close before. Sure, I'd seen Maori and Pacific Island people on the street, but I'd never dared look, really look at them. No one had ever said anything to me, but I knew to keep away, that somehow we were apart from them. Did anyone ever say we were better than them? I don't recall, but I do remember knowing that it was not the normal order of things for this man to be sitting next to my brother in such a genial way. Vaiuli was in the passenger seat of the truck, his arm resting on the open window, an arm as thick as my brother's thigh.

This is my friend Vaiuli, Joe said stepping out of the truck. *This is my sister Olga.*

Hello, he said looking down and almost bowing his head, as shy and embarrassed as a young girl.

I stepped back and mumbled something, it might have been hello, I don't recall. I was uncomfortable in his presence, this hulking man with his skin as dark as coffee beans.

Vai's come for dinner, Joe said and my eyes widened at this. *Don't worry, Ola,* he whispered, *he won't eat you.* He was teasing, of course, but I coloured nonetheless, for Joe knew me so well he could see plainly on my face what I was thinking.

Dinner was a strained affair with my mother disapproving, not in how she reacted to Vai or even in what she said, but more in what she didn't do or say. She'd never had a Polynesian (or a Chinaman, or Indian or man of any colour) in her house before and she seemed quite thrown by the whole situation. The dinner was laid out, and even though Vaiuli was our guest, it was the everyday cutlery and plates and saucers that were brought out, not the fine china that my father had given to my mother on our arrival. And another thing, she asked not one question of the young man, not anything.

My father, God bless him, asked questions enough for the whole house. We learned Vaiuli was Samoan and that he cleaned at the racecourse to send money home and to help pay for his night-school classes where he was learning to be a mechanic. I thought he sounded kind. Joe told us how they'd met and the men all laughed and everyone seemed very jolly.

But while all this was still going on my mother got up from the table and took herself upstairs without so much as a by your leave. Joe gave me a wry look, as if to say, *What can you do?*

○ʀ

Joe didn't bring him for dinner again, but I saw Vaiuli on and off when I was out and about. I guess he'd always been there; but now I'd met him I noticed him everywhere. I'd see him waiting for a bus, or carrying groceries or walking with purpose to who knows where. We'd acknowledge each other with a nod, neither of us stopping, but both of us happy enough to have seen the other.

I might have spoken to him then, or at least said *Hello* if I hadn't been so preoccupied. You see, my mother was back planning my future.

༄

His bell rang in the alleyway and I let out a groan. Mr Papić was coming to tea.

Olga! My mother yelled out for me.

I stomped down the stairs with a look on my face sour enough to kill someone.

Get the door, she hissed at me, *and call him Mijo.*

I felt sorry for Mr Papić. He wasn't to know the state of affairs in my head, and if I found him unattractive it didn't mean that he was an unpleasant man. I ushered him in, accepting the small box of toffees that had come all the way from England and would've cost a pretty penny.

I approached the table and, ignoring the conversation going on between our visitor and my mother, I stared at the china cups and saucers on the table. It was too much for me. I was not the daughter my mother had been and I couldn't do what she and my father expected of me.

Sorry, I said. I dumped the box of toffees unceremoniously on the table and ran out the door. My mother ran after me, shouting my name into the alleyway. But I kept on running.

༄

I met Vaiuli walking along Ponsonby Road.

I was puffing and I knew I must've looked a fright from the look on his face when he saw me.

Are you OK? he asked as he took my elbow and pulled me to the side of the footpath.

I nodded, because what could I say to him? Vaiuli didn't know me from Adam. He must've thought I couldn't speak because I was sick, and in a way I was. Before I knew it, he'd picked me up and was carrying me around a corner to his house. He sat me down on a swing seat on the veranda and was soon back with a glass of water. He perched himself on the top step and waited.

Did you really push Joe into a cupboard? I asked.

He smiled and nodded.

We sat like that for a while, and it was an easy silence, not strained as it had been with Mr Papić. At the thought of him, I felt guilty over what was certainly going on back in the kitchen.

I don't want to go home. Do you think you could get Joe?

He nodded again, and in one smooth unhurried movement set off in search of my brother.

☙

That night my happy-go-lucky father was in a furious rage that I've not seen before or since.

Where did you go? He grabbed the hair at the back of my neck. I thought he might throttle me.

Mijo Papić is a good man and you disrespect your mother and me by running off like a child. I realised then that he didn't care if I refused to marry the man; the sin was in running away and humiliating him.

I'm so sorry, so sorry, I pleaded. I only wanted to be left alone. I recalled my father's story about my mother and how she had followed her mother's wishes without complaint. Mama hadn't caused embarrassment or been disrespectful like I had. But I wasn't the kind of daughter who did as she was told.

He is a nice man, but please don't make me marry him. I almost said that I would do anything not to marry him, but I bit my tongue, for who knew what else my mother had in mind for me.

☙

It's difficult to say now how they managed to accept it, but Joe suggested it and my parents agreed to let me enrol in a college that groomed young women to be typists and secretaries. I'm not sure it's what I wanted, but as a default choice it was better than working daily in the fish shop next to my mother.

We settled into a pattern of mutual avoidance of each other. But although my father had been so very angry with me, his anger was of the type that comes and goes in a flash and it wasn't long before he treated me in the same easy way he always had.

The college was a short walk into the city, and in the afternoon Joe would pick me up and drive me home. Sometimes we stopped at Vai's house, where the two friends would talk while I studied and read endless books from the Auckland Library. It was the most relaxed I had felt in my whole life.

☙

I've never liked the way rain falls here in this country, the Land of the Long White Cloud. When it started to rain that spring I thought it would never stop. The streets were slick with it and one day I received a fright when I witnessed an accident while walking to college. A car taking the turn onto Symonds Street carried right on through the intersection with its tires slipping and turning the wrong way. It hit a truck coming from the other direction and both stopped dead, right there in the middle of the road, although there was no harm done to the drivers.

Joe left early on that Saturday morning to drive to the races in Hamilton. From upstairs in our flat I watched the houses and streets whipped by lashing rain and felt the biting wind whistling in through the gap in the window frame into the flat. By midnight Joe was still not home. My father called a friend to come with his truck so they could take to the road and look for Joe. My mother and I sat at the kitchen table waiting, the sound of the rain hammering *rat-a-tat-tat* on the tin roof so loud that it thankfully made conversation impossible.

As the rain eased and an uncertain light announced the start of day, my mother and I leapt to our feet at the sound of a vehicle in the alley. Within a few steps, my hand was on the door, tearing it open to find the truck leaving and my father making his way to the doorstep with leaden feet.

My mother pushed past me and we both waited, holding inside us the question we dared not give voice to. My father looked at us and shook his head.

I've been to the police station. Now we wait.

☙

Sunday was blanketed in thick grey clouds that appeared to be on the verge of bursting but never did. My mother took to her room with Pero, who was blissfully unaware of Joe's disappearance and was happy to read his English books and draw on a chalkboard. My father and I sat in the kitchen near the telephone and mirrored the weather by holding our emotions in check.

The telephone had barely rung once before my father had snatched it up. *Yes?*

I tried to read his face as he listened intently to the other end of the phone, but he turned his back to me.

I will come now, he said. He replaced the receiver in the cradle and turned to me.

They have found him and he is on the way to hospital in Hamilton. They couldn't tell me how he is. I will go now. He was reaching for the phone. *I want you to say nothing to your mother until I find out how he is, you understand?*

But . . .

Hello, Bartul . . . He organised his ride to Hamilton and within ten minutes he was on his way. As I watched him leave, I knew I couldn't stay there with my mother and Pero and pretend to know nothing. I wrote a hasty note saying Father was out searching for Joe and that I was going to Mass. Then I headed straight for Vaiuli's house.

❦

I didn't know what I was going to do there or for what purpose, other than to be near to the person that knew Joe the best. I knew how it would look, me going there, but what drove me was beyond any reason, as tired as I was. I suppose it was a need to be around someone who could tell me that clever, charming, happy Joe was going to be alright.

The rain had stopped. The only pair of decent shoes I had were soon spongy from the puddles left behind, but I pressed on. Before I knew what decision I'd made, I was in front of his house. At first there was no sign of life and I simply stood there on the footpath looking at the front door, willing Vaiuli to come out. I had been there a good while, leaning on the front gate and wondering which room was his when I heard the sound of a bike on the road – the gentle clicking as the wheels ground up the incline of Franklin Road. My first thought was to strike out across the road and back towards Richmond Road, but I knew then that I'd be in plain view on the empty streets.

Then there was a noise of someone unlatching the door at the same time as . . .

Ding, ding.

Mijo Papić looked right at me, his face red from the exertion of coming up Franklin Road while his clothes were as neat as a soldier's uniform.

I should have run back home then, before he could ever know why I was leaning on a fence on that gloomy Sunday morning, but Vaiuli had opened the front door and was standing there in plain view with only a lavalava wrapped around his waist.

Olga, Mr Papić called out to me. He rode onto the footpath and stopped in front of me, blocking my way. He reached out to take my arm but I hit his hand away before pushing the gate open and bolting up those steps as if I was being chased by the devil himself.

☙

It was a curious thing to be inside Vaiuli's house alone. It was like looking at someone's life without any of the rules that normally existed, and it felt suddenly wrong to be there without Joe.

I'm sorry, I said. *It was wrong of me to come here.*

Somewhere in the back of the house I could hear other people stirring, and I edged slowly back towards the front door.

I should go. And for the second time that day a man reached out to take a hold of me and this time I let him.

What's wrong, Olga? His voice was gentle like his manner and he opened his arms inviting me in. I told him then about Joe and he listened while I cried and talked and cried again and he led me into a room. It must've been his bedroom, for there was a bed and we lay there, he and I. I admit I don't rightly remember all of it, but I was desperate for him and I urged him on, taking him in my hands and guiding him inside me. I knew it was wrong. But I wasn't sorry then and I'm not now.

☙

He walked me home as it approached midday, and the rain held off right until we reached the shop. It was quiet. There was no sign of my father or Mr Papić, and my mother and Pero were still in the upstairs flat, my note untouched where I'd left it. Vaiuli kissed me on the forehead and said, *I'll be back later.*

No sooner had he left when the telephone trilled in its cradle. I snatched it up. *Hello? Hello?*

Olga, it's me. He's going to be alright. He's broken his legs, but he's going to be alright!

CHAPTER 23

PUALELE

Uncle Sam drops Pualele at the top of Richmond Road so she can go home and prepare dinner while he goes to the hospital to collect Sefi.

As she walks along towards home, she sees Ben. He is in the middle of the road picking up a rugby ball. He clutches it in one hand then spirals it through the air into a waiting pair of hands down the road. A group of young Samoan men disappears with the ball into someone's backyard and she listens as they shout and hoop as they tussle over the ball. She is dumbfounded that there can be such normality still around in a world in which her own has been so utterly destroyed.

Ben turns towards her.

I hear you've been getting adventurous, Pualele.

She stares back expressionlessly.

Who was in the car? You know that if the PIG patrol finds you out on the street at night they'll arrest you for being a vagrant. You know what a vagrant is?

The Queen appears on her porch and calls out to Ben. He looks over and shouts back to his mother and Pualele quickly walks away from him towards her home. She knows about the PIG patrol – the Police Investigation Group. She's heard the rumours. The PIG patrol picks up Pacific Islanders and takes them to jail. She doesn't know why, but she knows you don't do anything to get the patrol after you. This is why she is confused. Pualele doesn't understand why they'd want to arrest her for being *fragrant*? If she had stayed by Ben, she would've told him that she knows what the word means. It's how flowers smell. Maybe palagi don't like Samoan flowers? How odd New Zealanders are.

Pualele. Ben calls after her but she keeps on going. Mrs Magasiva is saying something to Ben now. Pualele feels his eyes on her and she doesn't look back because Pualele knows he will have his answer in the end.

☙

On Sunday night the sky is thick with stars as Ben steps out onto the street. He shuts the door to the house quietly and heads across to where he sees Pualele waiting by the crossing. He nods at her in greeting.

Can you help me find another after-school job? She has rehearsed the words in her head and they tumble out of her like a rush of water flooding the night. Ben doesn't say anything for a moment. He looks at her trying to determine why she would need another job. Maybe money is tighter than normal with her father and Kasi gone. Perhaps she wants to be more helpful. So many potential reasons why, but first . . .

Soon as you tell me what you were doing getting into that car?

She hangs her head and wills him to look inside her head and see what has happened. He watches her shoulders droop and feels bad for trying to manipulate the situation. She is only a little girl he says to himself, but he knows what he knows and he can't let it go.

I can't help you if you don't tell me.

Pualele circles her foot on the ground and swallows the lump in her throat. *Can't tell you.*

Then I can't help.

Pualele considers this. If Ben won't help her there is little chance of finding a new job, and without a new job she is stuck at the Davisons. She desperately needs him. But a burning shame and the fear that Ben will be repulsed by the truth keeps the words locked inside her. She is already at her limit asking for help to find another job. Anything else is too much, and she thinks about turning around and running home.

I don't like all the dead people. The words burst out of her before she thinks about what she is saying. She tells herself that it is not a lie because she truly doesn't care for the corpses and the ever-present embalming smells.

Ben laughs and the tension in the air dissipates. *Can't say I blame you!*

Pualele is embarrassed that he has believed her so readily.

You still haven't answered my *question, Pualale.* His statement hangs in the air like a thick fog that she cannot see her way through. She regrets having asked him to help her, but then there is no one else. He waits, but she won't look at him. Eventually he sighs.

I can ask around about a part-time job, but they're not exactly easy to come by, Pualele. Have you told Sefi and Sam?

She shakes her head.

OK. Leave it with me. He puts his arm around her shoulders and Pualele pulls way. *You're going home.*

Pualele doesn't move. Ben mistakes what lies beneath her actions for fear of what people will say about her leaving a good part-time job. He reaches out and hugs her to him. *It'll be OK. I think you were great working there in the first place, and I don't think anyone will care if you get a job somewhere else.* He gives her an extra squeeze and Pualele stiffens, panic rising within her at the closeness of his body.

Relax, Pualele, he says, patting her back. *It'll be OK. They'll understand about the job. You get home.* He ruffles her and releases her. She steps backwards, forcing herself not to run. He looks at her strangely, and she wonders if he has used his fa'afafine powers to read her mind and know her secret. She turns quickly and bolts the short distance back to her house, leaving Ben staring after her.

༺ ༻

In the following weeks she says nothing to her aunt and uncle about wanting to quit working for the Davisons as she waits on Ben to find her an alternative. She is unable to concentrate on anything and slips behind in her school work. Sefi notices that Pualele is nervous all the time; she jumps at every little sound and she no longer likes to be alone. She still works at the Davisons twice a week, helping Mrs D with the cleaning, but she has had tummy aches and has missed several days of work, much to Uncle Sam's chagrin.

The first time Pualele runs into Mr Davison is three weeks after that terrible night. She hears him before she sees him: he is whistling. She puts her head down and turns away as he walks through the door. He stops whistling and stands still. They are alone in the embalming room.

Make sure that floor's polished properly, he says in a clear loud voice.

She keeps mopping and nods in response.

Then, like an apparition, he appears centimetres away from her and cups his hand to her buttock. She holds her breath and waits.

Hhhmm, he murmurs.

At that moment Mrs D marches through the door, and Mr Davison's hand drops away. He walks towards his wife as she launches into a tirade.

You'll never believe it, Tom. Beryl Grainger passed away yesterday and her family are using someone else. Can you believe it! And we buried Bill... Her voice fades as Mr Davison guides her back into the offices, his hand in the small of her back, leaving Pualele shaking over the mop and bucket.

⌘

When she is not working, Pualele is the first to arrive home in the afternoon. She sets the house in order and cooks dinner. When Sefi arrives home and asks her she says school was good, she is fine and her homework is complete.

There is a veneer of normality that Pualele carefully constructs to keep her aunt and uncle happy and to ensure they ask her no questions that she cannot answer. She finds comfort in routine – and once inside the house she locks the door and feels safe from the things that lurk outside the bounds of Richmond Road.

One day, Sefi and Sam arrive home to find the front door locked. This has never been the case – once someone is home the door is unlocked. This is how it should be. But Sam reaches for the handle and the door resists his efforts. He tries again, shaking the door, thinking it has jammed shut. Pualele is crossing the hallway when the noise at the door starts. She freezes mid-stride. All she can see is a giant rattling the door from its hinges. She too begins to shake.

It is locked, she hears Uncle Sam proclaim.

Where is Pualele?

Uncle Sam calls her name. *Pualele?* He pummels the door with his fist. Pualele moves one foot forward and then stops. Her feet don't seem to want to go any closer even though she knows it is not a giant come to get her.

There. She can see Uncle Sam pointing through the glass in the door at her. *Is that you, Pualele? Open up.*

She creeps slowly forward. She doesn't know why, but in a tiny voice she asks, *Who is it?*

Ach, Pualele, open the door. You are not some palagi lady in a big house!

Pualele opens the door and the two adults search her face for answers. She gives nothing away. She has developed a 'day face' that she now shows the world. Sefi harumphs and pushes inside. *Come, come, enough of this.*

Sefi expects this to be the end of it, but every day when Pualele is home first, it is the same locked door that confronts them. Asked why she does this, Pualele tells Sefi that she feels safer locking the door now that Father and Kasi are gone. Sefi can't argue with this logic, but why Pualele has waited two months to start locking the door doesn't seem quite right to the hypervigilant Sefi. She worries about what this means and thinks she will ask the Queen, who must surely have experience of this kind of behaviour with her extensive brood.

☙

Before the opportunity presents itself to ask the Queen, Sefi runs into Sister Margaret walking along the street.

Sefi – nice to see you. Just finished work?

Yes, yes, just about home.

How is Pualele?

Very well, Sister.

The nun's eyebrows rise. *But she has missed so many days of school.*

Sefi's mouth drops open. She clasps her hands in front of her and begins to cough to conceal her shock at this news.

I mean . . . she's much better.

The nun pauses.

Ah, I see. Well, hope we see her tomorrow. She looks pointedly at Sefi as Aunty fashions her mouth into a smile of sorts.

As they part company, the smile drops and Sefi rushes towards home.

Aie, aie, aie.

☙

The man who comes to the door wears a full afro under an olive beret. From his T-shirt a stern Che Guevara looks out at Pualele, and not knowing who either man is she wonders whether the man on the T-shirt and the man wearing it are one and the same person.

Hello Sam. Been a long time.

Pualele watches from the doorway of the lounge and sees the fear in Uncle Sam's eyes as he glances quickly down the hallway towards the kitchen where Sefi is cleaning. Uncle looks back at the man and shakes his head without speaking.

Yes. Yes it has, he finally answers quietly, making no moves to invite the man in.

Finally, when it is clear that Sam has said all he's going to say, the man asks, *Can I come in, Sami?*

Pualele can sense Uncle's reluctance to let the man in by the set of his shoulders and the slowness of his manner. Finally he steps aside to allow the man in over the threshold, but before he gets two steps down the hallway Sam's hand shoots out and grabs the man by his upper arm. The man stops and looks down at the hand and then slowly raises his head so the two men are looking at each other eye to eye.

I better go first, Sam says, and the man nods in agreement as he follows Sam to the kitchen, oblivious of Pualele's presence.

As they approach the kitchen Sefi calls out, *Who's there?*

Sam doesn't reply, and he doesn't try and stop the man as he steps in front of Sam into the kitchen.

Hello Sefi.

Willi. Her reply is curt and it seems to Pualele that Sefi is not that surprised to see this man in her kitchen. She is intrigued. Who is he and why is he here? She decides to listen and find out, slipping into the kitchen behind the men and hoping all the while that none of the adults will notice her standing by the wall.

Sorry Sefi, says Sam apologetically, holding his hands up as if in defeat.

I invited him, she says simply.

Sam shakes his head and Pualele thinks he looks as if he is trying to recalibrate what Aunty has just said into something that makes more sense to him. *You what?*

You heard me. I asked Willi to come.

Yes Sam. It's true. She asked me to come and see if the brothers can help you.

Sam glares at his wife and in the silence that follows, Pualele remembers Ben's words on the night of the fire. *We should talk to Willi.*

So this is the man. Pualele is disappointed. She'd imagined a man of great height. A man who would arrive with an aura of power about him. Not this Willi. He couldn't be more than a centimetre or two taller than Pualele, slightly built and with that afro. Well, she thinks, he looks more like a rough village boy than a city man who can fix things. She lets out a loud sigh without thinking and all the adults turn to look at her. She wants to kick herself for being so indiscreet and waits to be told to go, but Willi speaks and Sam and Sefi turn their attention back to him.

Sam – the brothers, they can help you and Sefi. I'm sorry, I should have come before.

Pualele sees that Sam is still disbelieving of the whole situation. Willi in the house. Sefi inviting him. Pualele feels that something is very, very wrong.

You can't help, says Sam abruptly. *They're gone.*

I'm sorry. I know about the raid. But I'm not here about that. He pauses. *We can help with Mr Hanson, the landlord.*

Pualele watches her uncle and aunt, who are looking incredulously at Willi.

Hanson's got debts. He's a gambler and needs to sell some of his properties.

Sefi looks to Pualele to be utterly confused, but Willi continues on.

You should've let us help you way back when.

Way-back-when, Sefi spits the words back at him. *Listen to him,* she shouts at Sam. *Way back when you and Sam drank every cent we had. That's why we don't have no house. And Sam never would've got arrested if it wasn't for you.*

Sefi . . . Sam steps forward and takes her hand in his *. . . that's in the past now.*

Way back when, she mumbles.

Come on, Sefi. I got the brothers to get David Lange to get the charges dropped. I – WE helped Sam.

He's right, Sefi. It was me that was drunk. It was me. Not Willi. Not the brothers. I drank our money away.

Sefi looks down at her hand in Sam's and says nothing. Pualele leans on the wall, stunned at what she has heard. Uncle Sam as far as she knew was teetotal. And she is amazed he had once been arrested. And Mr David Lange, the politician man, had saved Sam. Now this is fantasy talk, she is sure.

You asked me here Sefi, and I've come.

Sam squeezes Sefi's hand and asks, *What's this about Hanson and the house?*

We can help you negotiate to buy this place. He waits for them to digest this information and then continues. *The word on the street is it was him who got your brother and nephew sent home.*

Pualele gasps as her uncle explodes with a stream of Samoan expletives.

Sefi leans away from Sam and gives him a look that Pualele knows only too well. Sam clears his throat.

He never did anything to this house in all the time we been here, he says, looking around at the tired kitchen.

We could've put pressure on him to maintain this house better. We done that for lots of families, you know. But . . .

You still run the homework club? Sefi cuts in.

Yes, Willi replies.

I want Pualele to go there.

Pualele? Sam says. *What about the house, the landlord! What are you talking, woman?*

That's why I invited him, says Sefi. *To get Pualele help.*

That's why, the men chime in together.

Of course. She's behind in the school. Finally, she shows her hand and everyone seems to relax a little.

But what about the landlord? Sam asks.

I don't know anything about this. This the first I hear about it, replies Sefi.

Well, if it's any consolation, I thought you'd asked me here because of Hanson, so I guess it's a nice bonus, am I right?

We'll see. But Pualele can go to this club, yes? Aunty obviously isn't going to be swayed from what she wants from Willi. He nods.

Another thing, this time Aunty is not asking. *I don't want her coming back with any of your ideas. She's a good girl.*

We only want to help, Sefi.

She stares back at Willi, narrowing her eyes, and Pualele hopes that this Willi is as good as his word.

Pualele melts away back into the hallway and steals back to her room. She has no idea what a homework club is, but perhaps this will all work out, and this Willi fellow might be the one to find her a new job. She thinks about what he said about Mr Hanson. As far as she is concerned, it makes no difference who actually owns the house, but she hopes that she never lays eyes on that landlord again.

ଓ

Uncle Sam places his hands on the certificate of title and reads their names aloud. The solicitor has come to their house at Sam's request, and as Sam holds the document in his hands with Sefi reading the words over his shoulder, he begins to weep. Pualele now knows what owning this house means to her uncle and aunty: they really are living in Rich Man Road.

ଓ

The homework centre is in Ponsonby, and Pualele reluctantly walks there the first day, careful not to cross the road until she is well clear of Dillon's Four Square. It is up a flight of stairs and she can hear the children before she puts her foot on the first step. A nervous trickle of sweat is running down her neck as she starts the climb. She reminds herself that if it were not for this homework place she'd be cleaning at the funeral home at this very minute, and this thought helps her up the stairs.

The door is wrenched open by a thin brown woman in jeans wearing an old anti-war T-shirt:

No Vietnamese ever

called me Coconut

Hello, the woman says in a friendly tone. *You Sami's girl?*

Pualele looks down and nods.

Come on in then. Pualele, isn't it? I'm Nita. I'm one of the tutors. Come 'n meet the crew.

And like that she finds a place with children like her, whose names are Tito and Mere and Malu and who also struggle to fit in to their New Zealand schools. If only she could stop the nightmares in her head long enough to concentrate, things would be better, but she doesn't know how to get away from the car that chases her inside her head. The tutors are kind and seem not to notice that Pualele is any different. Then again, they've only just met her.

❧

She hasn't seen Ben for many weeks, and while on the one hand she is happy to avoid his prying questions, on the other she is frustrated and frightened at still having to work at the Davisons with no indication that Ben is looking for another job for her. Sometimes, when she is desperate to be away from Mr Davison, she tries to convince herself to seek Ben out and confront him about whether he has been looking for work for her. She tells herself that he hasn't tried to talk to her again about that night because he has forgotten all about it. But she can never fully satisfy the voice in her head that tells her to avoid him for fear of what he knows about her and that night.

So when on her walk home from homework club one day she sees Koko run under the Magasivas' house, Pualele is paralysed by indecision. *Koko,* she calls out in a rasping whisper as she crouches on her haunches. She's angry with the cat for putting her in this position, and if he doesn't appear right now she will abandon him and run the rest of the way home. *Koko,* she says one last time.

She feels a large hand on her shoulder and she is now truly paralysed, unable to speak or move or breathe.

That cat of yours likes running away. Ben takes his hand away and Pualele breathes again.

I haven't seen you, Pualele. How's the homework centre?
Good.
And how's work?
S'OK.

They wait for the other to say something, staring at the spot where the cat has squeezed his overfed body through the running boards of the house.

My friend tutors there, you know, says Ben.

She nods but doesn't ask who his friend is.

Her name's Nita. He says her name Neee-Tah. *She's at university. But she goes out at night and patrols with some of the guys to make sure our people aren't hassled by the police.*

She wants to shout at him to stop telling her all this; she knows where this conversation is going and she doesn't like it. She makes no move or any acknowledgement that she has heard him. Koko pokes his head out from under the house and makes his way over towards Pualele and Ben.

You know what, Pualele? I think Koko's going to have kittens. Your Koko's a girl.

Pualele looks at Koko as he waddles towards them and she recognises that he is indeed a she. She thinks of Leti then, her belly so full to bursting with piglets that it swept the ground as she walked.

Why so sad, Pualele? Thought you'd be happy about kittens.

Koko lets Pualele pick her up, but once in the girl's arms she struggles to be free again. Pualele bends down to place the cat gently on all fours.

Hey, look. Ben looks over her back and points at a car coming down the road. *Sam's got a new car.*

It is indeed Uncle Sam, but it is not the hearse he is driving today but Mr Davison's own car. Pualele trembles at the sight – and loses control of her bladder.

Ben gives her an enquiring sort of look as he follows her stare and then looks back at the puddle forming on the ground at her feet. He puts his arm around her and nods to himself, for this confirms that the gossip from the street he has heard is true.

CR

Uncle Sam and Aunty Sefi do not know what to do about Pualele. They ask the Queen for help and she arrives promptly that same day to offer her expert advice. She peers down at Paulele lying on the couch, inspecting her as if selecting a cut of meat from the butcher.

It is hormones, she declares with authority. *She is becoming a young woman, and this is why.*

Sefi nods in agreement, but the Queen hasn't finished. *It may even be because of Koko. You know, Sefi, that sometimes women in the same house will have their monthlies at the same time?* Pualele places her hands over her ears in embarrassment but she can still hear the Queen. *It is the same thing here. Because Koko has had kittens it has upset her hormones. You must get the cat and her kittens away.*

Sefi is apoplectic at this idea and declares to Sam when he comes home that Merita has lost her mind. At least, Pualele thinks to herself, Sefi didn't try to get rid of Koko.

ଔ

Pualele refuses to sleep on her own, won't walk home from homework club unless someone will walk with her and, most disturbingly, refuses to work at the Davisons'. No Auva'a refuses to work. This is a serious illness that no one has seen before, and it is causing Uncle Sam great embarrassment.

The rain drums on the tin roof while Sefi and Sam discuss the problem that is Pualele. She pretends to be asleep on the couch while the adults talk, but she cannot hear what they say because the rain is so loud, it sounds as if it is in the room with them. It is Pualele who hears the telephone ringing in the kitchen and tells Sam. When he returns, they read on his face that it is not good news.

He stumbles over the words. *Mr D . . . Davison is missing.*

What are you saying? Missing where?

Uncle breathes through his nose. *Disappeared.*

Who told you this? This is not right.

His forehead wrinkles as he recalls the conversation. *Mrs Davison called herself. She has called the police. He's missing.*

Maybe he forgot to tell her. He gone somewhere.

I don't know, Sefi. She asked me to come. The police want to ask some questions. I better go.

ଔ

Mr Davison's disappearance is a mystery. Pualele hears Uncle Sam reporting back to Sefi and eavesdrops nervously for details from the other side of the door.

Mrs Davison told the police that Mr Davison, well, he goes out at night sometimes.

What for? asks Sefi.

To clear the head, he always says to her. He pauses and lowers his voice so Pualele can barely hear him through the door. *She tells them she suspicious that there's another woman, but they don't find this woman. He's just vanished.*

Pualele doesn't wait for any more news. She sneaks back to her room and gently shuts the door behind her. *This is good*, she tells herself as she climbs into the bed. Yes, this is very good news. As she waits for Aunty to come to her, she falls asleep without even trying.

༺ ༻

Police investigations continue for several weeks, and 'missing person' becomes a homicide enquiry. Pualele knows that the police have talked to the working girls and club owners and to Mr Davison's trusted worker, her Uncle Sam. But nothing of any significance is discovered.

Then one day at the homework centre she sees a headline in the newspaper. *Tip-off in Missing Funeral Director Case.* The report says that there has been an anonymous tip-off. Mr Davison was seen driving out west along Scenic Drive towards the surf beaches on the night of his disappearance. The focus turns to West Auckland away from the central city, and although someone else comes forward to confirm the sighting, no trace of Mr Davison or his vehicle is ever found.

༺ ༻

Pualele worries about what Mr Davison's disappearance will mean for Uncle Sam's job. It would make life very difficult. Pualele has heard that the work at the parlour has slowed with all the publicity around the disappearance. She feels guilty that this has something to do with her, and when Uncle Sam tells her to come with him to the funeral home she digs her fingernails into her palms.

Pualele, you come with me. If Mrs Davison sees you, she might feel sorry for us and I not lose my job. He looks at the ground when he says this to her and she knows that this is an act of desperation on his part.

Things have been tough, Sam, Mrs Davison says. *I know you understand that.*

Sam listens and Pualele wishes she would hurry up and tell him he has no job so they can leave quickly. Mrs Davison rifles through some papers on the desk in front of her and Pualele hopes that one is a cheque with Uncle Sam's name on it.

I don't think you'll like it. There's no support for what I'm doing, but I hope you can see that I'm doing what I think is best to honour what Tom and I have built here.

Sam nods. Pualele feels queasy.

The industry doesn't like it. They're saying it's not a job for a lady. She snorts. *Well, Sam, I'm no lady. I'm on my own and I've got bills to pay and I'm going to run this business better than Tom. There, I've said it.*

She sits in Tom's old chair, her head tilted up so Pualele can see the little hairs that stubbornly grow on her chin. Pualele clears her throat, discomforted by this sight.

I don't expect you to stay on – I know people think it's not right for a woman to run this business. But you know what? She almost roars the words. *I DON'T GIVE A DAMN.*

Sam is as pale as any Samoan man can be, and when Mrs Davison notices this she blushes.

I'm so sorry. I know how religious you and Sefi are and I totally understand that you can't keep on here.

No! Sam hits his hand on the desk and Mrs Davison jumps in her seat. *I mean yes. Sorry. Yes, I will . . . I will stay.*

It's Sam's turn to colour and Pualele understands his embarrassment at his own words. He tries to settle his features, but he is so visibly relieved to not be out of a job that he breaks into a goofy grin.

Well, she says. *That's marvellous. And you, Pualele. Are you better now? I'd love you to come back if you can manage it with your studies.*

She'll be here, blurts Uncle Sam before Pualele has a chance to take a breath.

༄

Pualele can't say exactly why she feels responsible, but she does. She knows she should feel happy he is gone, relieved even. He won't ever touch her or hurt her again. And she now works for Mrs Davison, who is as good a boss as anyone can have.

But there is a little knot of fear growing in her belly. She is afraid for Ben and has added him to her prayer list on her almost-daily visits to St Mary's. She will never ask him and no one will ever prove it, but she's sure that Ben or his friends know what has happened to Mr Davison.

CHAPTER 24

OLGA'S JOURNAL

Joe had lost control on a bend and it was a farmer who found the truck in a ditch off the main highway with Joe still inside it. Apart from bruises and the two broken legs, he was fine. My mother set up a bed for him in the kitchen so that he didn't have to negotiate the stairs. And I never understood why but Joe surviving the accident brought a kind of joy into the house as if we were so incredibly grateful to be alive that we couldn't hide our happiness. How different to surviving the war, I thought.

And that wasn't all. Joe had won the trifecta at Te Rapa and was flush with the winnings. It was hard to say whether the visitors who came to see him were there to celebrate his being alive or if they were after betting tips from the winner himself. Either way, my concern was with who was coming to visit. I had a feeling that one day Vaiuli would call on his friend, and I was afraid for him. Worse still, I was worried that one day Mijo Papić would visit and then the good humour that currently sheltered our family from ourselves would vanish.

∞

After a month in hospital, it was another eight weeks he was like that laid up in the kitchen, with thick plaster entombing each leg. In the first week Joe was home, I looked and looked for Vaiuli as I walked to and from college. I must've appeared mad to anyone watching me as I spun around whenever I imagined I had seen him. At first I was worried that Mr Papić had done something to him, but then I became angry that he hadn't been in contact. I didn't see him until the following week, when he was waiting for me outside the school.

How's Joe?

He might have been asking anyone that question and it so irritated me that I couldn't speak. Had Vaiuli forgotten what had happened between us?

He looked as if he might go if I didn't say something.

Ivan won the trifecta, I blurted.

Oh, he said, surprised.

And he's broken his legs.

I'll walk you home, he offered, holding out his arm for me to take like a proper gentleman.

Silly as I was I had the good sense to think about this. Mr Papić had stayed away, washed his hands of me and my family, I hoped. But to walk home with Vaiuli, well, that would be tempting fate, and hadn't fate already done enough? The irritation rose up once again.

Where have you been? I thought you'd have come by to see Joe, but I know you couldn't, but you know where I am and . . . Everything I was thinking came out at once, and to Vaiuli's credit he listened. When I'd run out of words and anger and was standing there with my head ringing, flushed with the heat of all the words and feelings, he took my hand.

I don't want to get you in trouble. When Joe's back on his feet we'll see how things are. And if it's OK with you, can I walk you home now and then?

◈

Maureen's told me her parents are coming to Auckland. She's in a state. She's trying to think of ways to dissuade them. I have been bold and suggested that she should be brave and tell them about the cancer. I'm scared that the real reason she's refusing to tell them is because she believes that she will die. But if she beats this disease there's no harm, only relief and elation if her parents know about the cancer. And she will, God as my witness, beat this cancer.

She thinks they will be disappointed because even if she doesn't die, they will never have grandchildren now. I asked about her brother, and she laughed. She said in a very nasty way, *He's gay*. Well, I can't profess to know anything about gay people or their wishes and wants, but I am fairly sure from what I have heard and read that even gay people have babies now. There was a magazine here a few days ago and there on the cover was Elton John, the singer (though I suppose you already know who he is), with his partner and baby. Well, I don't mind telling you it was a bit of a shock, and I thought it a joke at first until I read the article and they talked of surrogates and science.

I told this to Maureen, who I must say was quite upset at my mentioning it. She broke down and sobbed, *My baby, my baby*.

ଔ

I've got to the bottom of it now, and it is a sad story, Pualele.

Maureen was pregnant when she discovered the lump in her breast. It was early days and she hadn't sought confirmation of the pregnancy, or even told her boyfriend at the time. The doctors said that they could effectively treat her and not harm the fetus, but the wee life inside her did not stay, and before she could contemplate any decisions, she had miscarried and flown back to New Zealand where she could be treated.

So sad.

For I once carried a life inside me too.

ଔ

I'm not sure when I first felt unwell. It was like with the cancer. It was just a funny unsettledness somewhere in my belly. I remember that it had me running to the outhouse to dry retch.

It was my mother who saw it for what it was.

I came out of the outhouse one morning and almost fell on top of her. I can't be sure, but I think she'd had her ear to the tin door listening to my retching.

She looked at me and her hands were shaking – from the cold, I thought, but then she slapped me and I knew it was from the anger.

You little whore. My own mother said that to me as I clasped the side of my face. *Get inside before people see you!*

It was as much a shock to me as it was to her.

CHAPTER 25

AUCKLAND, 2000
PUALELE

She arrives at the convent by taxi. For a long time the new postulant has dreamed about this moment, and how excited and nervous and humble she will feel, but now that she is here she feels none of these things. She is instead paralysed by the thought that she doesn't belong here. It is one thing to believe inexorably in God, but it is quite another to give oneself over to the rigours of religious life. Her mother wrote many letters beseeching her to come home, that it is enough to be a pious churchgoer. She needn't give herself to the church. The letters lie neatly folded in the inside pocket of her suitcase. Maybe her mother is right – it is time to go home.

When she writes back to her mother she tries to explain that entering the convent feels right. What she doesn't ever say is that the psalms and gospel readings send a wonderful flush of calmness through her and centre her in this world in a way no place or person ever has before. She cannot tell her mother that Samoa no longer seems like home.

What Pualele wants is to always feel that glorious sense of peace that takes sway over her when she is praying. It makes her optimistic for the future when all around her life seems so damaged and bruised. Still, she is not without doubt, and she stands at the gate, her hand hovering motionless above the buzzer while the other remains in a fist around the handle of her bag.

Across the tree-lined road, a low-slung vehicle pulls out of a gated residence, the driver of the car barely registering Pualele's presence as he accelerates away. She turns to watch the car as it puffs exhaust fumes, ascending the hill before disappearing over the top. The sun bounces off the chrome bumpers, blinding her briefly. *Pride is an ugly thing.* It is enough to give her the courage she needs, and after smoothing the creases from her blue skirt and straightening the collar of her white shirt, she presses the button.

There is a low buzz and Pualele leans on the gate until it swings open. A thin path cuts its way through a wild garden where climbing roses wrap themselves around magnolia trees. Every inch of the garden is crammed with hebes and dahlias, and the edges are bursting out onto the path where a creeper crawls across, threatening to take over. As she walks towards the convent, the front door opens and a small figure emerges onto the veranda. The nun stops at the top of the stairs, slipping her hands inside opposing sleeves, only her pale face visible amongst the brown fabric that engulfs her. She is too far away to see the detail of her features, but there is something of Pualele's mother about her. Pualele feels comforted by this.

Welcome.

The nun's voice is melodic and Pualele detects the hint of an accent – big fat vowels and a 'v' where the 'w' should be. Here is someone who is different, just like her. Her fears recede a little and she walks up the stairs, stopping one step below the waiting nun. The older woman smiles at her, and when it seems she is about to speak she turns and walks inside, leaving Pualele to scramble after her.

The unmistakable smell of borax brings memories of the life she has left behind. She swallows, her heart beating nervously in her chest and her hands coiled into fists, her fingers worrying the scalloped scars.

Overlaying the familiar smell is a stillness. The only sound to be heard is footfall on wooden floors and the careful opening and shutting of doors as the sisters go about their work in silence. The walls are white – not a bright diamond white, but the kind that has had the shine taken off it. Here and there, along the corridor, photographs of nuns hang on the walls.

The nun stops and waits for her again. As Pualele catches up to her she notices the crêpe-like skin of her face and neck. Deep lines run from her nose down to her mouth and spread outwards from the corners of dark-brown eyes.

Mother will be with you soon. Her voice has a soothing quality to it and Pualele allows her hands to relax. The nun motions to a wooden chair leaning against the wall. To the left there is a door that reaches up towards the high-pitched ceiling. Pualele wonders about the woman who sits on the other side of the door and whether she will be as welcoming. She sinks into the chair, and thinks urgently what to say to the nun to stop her from leaving.

I don't mind waiting. Really I don't. I've been waiting forever to come here.

She bites her bottom lip and drops her gaze to the tongue-and-groove floor. She can't believe what's just come out of her mouth – a drizzle of nothing. She clenches her hands as she wills the words back, thinking how stupid she is to still be speaking without thinking. Tentatively she raises her eyes. The corners of the nun's mouth start to twitch, and the lines around her eyes crinkle before she turns away. These same undisciplined outbursts got Pualele into trouble as a child, but she isn't going to let impetuosity ruin this. She doesn't know the older nun's name, but she makes a mental note to find her later and thank her.

❦

It is hard to tell the age of the prioress. The hair that escapes her headdress is still dark blonde, and the skin that stretches over her cheekbones is pale and smooth. It is the eyes that suggest her age. Pualele knows better than to stare, but she can't help wondering if the nun is still able to see clearly or not.

Welcome, Sister.

The eyes come to life as she speaks.

Father Barry speaks highly of you.

She sits still in the chair, not knowing how to respond.

He says you have a great love for our Lord. Are you determined to persevere?

Yes, Mother.

Good. I understand that you wish to take the name Mary?

Pualele bobs her head again, her mouth barely open. *What if I don't love Him enough?*

That is the lot of a postulant – to learn to love with commitment and not be deterred. The nun's voice is firm as if there is no question that Pualele will not succeed.

Pualele wants to be committed, to persevere.

You've already met Sister Teresa and I have asked her to guide you. She has been with us almost as long as I have, and she knows how hard it is for a new postulant to make such a decision.

❦

Outside the door, Sister Teresa is waiting. She motions to Pualele to pick up her case and to follow her along the hallway and up a narrow staircase. Sister Teresa leads her to a room at the end of a long corridor. Pualele places her small bag on the end of the single bed that has a permanent depression in the middle as if some invisible giant is already sitting there. The sagging bed makes her think about all the other nuns who have lain there and she considers where they are now. The room is narrow with a small wooden desk and chair facing the wall below a window.

As Pualele peers out at the trees thick with leaves Sister Teresa whispers to her. *Come to the garden once you've unpacked. You can keep your city clothes on . . . you'll get new ones soon.* Her voice is so soft and conspiratorial that Pualele isn't sure if she has actually heard the words or if she has imagined them. She turns slowly away from the window to look at the nun to see if the invitation is real. But Sister Teresa has already slipped out of the room.

❦

Out of the back door she sees a raised vegetable plot running along one side of the property, while on the other side, exploding with new growth, is an orchard of plum, apple, peach and other trees she can't identify. At the back of the garden Sister Teresa leans over a low fence of chicken wire, scattering food scraps.

Pualele stands behind the older woman waiting to be noticed. Once the scraps are gone, Sister Teresa turns and, without uttering a word, hands Pualele the empty bucket. The nun walks on towards the vegetable garden, where she draws a short-bladed knife from her belt, bends forward and starts cutting large leaves of silver beet. Once she has a handful of the dark green leaves she holds her fist up and Pualele clambers over the raised edge of the bed, taking them from her.

Pualele is grateful for the quiet. Sister Teresa seems neither happy nor displeased with the company. She merely continues with her work, using Pualele to help when she thinks of it, ignoring her when it is too difficult. For the new Carmelite, Sister Teresa is a reminder of her Mama and Mrs Davison. Words are too important to fritter away on meaningless chatter; they are women who consider every word before they release them into the world.

A bell rings inside, and Pualele finds herself following Sister Teresa back into the convent and the kitchen.

Do you cook?

Pualele's throat is parched, unable to let the words out. She nods instead.

Potatoes and onions are over there in the scullery.

Pualele walks across a floor that has been polished until the lime linoleum is almost fluorescent. Through the walls of the kitchen she starts to hear people moving and the creaking of doors. She feels herself torn between wanting to preserve the companionable silence she is enjoying and a desire to meet the other nuns. When it is clear no one else is going to join them, Pualele sighs and a ghost of a smile appears and then just as quickly vanishes. This is exactly where she needs to be.

CR

That first lunch, like all the meals that are to follow, is served in a narrow room off the kitchen. On one side are French doors facing the garden, and on the other is a wall of solid wood panelling with a sideboard leaning against it. At the west end of the room is a door connecting the dining area to the kitchen. Pualele stands in the doorway staring at the longest table she has ever seen. Above it hangs a chandelier, casting refracted light over the mahogany table top so that the table appears to be teeming with silver fish dancing across a flat sea.

Pualele tries to count the number of chairs tucked under the table, but she jumps as the door at the other end of the room opens and a stream of nuns enters. Two go to the sideboard in front of the panelled wall and pick up cutlery, while another two gather white plates, glasses and napkins before setting them on the table.

A hand takes her elbow and she allows herself be shown to a seat. Standing behind the chair, hands clasping the back, she waits for a signal. She has a strong urge to return to her old ways and press her sharp filed nails into her hands. But instead she focusses on the gold line that encircles the white plate in front of her.

It isn't until the prayer giving thanks is over that she raises her eyes. There staring back at her are the twelve residents of the convent. Her gaze skips over the nuns, coming to rest on the prioress standing at the end of the table. Next to her is a pudding-faced nun wearing wire-framed spectacles. She finds Sister Teresa across from her, and is surprised at herself when she smiles back at her.

Sister Mary, we welcome you to our table. We hope you enjoy our simple fare and we look forward to getting to know you after lunch.

Mother Superior's words bring a rush of heat to her cheeks. She would rather they didn't *look* at her or try to speak to her. Pualele has spent many years perfecting the art of being invisible – in the classroom, at home and at the funeral parlour. She isn't sure her new incarnation as Sister Mary is going to like this attention, even if it means getting closer to God. Sister Teresa's eyes are on her as she starts to scratch at her palms. She has seen the expression before. It says *I know you*. Then without thinking, her fingers stop digging at her flesh. She finds herself following the older woman's lead and pulls out her chair, suddenly ravenous for her first meal as a Carmelite.

CHAPTER 26

OLGA'S JOURNAL

Oh, my baby, my baby. I have spent many years thinking about what has become of my child. I was only a bystander as my mother took charge, and what plans she made for my sweet child, well, I never asked and she surely would never have told me.

On the same day she had discovered me, my father came to my bedroom.

You've disappointed us, Olga. It was plain on his face and I did feel bad, not because of the baby growing in my belly but because I had not done as he'd asked me and fallen into line with Mama. There was nothing I could say that would make it any easier, so for once in my life I said nothing and allowed him to move me into Joe's room. He put Joe's things into the cupboard room, and left me with the makeshift bed on the floor and a glass of water.

I listened as he fixed a padlock to the outside of the door and snapped the lock shut.

※

I needed to speak to Joe. I waited and waited but couldn't hear my brothers in the flat upstairs. I strained to see if I could hear them downstairs, but my parents had shut the door to the stairs and I couldn't make out if Pero and Joe were home or not. I didn't know my fate then. My only thoughts were how to escape and find Joe, he would know what to do. Aside from my being locked up like a criminal, my biggest concern was that I didn't actually know how far gone I was – nor how I was to tell Vaiuli.

Considering what I have just written, Pualele, you will probably agree with my mother that I was no better than a common street walker. But no matter what my mother and the church thought about my unmarried status, I knew in my heart that to have conceived this child out of love was right.

ଓଃ

My brothers had been sent away. Joe told me later that Bartul had collected them and they had gone to his farm in the west for the few days it took my mother to find somewhere to send me.

ଓଃ

The morning sun came into Joe's bedroom early, casting a rainbow of light across the bed. I woke and thought I heard my brothers downstairs, so I quickly dressed and listened again. Someone came up the stairs, walking lightly and carefully unlocking the padlock. It was my father.

He had the truck at the door, my mother already in the front.

Get in, he said.

I wedged myself in next to her and we sat in silence.

Then it felt like a death march as we walked into the long dark tunnel of the hallway of the hostel for girls like me.

ଓଃ

The days were long and were spent cleaning and sewing (I guess preparation for married life) and praying for our souls first thing in the morning and last thing at night. But I was there for only a few months, not because the baby was ready to come but because they worked us so hard that the baby came early. That's what they said, anyway, and I don't know if that was the truth or not for I was never told anything about my own pregnancy or the baby. I was allowed no visitors (in fact it is probable that no one knew I was there).

All I know is that I was scrubbing floors when the pain caught me.

Lie down, the nun said, pushing my shoulders firmly back onto the bed. The pain was terrifying. They strapped my legs up and told me to push, oh the agony of it. It was so intense that I thought I was being cleaved apart by the devil. I blacked out, and while in that other place the vila came to me, dressed in white and calling to me as she held my baby, cherub-faced with thick dark hair covering her head. She looked like Mila. Or Kata. Or herself. And then I don't know. It was all over and I didn't know what had happened.

You're bleeding a lot, the nun said.

My baby, where's my baby, I wailed.

She looked me in the eye and said, *She's gone.*

My baby. I was crazed with fear. I'd known why girls came here, to have their babies and then go back to normal life and find a husband who need never know. But I'd thought that's what happened to other girls. I'd pretended that it would be different for me and my baby.

The nun looked frightened and tried to soothe me.

Now, now. She glanced towards the door as if looking for reinforcements. *No need to go upsetting yourself.*

My baby. Where is she? I put my feet on the floor and tried to stand, but my legs gave way and I fell on the floor. Another sister came into the room, grabbing me by my arms and pushing me back up onto the sodden bed. *Stop this now.* She didn't hide her animosity towards me, stabbing her finger at me, making sure I got her point. *She's not your baby. You just remember that.*

The first nun turned towards me and a look flicked across her face as if to say, *That is how it is.*

༄

Writing this down and reading it back to myself hurts me far more than any physical pain – more than childbirth itself. They took my baby. My mother and the nursing sisters, they took her away. Oh Pualele, I never did see her except the top of her head, so perfect and tiny.

And I heard her cry. It wasn't a mewling cry like a kitten, but a full angry scream, *Don't take me from my mother.*

Oh my child, what has become of you?

༄

So how did a girl of loose morals and reluctant faith end up more than sixty years in a convent? Well, it's funny how God comes along. Sometimes he waits a whole lifetime for someone to see Him and then He will take them in even after a life of the worst kind. Then, sometimes, he doesn't need to wait so long for someone to believe that there is more to life than they had realised.

While I recuperated after the birth my parents let Joe visit me. I told him everything. He listened without emotion while I told him about Vaiuli and me and how our mother had discovered my pregnancy. Then he became angry when I told him how Father had locked me in Joe's very own bedroom and then brought me to the nuns. He held me and we both cried and he apologised in advance of telling me that Vaiuli had returned to Samoa. He also told me that our parents had, unbelievably, told everyone I had gone to Wellington to work for six months – although, he said, no one believed that.

It was such crushing news on top of the loss of my baby. I could not see how I would ever find Vaiuli, or how it was possible for me to ever live in Richmond Road with my parents again.

I said to Joe, *Why is life so cruel?*

He shrugged his shoulders. *Life's like that.*

It was more loss than I had strength to cope with, and Joe's answer was so inadequate that I became angry. *There's got to be more to life than this. Isn't there?*

That's a question you'll have to ask someone else.

He was right. It was a big question, and it was my time to seek the answer. And there He was waiting for me. The reluctant parishioner. The disobedient child. The breaker of Commandments.

CR

Joe found me a room in a boarding house in Mt Eden and I took a job as a sales girl in a ladies' clothes shop. Joe handled everything with our parents. I never asked Joe about them, although I cried many tears, and I never asked to see Pero because I knew that they would never let Joe bring him to visit me. It was as if, for my family and my community, I had ceased to exist. We may as well have been living in different countries, and there was something mocking in the fact that we had survived a war but hadn't survived life.

I had no friends in Mt Eden, and in fact couldn't bring myself to make any. There was no simple answer to questions about my family and where I was from so it was easier to not bother. The only familiar and safe place for me was the nearby Catholic Church. I went to Mass each morning before the shop opened and it gave me a routine that helped me feel normal. Almost everybody was rushing off to jobs or to ready children for school, so it was easy to feel part of something without having to talk to other parishioners at length and expose my past.

⁂

There was no thunderbolt from the sky, or great revelation. God revealed Himself to me slowly over time. There is a line about the Carmelite nun and her mission, a line that I have never forgotten:

In Him we live and move and have our being.

I had read it on a church noticeboard and it became stuck in my mind while I grieved for my baby and the loss of so many people from my life. A tug-o-war raged in me between choosing a convent life and staying where I was, but I was terrified of remaining in the lay world facing a future of loneliness and banishment from my family and community. The convent seemed the better choice and I knew my mother would be against it, even though she no longer held any power over me. Perhaps not the strongest reason for taking Orders, but I can't deny it.

Almost two years after my baby had been taken away, the Carmelites took me in with open arms, and for that I am eternally grateful.

⁂

I'm sorry I never made it to America, although I travelled further than I ever imagined I would. Sometimes, I wonder what happened to Mila and if she ever made it. Whether she is still alive. And what she would make of me? A dried-up walnut of an old woman, deep lines on my face not nearly as deep as the crevices in my heart. There were rumours about her as the years passed. Some said she had been murdered by the Germans, her body thrown down a well. Others said that she had been shot by mistake by our own people and her death concealed. I don't know the truth, but I like to think she is a vila on our mountain guiding a new generation of young women into adulthood.

Joe kept in contact with Oliver in St Louis. Oliver eventually married and had a family. He had a thriving construction business and was kind enough to send money for the convent – guilt money perhaps for abandoning me when I needed him. But I know that what we had was not lasting love. It was the kind born out of mutual suffering.

And I know not what happened to Vaiuli. I pray he was happy.

So now you know everything, all my sins – the lying and deception, the disobedience, the cowardice. But my greatest sin was the crime I committed against myself. I never stood up for what I wanted. I thought I wanted to leave my home and family behind me – but I was wrong. I have hidden away from the world and have lived off the love and support of our sisters, these honest women who never knew my true feelings. I am sorry that I deceived them too, for they deserved much better than that. I guess you should add that to my list of offences.

I'm tired now and don't see that I need to bother with the pretence any longer, but like all lies, at some point, it is too late to make amends. I will be gone by the time you read this, but you, Pualele, have a choice. Find where it is you belong and go there, for He will be with you always.

CHAPTER 27

SISTER MARY

Sister Mary puts down the journal and looks around the simple room. Her head spins with Sister Teresa's life. Her mother was born in Auckland. Could Olga be the one who gave life to her? She feels a rush of love for her friend and places everything inside the envelope, suddenly exhausted and confused. She will talk to Mother Superior and seek her guidance.

She will know what to do.

ଔ

She left me these things, Mother.

The prioress opens the envelope and pulls out the journal, photos, doll and embroidered swatch.

Yes, I know.

Sister Mary's eyes widen at the admission as the prioress picks up the photograph of the young man.

I let her keep it because I could never decide whether to take it from her.

Sister Mary leans in towards her, peering at the man in the picture, comprehension dawning on her face.

Why did you let her?

A broken heart makes a good Carmelite, Sister. And, I'm a practical woman – the man sends us money from America.

But the journal, you let her keep that too?

It's better to write if you can't talk. Mother scrutinises the photo, her middle finger sketching the outline of the man.

Have you read the journal, Mother?

No. But I'm sure I know most of it. We were young here together, Olga and I.

Then you know of her child?

A fleeting smile flits across Mother Superior's face and she nods. *She was haunted by the loss of her child. Losing that baby was the greatest regret of her life, I think.*

But she didn't LOSE the baby, Sister Mary is shouting, *they took it away from her.*

Mother Superior's face hardens. *The baby wasn't hers to keep.* Her voice is implacable. *She was unmarried, Sister.*

I think she might be my grandmother. She feels relieved once she has given voice to a possibility that could change all their lives. She needs to speak to Papavai. To Mama.

Mother Superior looks at her for a long time, clearly scared of what either outcome might do to this fragile nun sitting in front of her.

You won't like what I have to say, Sister, but this is a ludicrous suggestion. I don't believe this at all and I can't imagine how you might think this could be true.

It's true! The girl is now the one who is adamant. *She told the truth so I didn't make a mistake. I think she told me so I can do what she was never able to and talk to my grandfather – she knew who I was. I told her all about my family. About Papavai. She didn't make it up.*

Perhaps not intentionally, Mother huffs. *All I'm saying is that Olga has never been averse to letting people draw their own conclusions about things, whether they be right or wrong.*

But Mother, she knew what she was saying to me.

Sister Mary, think about it. Why would a married man in St Louis send money to a convent in New Zealand if he didn't believe he had an obligation?

But it wasn't his baby.

Olga was a complex woman and I know she loved you like a daughter. But that doesn't make her your grandmother.

You're calling her a liar!

No. Not at all. Let me ask you something Sister Mary – why did you come here to this convent?

I came to be Christ's bride.

Mother Superior harrumphs, her lips tightening across her face.

Why did you really come here?

The answer is on the tip of her tongue, but the wrong words come out in a rush.

When Aunty died, Mama wanted me to come home. My brother bought me a ticket, but I couldn't go back. I belong here. Even to her own ears, the words sounded hollow.

The words aren't important, Sister. The prioress looks archly at her. *It is what you believe inside that counts.*

Sister Mary isn't sure what she believes any more as she rubs her palms back and forth across her knees. Sister Teresa had been her last anchor in this world, and now she is gone.

I came here because the world is so ugly.

But it can be beautiful too, Sister – the beauty in prayer. And don't forget, we're all on this earth to suffer.

Suffering is wrong.

God sent his son to suffer for all eternity to save our souls. I'm sure you don't mean that God is wrong.

The prioress has never been reproachful before and Sister Mary smarts at the words. The older nun exhales and bows her head over the photo.

You've much to learn before final vows, Sister. It is human to suffer, and we all do in our own ways. Sister Teresa suffered for her sins in the knowledge that someone else would raise her child. Whether that child is who you think it is, is not for you and I to debate. There are channels you can contact to try and find the truth. Your real decision is whether you are ready to commit to this Order.

I don't know any more. I don't know if I can stay, Mother.

It's human to doubt, but you should know: I will do everything in my power to guide you.

☙

The taxi pulls up, its front wheel rim gouging itself on the curb. The driver steps out, wearing a white kurta over jeans. He flicks a cigarette butt out into the road as he walks around the vehicle to Pualele's side. When he speaks, she is surprised at how confident his voice sounds.

Pualele?

She signals yes with a slight movement of her head, avoiding his eyes as she bends and winds her fingers under the worn handle of her leather carry bag. She lifts it by her fingertips and lets it swing out towards the car. The driver reaches to take the bag from her, his hand grazing her forearm. Unconsciously she moves away and the bag slips from her grasp, her open hand exposing the raised purple scar on her palm. The driver says nothing as he picks up the bag and opens the passenger door for her, glancing discreetly at the simple, neat package of the woman standing by the car.

Aware that he is waiting for her, Pualele looks at the driver. She notes the frown on his face as she massages her hands.

You OK? His voice is nervous and thin.

Pualele swallows and looks back at the walls surrounding the convent. She could get in the taxi. Or she could go back into the convent. All she has to do is press the intercom and walk through the gate, follow the path and run up the steps to the front door, which would open again without question. If she goes back in she can leave the leather carry-all behind on the grass verge for the rubbish men to collect, and then there will be nothing physical to remind her of her other life.

I will do everything in my power to guide you.

But there is what she knows – or thinks she knows – about Olga and her own mother, and it niggles at the edge of her mind.

Miss, are you OK?

Pualele wants to tell this stranger what has happened to her. Not just about Sister Teresa but about her own life. All of it. It is such a simple question he asks, but there is no easy answer. She lets her hands hang free as she tries to settle her thoughts, the voice in her head growing stronger.

It is always there. In every soul. The very essence of where we belong.

He has her by the arm and she lets herself be led until she is sitting in the taxi, her feet still on the grass verge. The taxi can take her anywhere she wants to go. She just has to say. She takes a deep breath and peers at the gabled roof of the convent over the wall. Her arm presses against her thin coat and in her breast pocket she can feel the outline of the kauri gum, the winged insect suspended within it. The man waits for her to answer, and later she will take the memory of this moment and weave these few minutes into the fabric of her life so that she will always remember this day.

I'm fine, she whispers as she examines the kikuyu grass creeping over the concrete at her feet. The driver bends his head towards her, not sure of what she has said. Then, in a much stronger and clearer voice, she lifts her chin until she is looking directly into his almond-shaped eyes and says to the man who still doesn't know if he is driving her away or not, *I'm going to be fine.*

Acknowledgements

With grateful thanks to my lovely family (Phil, Harry and Frano) who always believed in my writing. In particular, to Phil who ensured I had space and time to write in our busy household, and Julie Glamuzina who inspired her youngest sister to start writing.

Thank you to those who read the manuscript in progress and offered advice: Karen Breen, Michael Botur, Amanda Coyne, John Cranna, Rod Fee, Judith White, Nina Nola and my editor, Geoff Walker. Thanks to my Uncle, Ned Glamuzina for sharing his personal story about evacuating from Dalmatia in 1944 and his recollections of being a refugee in El Shatt. Thanks also to Andrew Ta'afuli Fiu for sharing his family history about growing up Samoan in Auckland in the 1970s, Pip Cobcroft for providing me with some of her Samoan stories and Tim Heath for answering my questions about Samoan language and custom.

I consulted a number of texts regarding life in El Shatt including Šimun Ujdur's essay *From Gradac Dalmacija, Hrvatska via El Shatt 1944 to New Zealand 1946* and Mateo Bratanić's Doctoral thesis *El Shatt – zbjeg iz Hrvatske u pustinji Sinaja, Egipat (1944-1946)*.

And the documentary *From the Dawn Raids to Bastion Point & the Springbok Tour* by Nevak Ilolahia gave me great insight into the Polynesian Panther movement.

Finally, my deepest gratitude to Karen, Rod, Katie and Judy – to paraphrase EB White, *it's hard to find someone who is both a true friend and a good writer* – and all of you are that and more.

Author photograph
by Amanda Coyne

Ann Glamuzina is of Croatian descent and grew up in Auckland. Ann's paternal grandmother, uncle and aunts were evacuated from Dalmatia to El Shatt refugee camp in Egypt during the later stages of World War II. Her father, Stipe arrived in New Zealand from Dalmatia in 1940, working initially as a gum digger with his father. Ann's mother, Sylvia was born in Auckland to Croatian immigrants, and together, Stipe and Sylvia owned and operated Pt Chevalier Fisheries for 34 years.

Ann graduated from University of Auckland Law School in 1992 and then from AUT University with a Master of Creative Writing in 2009. She now writes full time.

She lives in Takapuna with her husband and son.

www.annglamuzina.com